ADV
HEA

MW00916710

"The latest from GG nominee Jo Treggiari manages to be many things at once: a thrilling, twisty mystery that I couldn't put down, a high school ensemble featuring a large and compelling cast of characters, and an incisive but sensitive piece of social commentary. In Treggiari's deft hands, this skillfully crafted multi-voice thriller keeps readers guessing, while providing nuanced insights into the emotions and backstories of her complex main characters. An absolute must-read from one of the best writers of teen thrillers working today!"
   –Tom Ryan, award-winning author of *Keep This To Yourself*

"A tense, riveting murder mystery...that also invites readers to look beyond the surface."
   –Atlantic Books Today

"A complex and twisting story featuring an engaging cast of misfits and a thrilling reveal. Riveting!"
   –Vicki Grant, bestselling author of *36 Questions That Changed My Mind About You*

"Polished prose, a trio of finely crafted narrators, and the best sort of finale: one that sits in the rich spaces between black and white, tailor-made for meaty discussion and passionate opinion. *Heartbreak Homes* confirms Jo Treggiari's place in the top tier of YA mystery writers."
   –Darren Groth, author of *Boy in the Blue Hammock* and *Munro vs. the Coyote*

PRAISE FOR JO TREGGIARI

The Grey Sisters

- Finalist, Governor General's Literary Awards, 2019
- Shortlisted for the 2020 Crime Writers of Canada Awards
- Shortlisted for the 2021 Ann Connor Brimer Children's Literature Award
- Nominee, Arts Nova Scotia, Emerging Artist Recognition Award, 2020

"Treggiari offers chills both subtle and shocking, and readers won't be able to turn the pages fast enough. Jaw-dropping twists and a distinct *Deliverance* vibe elevate this riveting thriller."
　–Kirkus Reviews

"...a well-developed psychological thriller filled with unexpected plot twists that will leave readers guessing right until the very end. The book speaks to many important topics of interest relevant to teens, such as family, friendships, grief and loss, conflict, survival, identity, resilience, and growth and change."
　–Canadian Review of Materials, highly recommended

"*The Grey Sisters* is a thrilling ride, an unrelenting narrative in which the suspense tightens to the breaking point."
　–Quill & Quire

Blood Will Out

"A heart-pounding psychological drama...this book slowly, steadily works its way towards its climactic—and surprising—conclusion...."
　–Atlantic Books Today

"A striking young adult thriller that reads like adult fiction with its complex and involving story.... *Blood Will Out* is involving, well-constructed, and hard to put down."
　–Midwest Book Review

HEARTBREAK HOMES

HEARTBREAK HOMES

JO TREGGIARI

NIMBUS
PUBLISHING LTD.
—— NIMBUS.CA ——

Nimbus Publishing Limited
3660 Strawberry Hill Street, Halifax, NS, B3K 5A9
(902) 455-4286 nimbus.ca

Printed and bound in Canada

Design: Heather Bryan
Editor: Whitney Moran

NB1647

This story is a work of fiction. Names characters, incidents, and places, including organizations and institutions, are used fictitiously.

Library and Archives Canada Cataloguing in Publication

Title: Heartbreak homes / Jo Treggiari.
Names: Treggiari, Jo, author.
Identifiers: Canadiana (print) 20220233950 | Canadiana (ebook) 20220233969 | ISBN 9781774711163 (softcover) | ISBN 9781774711361 (EPUB)
Classification: LCC PS8639.R433 H43 2022 | DDC jC813/.6—dc23

Nimbus Publishing acknowledges the financial support for its publishing activities from the Government of Canada, the Canada Council for the Arts, and from the Province of Nova Scotia. We are pleased to work in partnership with the Province of Nova Scotia to develop and promote our creative industries for the benefit of all Nova Scotians.

For my wonderful, inspiring, and loving children,
Milo and Lu

And to all the beautifully non-conforming kids who feel lost,
unsupported, or ignored, especially those who identify as
2SLGBTQIA+. I see you and I love you.

Please visit jotreggiari.com for content notes.

FRANKIE

This was not my scene.

We stood, gasping for breath, at the crest of a long upward climb over rocky soil peppered with potholes that could have sunk the *Titanic*. For the most part it had been straightforward: park at the bottom of the hill near the big sign some graffiti artist had altered to read *Heartbreak Homes*, then walk straight up the unpaved road. Jessa had already consulted her phone twice, looking up the text invite Suzie Jackson had sent her. I certainly wasn't going to voice my fears, but it had crossed my mind that this might be an elaborate set-up—that we had received a set of alternate directions to this so-called "back-to-school rager," designed to send us on some wild goose chase into the wilderness.

I clicked on my flashlight app. The watery beam picked out the iron-hard earth, gouged into deep ruts filled with muddy water, and a landscape violently cleared of trees and brush. The early October wind cut straight across our path, chill with the threat of rain to come, and sadly, Jessa's second-hand Golf was already out of sight.

"How did they even get permission to do this?"

"I guess his dad just doesn't care," said Jessa. She gripped my arm. "Listen!"

I sharpened my ears. Barely discernible over the sound of our heaving lungs was a low hum, a droning consistent enough to register as human-made. Bass-heavy music surging and ebbing in a long wave. Still far off, tucked in next to a thicket of trees, a faint glow indicated lights, and most tellingly, a whiff of weed smoke drifted on the cold air.

"Oh thank the gods," Jessa said, threading her arm with mine. "It's really happening."

Soon enough, we came to a row of vehicles on the shoulder. "Looks like we could have parked a little closer," I said, scowling at the gunk packing the treads of my Blundstones.

"I was feeling a little bit nervous." She inhaled deeply, relaxing her shoulders. "The fresh air is good."

"Why would you be nervous? These are your friends." I tried to keep the bitterness out of my voice. My fervent wish was that instead of shivering on a hillside in the middle of nowhere, we could be curled up on Jessa's bed watching movies in our pajamas, surrounded by bountiful snacks and drinks. Our regular weekend routine.

"Yeah, but it still feels new, you know?" Her forefinger went to the bridge of her nose. A nervous habit from when she'd worn glasses that were always slipping down.

I summoned a smile. "What did you tell your mom?" Jessa's mother, Casey, was Lincoln's chief of police, and to say she was overprotective would be an understatement.

"The usual." She placed her hand over her heart. "That

I solemnly swear I will not do any drugs. I will have a single beer and then water for the rest of the night. I promise to call if anything goes remotely wrong, and"—she pinched my elbow—"that I'll let you keep me on the straight and narrow, and drive us home. She's at work tonight and I'm praying she doesn't get a noise complaint. How about the elderly relations?"

My parents had both died when I was four. My grandparents didn't like to be bothered by anything untoward, so the mutual understanding was that I didn't tell them much about what was going on in my life. Like my photography. Or tonight. Or the fact that I was into girls. I liked to imagine that my parents would have approved of everything.

"Sleepover at your place. Back home tomorrow by lunch. I may have left out any exciting middle bits."

She smiled up at me. "An omission rather than a lie, Frankie."

"That's right, future lady Supreme Court Justice."

"So, c'mon then," Jessa said, hauling at my arm with fresh enthusiasm. "Let's get to the middle bits."

I admit I gasped a little as we finally rounded the bend. The rough track opened up into a graceful circular driveway, paved with red bricks and lined with inset solar lighting. At the end was a garage bigger than my two-bedroom. And rearing up from the earth was a jewellery box of a house, like some giant had just plonked it there. A two-storey mansion, tiered and turretted like a wedding cake, pristine white stone pillars with gold-flecked marble steps, glossy black wrought iron railings, an excess of polished golden wood, and a wide front door, lacquered a rich red like a poisoned apple. It all screamed for a row of maids bedecked in starched white linens, plump-faced cooks, and a stern-yet-kindly butler with a chest puffed out like a pigeon.

It was the perfect clandestine party location.

"Wowza." I sped up. I couldn't wait to see if the interior matched. It was over the top in a way that was both fascinating and repellent. As if Donald Trump had designed a luxe ski lodge. This was the showroom home of the Heartwood Development, and the only residence that had been completed before the project went bust.

"Hold on," Jessa panted, hanging back. "I can't go in like this."

I fanned her flushed cheeks with a bookstore flyer from my jacket pocket, wishing my entire head didn't turn brick-red when I was hot. Jessa was lighter-skinned than her mom and our exertion had given her a peachy-warm glow.

"I didn't want to be so late," Jessa said, fiddling with her neckline and pulling at the hem of her short skirt. Her eyes went to the black Mercedes coupe crouched like a panther in front of the steps: Malcolm Bradley's status object.

"Why didn't he have to—" I swallowed the rest of my sentence. Of course he wouldn't have to trudge up a monster hill.

"It's his party," Jessa reminded me. Her warm brown eyes had that shiny thing happening. As if she was all lit up from inside.

I remembered finding a postcard once when I was seven or eight; it had slipped down behind the china cabinet in my grandmother's formal parlour. The tiny room was cold year-round and smelled like mothballs, but my dog Bumble and I were playing hide-and-seek and that's where I had chosen to conceal myself. The photograph was of frothy waves rolling onto a golden beach edged by high cliffs. It looked nothing like the gentle green hills and old pine forests of Lincoln, and I could almost smell the fresh salt tang. On the back in looped cursive were the words *The heart wants what the heart wants*. It was signed *Marie*. My mother's name. She and my father had died in a car crash when they were twenty—barely older than I was now. My grandmother found me holding it to my chest and snatched it away from me. "Does the heart no good to stay stuck in the past," she said while I cried. She never spoke about my parents again. And I never asked about them. Still, I wondered what they would think of me.

I couldn't stop Jessa from feeling her feelings, but I could stand up for her no matter what happened.

"Well, at least you know he's here," I said, indicating the sports car.

She shot me a stern look but I saw her dimples peep for a second before she sighed. "I know you don't like him."

Even if I weren't gay I wouldn't like him. "Yeah, well he passed you over in ninth grade, didn't he?"

We'd been at a party. Spin the bottle. Mal had demanded a re-do when it landed on Jessa. And then he'd gone and spent way more than seven minutes in the closet with Anabel Stevens.

She raised her eyebrows in mock outrage. "That was a long time ago, Frankie." She pulled out her phone again. "Hey, give me a second."

"What are you doing?"

"Checking Missy's Instagram." She exhaled in relief. "They're inside." Her smile slipped. "They've all got their hair up." She showed me the screen. A row of girls who looked cast from the same mould, even if their hair colour and skin tone differed. They held an identical pose, arms bent in triplicate, leading with their chins. Their long hair was piled up in artful topknots, deceptively messy, held in place with jewelled clips. Suzie's were blue. I remembered Jessa had given them to her for her birthday.

"I should have worn mine like that." Her woebegone expression almost made me laugh out loud but I bottled it up. I also restrained myself from pointing out that Suzie's sparkly pink lipstick made her mouth look like it was open for business. Instead I made some kind of noncommittal noise.

"Don't be like that," Jessa chided. "Like everyone else who judges on appearance. You have to trust that I can make good decisions." Her lips quivered. "They have hidden depths."

I swallowed my snort with difficulty. "Just remember you're one of a kind," I said, reaching out to intercept her fingers before she ruined her sleek chestnut tresses. "You look amazing."

I sensed people arriving behind us, but before I had a chance to stand aside, I was jostled hard. A short, sinewy girl pushed by me, followed by two more girls. I caught a glimpse of hooded eyes, straight black brows, and a wide, generous mouth as she shot me a challenging look. She wore an orange bandana tied tightly across her close-cropped head, a black hoodie, and jeans. The other two were tiny, dressed in black with plaid shirts tied around their waists and raggedy high-tops. A blond with a shaved head, the other a brunette with hair spiked up as prickly as a cactus. I really wanted to take their picture.

Jessa wrinkled her nose as they swung the door open, unleashing a maelstrom of noise.

They smelled bad. Like they hadn't showered in a while.

I could smell her on me now, the strong-looking one, where she had brushed against my sleeve. A ripe mixture of BO and woodsmoke that made me want to sneeze.

"Who was that?" Jessa asked, glaring at their backs disappearing into the crowd.

I shrugged. I'd never seen any of them before. There was a wildness about them. An edge of danger. Maybe this party would be more interesting than I'd thought.

MARTIN

What the hell was I doing here?

It was my first free Saturday since the beginning of summer, but as soon as I walked through the door, all the bad feelings came rushing back. DISGRUNTLED TEEN SABOTAGES GREAT PARTY VIBE, screamed the headline in my brain.

It had seemed like a good idea. Charlie, my boss at the Quik Stop, had refused to let me work another double night shift. "You're gonna kill yourself, kid," he said, shaking his head. "And for what?" He was a good guy, but he paid me minimum wage and all the shitty coffee I could guzzle. Question was: how else was I going to raise enough money for college tuition and avoid being home at the same time? The landscaping company I worked for on the weekends was winding down after the frenzy of the summer season, which meant that outside of school I had nothing going on but the daily torture of having to face my dad.

I couldn't take his sad-guilty routine anymore. He'd drained my college fund—the one my mother set up on the day I was born—without telling me, and lost just about everything we had in a bad real estate deal. This very mansion I was standing in, as a matter of fact. I'd heard about what an amazing opportunity Emerson Bradley's Heartwood Homes development was for months, how my dad was going to triple his investment, and then wouldn't you know it? Eight months after the first joist was laid, crickets.

Dad had been too ashamed to talk to me about why we had to sell the house I grew up in and move to a rental on the other side of town, why I had to change schools, and why there was no money left. He'd let me figure it out by myself, the only clue being the bottle of pills and quart of whiskey he'd downed trying to bow out.

The new house was cramped, my room little more than a shoebox. Wood panelling, curling, mildewed wallpaper, bad plumbing, the stink of ancient cigarettes wafting up from the shaggy carpets. And my dad was always home, pacing and muttering, or slumped on the couch with his arms over his face. His accounting job allowed him to telecommute as long as he kept up with his therapy. I spent as little time there as I could.

This felt like a world away from that.

The place was wall-to-wall jammed. The energy was high. People were shedding their clothes. It was the kind of party where the ceiling starts to sweat and the windows fog up. First thing I did was find a beer. There were four kegs in the kitchen. An assortment of hard liquor on the counter, bags of chips, brownies, and deli trays. The Lincoln Academy drug dealer was there, peddling his wares. The air was thick with smoke. I felt my shoulders relax from the contact high.

Second thing I did was go looking for my friends. Maybe this was exactly what I needed to set me straight again. Maybe I hadn't lost everything. I might be graduating from Crestview now, but surely that didn't negate three years at Lincoln Academy?

Most people were in the living room. Couches and chairs had been pushed back and the floor surged with dancers. Over on the far side, lounging on a white leather sectional that took up almost the entire wall, I spied my old buddies, Mal Bradley, Drew Marshall, and Simon Bonneville, and a group of attendant girls.

Drew let out a yell that cut through the bass: "Hey, loser!"

"Good to see you, man," Simon said, giving me a hearty slap on the back. After a flurry of pounds and fist-bumps I found a spot on the armrest, leaned back, and took an appreciative sip of my beer. It was premium stuff. Nothing but the best for Mal's parties.

"Didn't we get rid of you?" Mal said with an edge to his lazy smile.

"Not that easy, bro."

All these months and I hadn't heard from him until I'd gotten the invite via Simon.

"Gang's back together," Drew said, trying to cheers his red Solo cup with mine. He already had quite a lean happening, as if his centre of gravity had shifted to his left foot, and frothy beer sloshed all over his jeans. I couldn't help but notice how much he'd bulked up, his baseball-sized biceps evident even under his thick woollen shirt.

"I think you know everyone," said Mal.

I nodded at the girls. "Hey, Missy, Anabel, Suzie."

It was funny: sitting there with all of them staring at me, I felt for the first time that I was no longer a part of the group. Simon caught my eye and grinned encouragingly, as if he could read my mind. Surely not that much had changed?

"You remember Jessa?" Mal said, slipping an arm around the shoulders of a startlingly pretty girl with dark eyes, warm brown skin, and shiny hair. Her name rang a bell. I managed to bite off a "Wow" as recognition set in. I *did* know her, but she'd changed a lot.

"Nice to see you." She shook hands, which seemed kind of sweet and old-fashioned. Mal's arm tightened and he met my gaze. Laying claim. *Fine by me.* And fine by Suzie, too, apparently. I hadn't realized they'd broken up. She was staring intently into the crowd.

I checked Mal out surreptitiously. The expensive haircut, the giant watch. *Must be nice to be so wealthy that losing millions barely makes a dent.* I gulped down the sour thought with another big swig from my cup. *Relax*, I told myself, leaning into the soft expanse of the couch, *just try and have a good time.*

Everyone from the senior class was here, and probably most of the lower grades as well. I spent so much time nodding and smiling that my neck cramped up and I thought my face might crack. It was almost like the night was following a script, each character behaving exactly the way I expected them to, down to who was going to end up puking in the bathtub and who was going to hook up with whom. I was kind of enthralled by the familiarity of it all and disgusted at the same time. Everything had changed for me and nothing had changed for anyone else. Or were they just better at hiding it?

"Lincoln's in the house!" Mal yelled as a pack of guys spilled into the living room from the kitchen. Guys from the wrestling team, jacketed in red and gold, *whoot whooted* and chest-bumped. The entire football team, the Razorbacks, followed them, instantly taking up space and, it felt like, most of the oxygen in the room.

Drew thumped me on the shoulder again with such exuberant force, he almost sent me flying. "I'll grab you another one," he yelled. Drew always operated at full volume. I raised my cup in thanks and he swayed away, bulldozing through the crowd. There was a smear of glittery pink lipstick on his shirt collar. I looked from him to Suzie and back again. Her lips were painted in the exact same colour. As I watched, Mal made a grab for Suzie and she glared, shook off his arm, and stalked away. *Interesting.*

I downed the rest of my beer, feeling my nervousness dissipate.

Simon leaned over. He followed my eyes to where Mal sat cuddling with Jessa.

"What's going on there?" I asked.

He shrugged. "It's new, I guess. I'm glad for him. He's been pretty down. Things good with you?"

"Yeah, busy. How about you?"

"Same old, same old. Crestview okay?"

I grimaced. "Just trying to get through." All I was focused on was keeping my GPA up. College would be the great leveller as long as I could get my foot in the door.

LOCAL BOY COURTED BY TOP FIVE UNIVERSITIES.

Simon glanced at me. He seemed embarrassed. "You know I got the *Progress* editor position? Since you couldn't..."

That was the school newspaper. I'd started on staff in freshman year, doing layout, writing opinion pieces and movie reviews—whatever I needed to do to get a byline. My dream was to pursue investigative journalism. Correction: had been. DISAPPOINTED TEEN EMBRACES MEDIOCRITY. Crestview didn't even have a school paper. I'd lost my only shot along with the move.

"It's fine. No big." It wasn't true, but I couldn't stand that pitying look in his eyes.

"Not the same without you," he said. "Mr. Harris is constantly praising your stellar interviewing chops." Mr. Harris was the teacher advisor. He was always talking about that movie *The Post* and encouraging us to go deeper, like we were going to stumble upon some deep conspiracy.

"Thanks, man." We cheersed.

"Did you go out for soccer this year? Thought I might see you at a game." Simon played defense.

I winced. He was only being friendly, but every question felt like he was salting an open wound. I couldn't commit to a new team, not with my free time eaten up by work.

"No." The word came out harsher than I'd intended. "But I'm too busy anyway."

I washed down the lump that had been building in my throat and started thinking about the next beer and the one after that. Where the hell was Drew with my refill? He was probably so drunk he'd forgotten.

"Wouldn't like to be on the receiving end of one of your power shots anyway," he said with a little smile. My shoulders released.

"We should hang soon," I said.

"No doubt." He gave me a fist-bump and disappeared back into the crowd.

"Haven't seen you around much," Mal said, sliding in next to me. I followed his gaze to where Jessa was dancing with Suzie and the other girls. "You too good for us now?" His face above the fading tan was flushed and a little sweaty. From his breath, I guessed he'd started chasing his beer with hard liquor.

"You lose my number?" I countered.

He guffawed. "You know how it is."

I held his gaze until he looked away. "I've had a lot going on," he said, tossing back his drink. He crushed the cup and threw it behind him. "You?"

"Been working," I said finally.

"Oh yeah, right right. Member of the proletariat." Something flickered in his eyes, carved a notch into his forehead. "Me too," he said.

"Really?" I couldn't keep the incredulity out of my voice.

"Yeah, at my dad's firm." He pulled a quart of whiskey from his jacket pocket and offered it to me. I shook my head.

"They gave me a corner office on the fourth floor." He gulped down a double shot, his voice relaxing into his usual boastful cadence.

Of course they did. I bet it had a view and a private bathroom. I felt like I already knew the answer, but I asked anyway. "What are you doing? Filing?"

"Nah, they've got a girl for that," he said, totally missing the sarcasm. "Mostly sitting in on meetings. Getting a feel for it, ya know? My dad"—he paused, swallowed another slug—"he's grooming me to take over."

"Sure." *That's the way nepotism works.* I bit back the boastful words that wanted to spill from my lips. How Charlie trusted me with the bank deposit. How clients praised my meticulous pruning abilities and my skill with their prize dahlias. Achievements that now felt laughable. I cracked my neck.

"I don't recognize half these people." I had no trouble hearing the self-satisfied note in Mal's voice. They all knew him, though. Was that how it was for his father too? He spared no thought for the people whose lives he'd ruined. Why did Mal's family get to be happy when the rest of us were barely making it? I felt a surge of rage so strong it was incandescent. Surely Mal would notice? I locked eyes with him. His face was even redder, his gaze unfocused.

"Later, bro," he said, giving me an uncoordinated slap on the back as he moved towards the dancing group of girls. "Enjoy yourself," he added with a magnanimous flourish.

Sitting there on that huge couch, holding onto my empty cup, I had never felt so out of place.

LONELY GUY THROWS PITY PARTY; NO ONE COMES.

After a minute, disgusted with myself, I got to my feet. Weaving through the crowd, I wandered, mentally checking off the luxury details: the sunken sitting room, the massive kitchen with stainless steel appliances, the dining room with the requisite chandelier, fine art on the walls. I picked at the gilded frame of a Chagall. It was foam, plaster board, the bold splashes of blue, purple, and red a little too vivid. It wasn't even a framed poster. It was like they'd tried to pretend it was the real thing. That was when I began to notice all the fakery around. Faux leather, dark wood veneer, bowls of glossy plastic fruit, and vases of opulent flowers that needed no watering. This was what my father had invested so heavily in. And none of it was real.

The lump in my throat swelled until I could taste the bitterness on my tongue. I went to the kitchen to get a refill. Maybe getting good and drunk would help me force it back down.

CARA

It was the perfect night to rob rich kids.

Pitch-black. The moon skinny as a fingernail clipping, stars shrouded by clouds. We knew this rough ground well, and once we emerged from the dense trees it was easier to see where we were putting our feet. The big house was hidden in a hollow, but we could hear people—that low hum that sounds nothing like insects—and see a faint glow hovering above the horizon.

"What do you think they're doing up there?" Toni asked. She wore a black woollen hat pulled down low over her kitten-soft buzz cut. It was chilly and we were all wearing triple layers—T-shirts, flannels, and hoodies—dark colours, so we blended in with the gloom. Normally Toni and Iggy sounded like water buffalos in a stampede, especially if they were goofing off, but even they were treading lightly tonight. Still, none of us could compare to Shadow, who had earned her nickname over countless nights.

"Birthday party? Satan worship?" said Iggy. She rubbed her hands together with glee. "Either way I hope there's snacks."

We hadn't seen anyone yet. Only a few headlights in the distance, the hum of engines suggesting faraway cars trundling up the muddy hill. As we got closer, the earth became packed dirt, the deep tracks of heavy machinery stamped into the earth catching our boots in ruts and ridges. And slowly, the house revealed itself.

Shadow crouched and I got down next to her. I whistled low to Toni and Iggy and they dropped bonelessly a few feet away. I lifted my finger to my lips to shut them up, but I could sense giggles not far off. Although Toni had blond hair and Iggy's was dark, they were one of those couples that had grown to resemble each other. They were both small-boned, with pointy chins and wide-spaced eyes that made them look a lot younger than their seventeen years. They ruled at panhandling, bringing home in a single day more than twice what Shadow and I could in a week. This was still a game to them. They hadn't experienced a really hard winter yet or done without food for more than two days in a row. They spooned in a shared sleeping bag every night. Part of me wished they could stay the way they were. Trusting and innocent.

Or at least, as innocent as they could be given what they'd gone through. How could they look so fragile and yet be strong enough to survive it? That was the same for all of us, I guess. I'd never understood why girls were considered weak. Girls were the strongest people I knew.

I crouched down closer to Shadow. She was quiet, but I could feel her whole body shivering.

"Are you cold?" I had my sleeves pulled down over my

hands, and still my fingertips were tingling. There wasn't much cover out here and the wind cut straight through our worn clothing.

Shadow made an imperceptible sound, but I knew her so well by now. Never being warm enough was something we'd gotten used to in our stripped-down house. This was not cold, but fear.

Slowly I made eye contact. "You don't have to come. You wait out here and we'll do what we have to do. You can help us carry everything back. Or you could even head home if you wanted." I knew she hated being around big groups of people.

She made a different sound, a choked cough like a pissed-off cat. Angry, as if I were giving her an order. "I am fine," she said. Her grey eyes were bright lights, the sharp planes of her high cheekbones peeking out from the black bangs she hid behind.

"Okay." I risked pressing my hand against her forearm for a brief second but she shook me off. It made my heart squeeze the way she drew me in, pushed me away. Just when I hoped we were getting closer, sharing more.

When I first met her on the street a few towns away, it was days before she'd look directly at me. Longer still before she spoke. It was like taming a cast-off bait dog. Gentle words, not too loud, the offer of a place to sleep, some food, slowly proving to her that I wanted nothing she didn't want to give. When Toni and Iggy had joined us in the abandoned Maersk shipping container we'd been living in for a few months, Shadow had to start all over before she got used to their high energy and raucous voices. Now, they teased her sometimes and she suffered their casual affection.

I knew that at some point in her life, Shadow had endured something terrible. Something unspeakable that hadn't broken her but had reshaped her. She'd told me some of the more recent stuff but there was plenty more buried deep. No one chose the streets unless the alternative was worse.

I stood up slowly and glanced down the hill. A break in the cars heading our way. We could take the road until we got closer, then go full sneak mode and see what we were dealing with.

"Who do you think they are?" Toni asked.

"Kids," I said.

Iggy nodded her spiky head vigorously. "Those boys have been coming around all summer in their fancy cars," she said. "Drinking, mostly. Doing stupid stuff."

"Any adults, you think?" I asked.

"Doubtful."

"They've got money," Toni said, indicating the cars parked along the track.

My smile grew wider.

Wealthy teenagers were perfect targets. They thought they were safe from all the bad shit. That they were above all the hardships of life. And the ironic part was, they wouldn't miss anything we took from them. They'd instantly replace it with the newer model.

"Let's go," I said.

The whole house was lit up like a Christmas tree. We were all wearing empty backpacks stuffed with more bags, and the plan was to leave with them full. More than full. I wanted to have to drag mine behind me like Santa's sack of presents the whole five-kilometre trek home.

"Food and water. Lights. Tools. Blankets," I said, beckoning Toni and Iggy closer. Those were always top of the list.

"Anything else is a bonus, but—" I made eye contact with both of them—"we don't draw any unnecessary attention to ourselves." Bonuses included wallets, purses, and drugs we could resell.

"Go 'round the back?" Shadow suggested.

I nodded. We would scope out the situation before making a move.

It was amazing how hidden the house was. We knew, because we couldn't see anything other than the water storage tank and the cell tower from our spot, that the way the land rose and fell shielded this whole area from the town below. There were days when we felt like we were all alone in the world, until hunger drove us to hit the dumpsters behind the restaurants in town or beg for money. It was like being in a bubble. Although I was aware—from the shipping container, the lean-to under the bridge, the old garage scheduled for demolition, and all the other places I'd lived for days, weeks, or sometimes even months—that like a bubble, it could all be popped in a breath.

Now that we were close, it was obvious there were tons of people here. Cars parked nose to tail all the way up and down the road. Music shaking the windowpanes. *Safety in numbers*, I thought to myself. *Easier to disappear in a crowd.*

Shadow had already moved on, travelling in a wide circle that would take her to the back of the house. We followed, quicker now. There were dry-looking shrubs in planter boxes along the edges, blocking off a gardening shed and a dumpster filled with mouldy plasterboard and lumber. A blue Porta Potti tucked up against it gave off a stench that could strip paint. A stack of planks rested against the side of the house, abandoned. I toed them with my boot. Good solid pine, hardly warped at all. They'd come in useful for shoring up our windows and doors but they'd weigh a ton. I added them to the bottom of my mental list. If we decided it was worth the risk, we could come back for them.

There was a row of grimy windows at ground level. I spit on my sleeve and wiped a spot clean. A basement. Further along was one of those hatches that look like a cupboard built into the ground. Locked, which meant there was something worth stealing inside. The padlock was small, though. Easy enough to pick or smash open with something heavy.

"Okay, once we're inside let's spread out," I said, nodding to the others. Shadow, I knew, would stay clear of people. "Basement?" I said to her. "Through the hatch?" There could be tools left behind. It was obvious that work had stopped suddenly. "Want me to magic it open?" I dug a paperclip out of my pocket and shot her an inquiring look.

She hefted a rock in her hand. "No need for finesse." Her mouth quirked in what passed for a smile. It wasn't much, but it warmed my heart.

I caught Toni and Iggy's eyes. "And you two, why don't you check out the kitchen and I'll work my way through the other rooms on the bottom floor? Make sure you know where all the exits are."

"Speedy getaway," Toni said.

"Can we, you know, relax a little?" Iggy said, pulling her fingers through her crumpled black spikes until they stood up again.

"Yeah, like mingle?" Toni chimed in.

"Fine, but no conversations. We're invisible, right? And don't get too drunk," I warned. "We're going to have to lug everything we can lay our hands on across all that rough ground."

I cast a quick look around. "See those trees in the planters? Cache your loot behind there. We'll meet back here at midnight."

We left Shadow with her rock and made our way to the front of the house. I gave Toni and Iggy a once-over. We were all pretty grimy. Necks grey, fingernails black. Probably nothing short of a power hose would clear the dirt buildup. During the summer we washed in the creek, but for the last few weeks it had been too cold to do more than jump in and get the hell out. We looked rough.

"Come here, you," I told Iggy. She slouched over, rolling her eyes at Toni, and submitted to my wet finger attacking an oily smear on her cheek.

When we got to the stairs, there were a couple of lost-looking high school girls standing on the porch. Waiting, like they expected some old white dude in a stiff black suit to invite them inside.

I pulled Toni and Iggy into a quick huddle.

"Act like we belong here. Be ballsy about it. If you look like it's yours, they won't question anything," I told them. "Any trouble, you split up, run, and hide. I'll find you."

They nodded and grinned in unison. That was always the routine.

"Possession is nine-tenths of the law, right, Mom?" Iggy said with a smirk. I popped her one on the arm. The "Mom" thing got on my nerves.

When opportunity knocks, you open the door, as Tick Tock used to say. But I always added the word *carefully*. You never knew who was on the other side. Sheep or wolf.

I squared my shoulders, said, "Quick and easy," and we stormed the steps, pushing the girls out of the way.

FRANKIE

I kept losing Jessa. Hardly surprising. The house was cavernous, with a long wide hallway like an aorta, splitting into branches leading back to the kitchen, a large pantry, and a small bathroom, and then sweeping up to the second floor via a graceful curving staircase, and down a few shallow steps into a sunken living room with colour-coordinated wall-to-ceiling bookshelves on either side of the fireplace mantel. A dining room mirrored it on the other side.

The battery-powered lanterns didn't give off much light, and the pillar candles in the fireplaces and alcoves threw dizzying shadows against the walls and high ceilings. It felt like a fever dream. And it was stifling. People lined the hallways and massed everywhere. A lot of them were strangers, a clear indication of which layer of social strata I inhabited. Let's just say I wouldn't be having a heart-to-heart with anyone here about Diane Arbus or Chinese dragon kites.

As we followed the bass thump to the living room, Jessa was engulfed almost immediately. Suzie sashayed over, gave me the briefest of nods, and then pulled Jessa into a blatant lovefest in the middle of the dance floor, leaving me stranded. They were all wearing matching black denim jackets, like they belonged to some kind of secret club I'd never be invited to join.

Swallowing my hurt, I dragged my attention away. The furniture was pushed back against the walls, but most of it was occupied by couples making out and a squad of boys holding court on the massive sectional. Mal was one of them. I'd recognize his pale blond crewcut and domineering voice from a mile away. He was wearing a leather moto jacket with white stripes on the sleeves, as if that made him a badass or something.

Suzie's group picked a spot right in front of him and his friends to begin their stripper-like gyrations. I knew Suzie was a gymnast, and seeing her in action, I had to admit she was limber. I saw Mal's baby blues fix on Jessa, and his patented smile—the one I found smarmy but she probably found charming—oozed across his face. And then, like an amoeba eating a paramecium, the two groups merged.

The next time I saw Jessa she was swaying in Mal's arms. She seemed so happy. I sincerely hoped she was, but I wondered if this was the beginning of the end of us. Spitting on each other's palms in third grade and promising forever friendship no longer seemed as ironclad as I'd always believed.

Suzie caught me staring and nudged Missy, who elbowed Anabel, and then all three of them had me under their laser gazes. There was something so accusatory in those thick-pencilled eyebrows. I felt my cheeks grow warm. I couldn't see Suzie without thinking of the conversation we'd had just a month ago at the beginning of the school year. She'd suggested, not-so-subtly, that maybe I wanted something from Jessa that she couldn't give me, and that made me controlling and possessive. Her face had been sympathetic, her voice soft and caring, and the knife had slipped in without me even realizing it. Not until she'd flashed a bright smile and walked away.

She had no idea. I loved Jessa but I wasn't *in love* with her. I wasn't deluded. I might not have had that much experience in romantic relationships, but I knew better than to fall in love with a straight girl. Plus, Jessa was my best friend. Which was why I'd stood down and given her space. And it was why, right now, the only thing I could do was leave the room—though not before flipping off Suzie's back.

I tapped the keg and filled a cup for appearances' sake, and then I spotted Lorelei.

"Hey," I said. Our eyes met and then darted away. Just like they did sometimes in Advanced English. I felt my cheeks heat up even more. Lorelei intrigued me. She had a kind of buzzing energy that manifested in an angular body, a sharp, bleached-out bob, long thin fingers, and, most alluring, two moles—one on the kissing spot by her upper lip, the other on her jaw.

We'd fooled around a couple of times but things had eventually fizzled. Maybe because I wasn't officially out. I figured she was trying me on for size. Using me to answer all her *Am I gay? Am I bi?* questions. I'd known I was a lesbian since the days of playing with mud, but I still felt weird about putting my sexuality front and centre. It seemed a little risky to me in a small town where people assumed that all female coaches and male nurses were gay.

"Frankie," she said with her crooked grin. We hugged quickly. I wondered if she could feel my heart beating against her chest. My eyes went to her mouth and that tantalizing beauty mark. Could she tell I wanted to play connect the dots with my lips?

"Surprised to see you!" she said. "Didn't think this was your scene."

"Are you having a good time?" I tried not to stare at her breasts, but her grey shirt was worn thin and I could see the outline of a plunging black bra.

She leaned in, warm breath against my cheek. Her hair swung forward. She smelled of citrus and cigarettes and my head began to swim. "Just watching football players puking into plastic plants," she said with a sly smile. "If that's not a good time, I don't know what is."

"Did you come here solo?" The words burst out of me before I could stop them.

"What?"

I eked out another smile, nodded, and moved away. I was glad she hadn't heard me. I sounded like some douchebag trying to pick up a girl at a bar; for some reason, witty repartee failed me when I was in her presence.

For the next while, I wafted in and out of rooms like a ghost until I made my way back to the sitting room. I zigzagged around, moving the empties off a windowsill and then perching on it. I skated my eyes over people, not letting my gaze land anywhere for too long. A few familiar faces popped in and out, but mostly it was like looking at an impressionist painting close up. Blurry and polychromatic.

I considered making the trek home. It was doable. Bumble and I walked miles every weekend if I wasn't working at the bookstore. She was a rescue and almost nine but she still acted like a puppy. This meant she chewed stuff when she was bored. My books. Candles. Cushions. She'd even managed to gnaw a hole in the middle of my bedroom wall. In accordance with the house laws, I kept her shut in there when I wasn't home for the sake of my grandmother's embroidery and crocheted throws.

Give me a low morning mist drifting in off the river and Bumble chasing invisible rabbits, and I was at my happiest. Striding across the moors like a brooding Darcy. Searching for my Lizzie Bennet.

Two people stumbled past me, mouths glued together, and collapsed, still kissing, onto the carpeted floor. I shifted my eyes away. Maybe everyone but me was on some amazing new hybrid drug.

The energy in the room was strange. Like people were trying too hard to have a good time. I thought of the *FOR SALE* signs sprouting all over town like an invasion of knotweed. Small businesses closed and boarded up. How many of these kids had parents who were broke and desperate now? When Heartwood Homes imploded, it cast ripples far and wide, and underneath all this determined wildness, I sensed desperation and maybe a little fear that nothing was certain anymore.

That life wasn't tracking in the way we had all thought it would. Or maybe it was just hormones going haywire.

A sound like breaking glass on my left. An "oops" followed by laughter. A pale face with hair like black wings appeared at the side window. I snapped a quick photo with my phone. A girl shrieked Suzie's name a few times and I saw her in the crowd, arm raised as if in greeting, pushing against the surge of bodies but unable to move forward. I took another photo. There was something intriguing about freezing that moment, all that chaos contained for an instant.

The thick carpet was tracked with muddy footprints, spilled soda like bloodstains, ground-in pretzels and chips. The candles blazed in the fireplace, adding to the heat of sweaty bodies in the room. I tried to open the window to let in some air but couldn't. The loose hardware sat on top discarded, latches and pulls uninstalled. Maybe they'd nailed it shut for security.

Jessa danced by, closely followed by Suzie and the others. Even if I'd wanted to join in, I wouldn't have been able to get near her. Lorelei had vanished. Out of curiosity, I looked for the strange girl who'd jostled me and thought I spied her once or twice, but she was constantly in motion. Diving in and out of the crowd like a fish swimming upstream, too fast for me to capture. There was something mesmerizing about the way she moved. Powerful and lithe. *Maybe more like an otter chasing a fish*, I decided.

Bored, I slunk out of the room, keeping to the wall where the crowd was thinnest, until I got to the elegant staircase. I went up, stepping over and around people hanging out and hooking up. All these relationships seemed so transitory to me, so erratic and intense. It was almost incestuous the way people got with their friends' exes. Like they were all taking baths in the same water. I imagined Lorelei telling some other person how I kissed. Would she say bad or good, dry or sloppy? The only other girl I'd made out with had pursed her lips hard like a bird. Pecking, pecking. I shuddered and another thought assailed me: *Maybe I'm a shitty kisser.*

Upstairs, all the doors were open, but I knew that pretty soon they'd be occupied. Closest to the stairs were two bedrooms, identical and fully furnished with tall mirrored closets and sleek dressers, luxurious rugs, bold abstract wallpaper, big beds with thick quilted mattresses. Next up were a couple of bathrooms across from one another. A handwritten sign was posted on each door, warning that the plumbing wasn't hooked up and to use the Porta Potti behind the house. From the eye-watering stench, I was guessing no one cared. A neat tower of square porcelain tiles and a clutch of tools were stacked alongside the wall. Evidence that construction had shut down in a hurry.

I checked out the master suite at the very end of the long corridor. An Art Deco mirror above a wide dresser painted in matte black made the room appear even larger. The floor-to-ceiling shelves on either side of a gaping fireplace were stocked with books, organized by colour. Bands of rose. Turquoise. Dove grey. A thick section of red leather like an open vein, with titles embossed in gold. I pulled out a copy of *Jane Eyre*. It felt almost weightless. I opened it up: hollow. Nothing but two covers with no pages between them. I rapped my knuckles on the next spine and heard a thunk. Design without substance. *Who came up with that stupid idea?*

The king-sized bed, though. That was the real thing. Firm and springy. I bounced on it for a while, shaking the fidgets out before continuing my exploration. No surprise, there was an en-suite bathroom. Huge shower, soaking tub, bidet, toilet. Another ignored sign on the door saying not to use the facilities. High school kids were gross.

Back out in the hallway, I opened the door opposite. A battery-powered lantern sat on the dresser. By its light I could see that the room was decorated a silvery pink with floral wallpaper, the carpet a light blue with puffy white clouds. A kid's bedroom, I guessed. The blinds were drawn, but slowly I realized there was someone tall standing by the four-poster bed, in front of a mirror. Their clothing was dark and I couldn't make out their face. A pungent odour crept into my nostrils, like when wet clothes are left too long in the dryer.

"Sorry," I mumbled, backing out of the room and closing the door behind me. It seemed almost as if I'd interrupted something deeply private.

I wandered back downstairs. It felt disquieting being in this family house that would remain unoccupied, unloved. Never become a home. Such a waste. Looking down into the entrance hall I picked out a few more classmates, including some students I knew had graduated the previous year. What made them cling to their high-school days? If I were ever lucky enough to leave this town, I would never come back.

I resisted the urge to slide down the polished handrail, and instead wove my way down the steps. As soon as I got to the bottom, Jessa bounced up. "I found you!" she yelled, pulling me into a tight hug, her eyes aglow with happiness. We swayed back and forth, her drink sloshing in her cup.

I laughed back at her. "I've been right here." The baby curls around her temples were all springy. I smoothed her hair away from her hot face.

"Did you see me dancing with Mal?" Her fingers pinched my arm in excitement. She'd done that ever since we were little. I wasn't sure if she knew how much it hurt. "He's been by my side the whole time," she said, nearly breathless.

Twisting my reluctant mouth into a grin, I said, "Yeah? Where is he now?"

"He went to get me another drink."

I felt a twinge of annoyance. "How drunk are you?"

"Not so much," she said, batting my hand away. "This is still my first beer." She took a noisy gulp. "I promise I will politely decline another."

Her name was written on the Solo cup in black marker. Trust Jessa to do that.

"And what about him and Suzie?" Their vibe was weird. Slightly proprietary.

"She says it's ancient history."

"Hmm." I was sceptical. Their social groups revolved around each other, both vying for the sun position in the school's solar system.

"I think there's something going on with her and Drew anyway," she said.

I searched her face.

"Don't fuss. I'm fine. Having fun! It's hot and I've been dancing non-stop."

Someone yelled Jessa's name, and I saw Suzie and Missy waving their hands at her.

"Your friends want you," I said pushing her towards them, soothing her worried expression with the biggest smile I could summon up. Ignoring how my lips caught on my teeth.

MARTIN

The crush in the kitchen was suffocating. Beer pong, Never Have I Ever, and Beer Jenga were happening all around the massive island. The tile floor was sticky with spilled booze and crunchy from all the chips scattered about.

PARTY ACCURATELY RECREATES THE VOMITORIUMS OF ANCIENT ROME.

As I attempted to navigate the press of bodies, I felt a tentative hand on my arm. Turning, I looked down into pair of coppery-brown eyes, black-rimmed spectacles, and shaggy red and orange hair wafting like a halo around a long-nosed, freckled face. For the first time since my arrival, I felt genuine pleasure.

"Frankie!" I said with a broad grin.

I was maybe a little too excited, because her forehead wrinkled in confusion. The thing was, I only knew her as one of the photographers for the *Lincoln Progress*. We'd pulled a couple of late-night editorial deadlines with a few other keeners, and Mr. Harris had often referred to the two of us as his "dream team." Me handling the investigative articles, and she, the photographs. We'd never been close, but she felt like a piece of the past, and her smile when it came was friendly and open.

"Hey, Martin, I haven't seen you in so long," she said.

"Moved. Switched schools. You know, after everything came crashing down."

She grimaced. "I'm sorry. Must be hard to transfer in your last year. I know you had to give up the editor position at the *Progress*. Simon's doing his best, but he's not you."

I felt a flush of warmth. "They don't have a paper at Crestview," I said.

"Maybe you can start one?"

"Yeah, maybe." It was nice that she thought so. For some reason I didn't feel the sting of failure as much when talking with her.

"I suppose it would be impossible to compete with some of our hard-hitting stories." Frankie met my eyes. Hers were dancing. "Like, the Cafeteria Macaroni and Cheese Incident."

"But was it ever truly..."

"Cheese?!" we both finished.

I laughed, and felt my body relax. "Yeah, that was my hour of glory," I said.

Student Journalist Uncovers Cheesegate.

A heavy warm hand buffeted my shoulder. I turned around to see Drew's face, shiny and flushed and way too close. "You waiting for the keg, my man?" he said.

I stepped aside but he leaned in, slinging his beefy arm over my shoulder, leering at Frankie and then at me, eyebrows waggling like a cartoon wolf. "Soooo, what's with you two?" His insinuation was like a film of grease on my skin. How did girls put up with this shit all the time?

"I'm going to go find Jessa," Frankie said in a flat voice, and disappeared.

"Pretty sure she's a lesbian, dude," Drew said. His hot, beery breath stung my ear. "You're swinging at a fly ball."

I ducked under Drew's arm, dropped my empty cup on the kitchen table, and made a quick exit, ignoring the "Have you seen Suzie?" he yelled after me.

I headed for the relative quiet of the dining room. The giant table with curved legs was piled with more snacks and bottles of booze. A tough-looking dark-haired girl was grabbing handfuls of food, wrapping them in napkins, and dropping them into a backpack. When she noticed me watching, she stepped towards me with her lower lip out like she wanted to fight. I raised my hands in surrender and withdrew to the living room.

One end seethed with dancers and at the other, Mal and Drew were pegging bottle caps at a portrait of an old man that hung over a second fireplace big enough to roast a cow in. The painting looked familiar, like something I'd seen in a museum or an art book. Downing his beer, Drew picked up one of the burgundy velvet chairs and held it over his head like he was going to throw it. I eyed the glass picture windows on either side and took hold of the ornate wooden legs.

"Drew. Cool it," I said as friendly as I could. For a moment he hung on and we wrestled for control, lurching in a clumsy two-step. He gave up suddenly, pushing the chair into my chest with all his body weight. I staggered but kept my balance.

"Why do you even give a shit?" he shouted. Some of the dancers stopped to watch him.

I set the chair down down and sat in it, scraping the hair off my sweaty forehead and trying to force a laugh that died in my throat. I couldn't really explain why. Trashing this place just felt like a giant fuck you to my dad and all the other people who'd lost their life savings.

"You need to relax, Weber," Mal said, "Maybe find yourself a girl."

It was probably the drink talking, but I shot back with, "I see Suzie finally came to her senses."

"Oh snap," yelled Drew, high-fiving anyone in within range.

"Instead of talking crap, Weber, maybe you should go ahead and break something. Get it out of your system." Mal's words were easy but his expression was stony. Eyes gone flat and dull. I felt like I was being tested in some way I didn't understand. He spread his arms wide and raised his voice. "I give you my permission. Bring it on. You know you want to." He banged the table beside him after each word he spoke next: "Fuck. Shit. Up." His foot shot out, kicking the leg of my chair, and I went sprawling backwards.

The air in the room altered instantly. A charge raced through my bloodstream and my heart thumped in my ears as I got to my feet.

I scooped up a tray of deluxe cupcakes and hurled it at his face. It weighed barely anything, but the look in his eyes when it hit him was worth everything.

Until his meaty fist found my jaw.

FRANKIE

From my corner, I watched the flow of people from room to room and up and down the stairs. I tried to find patterns in it, like I was observing migrating birds, but this was not a mumuration. Only people talking, dancing, hanging out, hooking up, swarming. Why couldn't I just be one of them? What the heck was wrong with me? Lorelei had walked by a few times, paused, smiled even, but my tongue had tied itself into knots and eventually she'd abandoned me to join the whirling chaos on the dance floor.

I put my still-full beer cup down in an alcove ornamented with a bouquet of artificial calla lilies, and wondered whether it was too cold to wait outside until Jessa was ready to go. At times like this I wished I had my own car. But my weekend job at the Book Nookery didn't pay much, and every week I bought more books, completely wiping out what I'd earned. Plus, even if I could afford a vehicle, my grandparents would never add me to their insurance. They were convinced cars were for two things: underage drinking and making babies, which, incidentally, is how I came to exist. So I was dependent on Jessa.

The last time I'd spotted her, she'd been in the dining room. Suzie and the others were clustered nearby but all Jessa's attention was on Mal, who was squished beside her in an oversized armchair, playing with a shining lock of her hair as he looked deep into her eyes. A manoeuvre I figured he'd practiced countless times.

I sighed and checked the time. Eleven-thirty. We'd been here more than two hours and I felt every one of those seconds in the tightness of my jaw. I continued to circle the rooms, feeling invisible. I snapped a few crowd scenes. Couples on the stairs. The surging mass of dancing bodies visible through the arches. One long view that showed Jessa in the middle of the throng, her Solo cup held high. Mal pressed up close behind her with his paws on her hips. A close-up of Suzie's frowning face looking like someone had peed in her beer.

Turning away before she could catch me, I pointed my phone into the shadows, clicking at random. Two guys who looked way too young to be here had set the bowl of plastic fruit on fire. Black smoke plumed, and a sharp chemical smell tickled my nose, until someone else had the smarts to dump their drink on it. I felt a little like a voyeur but I was less anxious with something to focus on. I found the cute girl in the orange bandana again, her head bent close to another girl with a light fuzz of shorn blond hair, and I wondered if they were together.

When the background noise changed, I was absorbed in framing the profile of a girl with her hair braided in exquisite cornrows. The sound of yelling merged with the hip-hop mash-up playing through the speakers—until it didn't.

That's when I heard the shouts. Some gruff, some high-pitched and tinged with panic. At the same instant it seemed like everyone else downstairs noticed too, and I was carried forward in a swell of people to the dining room. It was as if I was being lifted by a huge wave.

And there in the middle of the floor, amidst a bunch of chairs that had been tossed aside, was a heaving pit of flailing limbs and fists. Some people were trying to stop it, but just as many were egging the fighters on. I saw the green and silver jackets of the Razorbacks team. Recognized Drew Marshall's dark head and Mal's light crewcut, his face oddly jubilant as he struggled against the bodies pushing back at him. There was a creamy substance smeared across his forehead. *Frosting?* I looked for Jessa and saw her huddled with Suzie and the others. Missy and Anabel had their arms around each other, mouths wide as they pleaded with the guys to stop. And then I caught sight of the person on the receiving end of Mal's punches.

What the hell is Martin Weber doing in this dog pile?

I tried to work my way around the circle to Jessa but the crowd was too thick.

Food was soaring now, too. Peanut butter squares, cake pops, and pizza slices hit the white walls, the paintings, and the windows, leaving Jackson Pollock–style smears of brown, yellow, white, and red.

As with most fights, it de-escalated suddenly and there was a period of embarrassment as everyone assessed the damage and tried to remember why it had started. Boys slapping each other on the back, laughing and holding paper towels to their bloody mouths, some shame-faced. People picked themselves up from the floor, brushed themselves off, handed around bottles and cans of beer. Slowly, the crowd dispersed and the music started up again in the other room.

"Jessa," I said, hurrying to her. She was alone for the moment and clearly upset.

She gulped at her beer, drinking half of it on autopilot and then coughing as it went down the wrong way. I patted her back and smoothed her hair.

"This isn't even mine," she said, looking at the cup.

I took it from her and put it down on a side table.

"That was so awful." She gripped my hands, her mouth twisting in distress. "It was so vicious. They were kicking him!"

"What even happened?" I'd tried to find Martin in the melee but couldn't spot him.

"I don't know. It was so sudden."

"Well, at least it blew itself out."

"I should check on Mal," Jessa said, giving me a sloppy kiss on the cheek.

She went to him, stumbling in her haste, and Mal slipped his arm around her waist. The frosting had migrated to his hair, and angry red marks showed along his jaw and cheekbone, but he was grinning from ear to ear. She sank into his shoulder and I heard him say "Lightweight" to her teasingly.

Martin had dragged himself upright. He looked as if he had been on the very bottom. His hair was rumpled, his shirt ripped at the collar. As I watched, he aimed a hard punch at the nearest wall. "Fuck!" he said, shaking his hand.

"Martin!"

He picked at his raw knuckles, winced, then gently ran his tongue over his fat lip. His furious expression eased and he looked at me sheepishly. "Witness my humiliation?"

"Are you hurt?"

"Not so much. That got out of hand." He tried a rueful smile, teeth bloodied, and the movement made his lip break open again.

I folded a napkin and handed it to him. He pressed it to his mouth with his good hand.

"What was it all about?"

"Stupidity. And a surge of testosterone."

"You weren't trying to impress some girl, were you?" I asked, half-joking.

Martin looked thunderstruck. "Do you think I'm the kind of guy who would do that?"

"No," I said, "but some guys are."

CARA

I was watching the aftermath of the fight when I was grabbed from behind. Turning, fists cocked instinctively, I relaxed when I recognized Toni's cheeky grin. Her backpack was stuffed to overflowing, her small frame slouched under the weight.

"Donuts and beer," she said triumphantly. "Iggy got a swanky leather jacket some fool left on a chair. She's already stashed it."

My eyes zipped around. The atmosphere had shifted. A crackling energy like the buzz in the air before a summer storm. People were drunk and out of their heads. It was time for us to go.

"Where is she now?" I asked.

"In the kitchen. There was a knife block she had her eye on. Some pans."

I didn't know what we'd do with fancy knives. It wasn't like we ever had meat to cut, but maybe we could sell them. The pans would be a good addition. On the rare occasions we cooked rather than eating right out of the can, we did it outside on a campfire. All we had now were some flimsy aluminum trays crusted with old food and blackened with use. We ended up eating plenty of charcoal with our canned beans and potatoes.

"Is Shadow getting antsy?" I asked as we made our way towards the kitchen exit.

I didn't want her anywhere near these people. I scanned the room for Iggy but couldn't find her either. There were more unopened bottles on a table. I grabbed a pint of rum and tucked it into my hoodie pocket.

"Dunno." Toni shrugged. "Haven't seen her for hours. Maybe she headed home?"

I was certain she wouldn't do that, leave us to carry everything without her.

When we got to our hiding place, there was no sign of either of them but there was a bunch of stuff heaped behind the planters.

"Wow," I said. "This must be what birthdays feel like."

It looked like items had been tossed in makeshift piles as each person quickly darted out and dumped their haul. I picked my way through it, making stacks, assessing everything. There was a whole heap of those thick blankets moving companies use to pad furniture, boxes of nails, random tools, a couple of hooded sweatshirts, extra big and smelling of boy sweat and cologne, some family-sized bags of chips, and plastic trays of cupcakes and donuts.

I unloaded my pack. Toni took a dive onto the blankets and rubbed her cheek against the greasy material. "Mmm," she said. I knew what she meant. They were dirty and gritty but they were also thicker than our mildewed sleeping bags, and there were enough of them for each of us.

"Shadow must have gotten these out of the basement." I wiped the cobwebs from my fingers and looked up at the house looming over us. The windows upstairs were closed, the rooms beyond dark or lit by flickering candles.

"How are we going to get all this stuff home?" Toni asked from her nest on the ground.

"Two trips, maybe?" I wondered whether we should get a start now. Wouldn't do to get caught taking something that didn't belong to us. Especially with this new tension in the air.

I had that itchy, crawling sensation on the back of my neck. Tick Tock always said you had to listen to that feeling. It warned of trouble to come.

FRANKIE

Amazingly, the brawl didn't break up the party. A few people left, but pretty soon everyone was dancing again. I found some chunks of ice in a cooler for Martin and we sat outside on the front steps for a little while. His lip had stopped bleeding but it had puffed up like a mushroom, and the beginning of a bruise was showing on his cheek. His knuckles were oozing, and from under his jacket I could see some blood on his shirt. He blew out a big breath, shook his shoulders as if shrugging off some great weight, and stretched his legs out. A second later, he was on his feet and pacing.

"How are you feeling?" I asked.

"Sore. Dumb. Really pissed off." He tried a smile, which looked more like he was baring his teeth, and winced. I pointed to the ice I'd wrapped in a paper towel and he pressed it against his lip, sighing. "I don't even know what happened in there. I mean, I get how it set off. Beer, hard liquor, idiots jumping in. But Mal...maybe I should go back in there. Have it out with him."

"Tonight might not be the time. He's got all his goons around him," I said, gesturing for him to sit down.

He did, with another big exhalation. "He can be kind of jerky, but I've never seen him like that."

"Yeah, you guys have been friends since childhood, right?" *Like me and Jessa*, I thought. But even that had changed, hadn't it? Which was why I was sitting out here while someone else was comforting her.

"We are. Were. I don't know. Maybe it's me," he said with a groan. "Got to admit I'm pissed off that he still gets to leave this town, move on with his game plan for world domination like nothing has changed. I might have lost my temper, but *he* was throwing out bait. I was just dumb enough to swallow it."

I had no idea how people like Mal operated, but I could see how things were stacked in his favour.

"You think he was trying to start something?"

"My jaw believes it." Martin's forehead crinkled. "I haven't seen him for months, though. I have no idea how I could have pissed him off."

"Could be it was more about letting off steam? Maybe he's going through something?"

"Yeah, I guess. Simon mentioned he was having a hard time." He examined his shredded knuckles. "This whole town feels like a powder keg."

I looked down the hill. Far off, I could see a sliver of moon like a silver eyelash, the ugly hulk of the water storage tank rearing above the treeline. There'd been some talk of painting it up to look like camouflage but for now it remained white. Any emergency funds the town still had in its coffers were going into small business incentives to help retailers keep their doors open. I knew that Lisa, the bookstore's owner, was subsidizing the business with her retirement fund and hanging on by her fingernails.

"You can't even see it from here," I said. "The boarded-up windows. The foreclosure signs."

"That was the Heartwood promise, right?" He made air quotes. "'A champagne lifestyle.' All the amenities, but no distasteful rundown neighbourhoods or hard-working lower-class people to look at. Nothing but nature's glory and swimming pools." He shrugged, wincing as the movement jarred his body. He dropped his head in his hands.

Out of the corner of my eye I saw a girl, all in black, slink around the side of the house.

Martin thumbed his lip and tossed the ice cubes into the bushes. "Maybe the simple lesson of the evening is: You can't come back."

I could feel the frustration steaming off him and it mingled with my own, which gave me the guts to say out loud what I'd been thinking about all night: "Do you ever worry that this is it? The sum total of our existence?"

He snorted. "All the fucking time. Without money, you're trapped."

I nodded. That, I could understand. My parents had tried to leave. They'd made it all the way to the coast. And then one night, a dark road, a blown tire, and a large tree had ended everything for them. As far as my grandparents were concerned, it was the ultimate cautionary tale. To add further insult, my parents were now buried in Lincoln. The thought of being stuck like that made my lungs feel too small.

"What if we don't ever get out?" I said.

Martin rubbed the back of his neck and shot me a pained look. "I can't let myself think that. It would...I don't know what it would make me do, but I think I might lose my mind."

I groaned. What were the options? Pray for a scholarship? Or a job that paid enough? Or just pack a bag and hit the road and trust that it would all work out somehow?

"Want me to give you a ride home?" Martin said, interrupting my dismal thoughts. "Hazel Lane, right? You're a few blocks over from the shithole I live in now."

I raised an eyebrow. Hadn't he been drinking?

He coloured a little. "I'd sober up first. Take it really slow. My clunker's parked about three kilometres away. Couldn't make it up the hill."

"Thanks, but I'm staying over at Jessa's."

"Will she be okay to drive?"

"I think so. If not, I'm good. I've driven her car tons of times and I've only had water. I should go find her probably," I said, getting to my feet. "Make sure she's staying out of trouble. You going to be all right?"

"Yeah, for sure. Thought I'd sulk for five more minutes. Go, go," he said, waving me off dramatically. "Save her from complete indoctrination into the vile Church of Suzie."

That made me laugh out loud. "Later," I said and went back in.

After the cool of outside, the house was almost unbearably hot. The candles sputtered, reduced to pools of melted wax. Some of the lanterns had run out of batteries and the lighting was dim. Slow, moody music was playing. There were people on every inch of the furniture, wrapped in each other's arms. Feeling like a pervert, I quickly scanned faces and hair, but I couldn't spot Jessa or Suzie or her cohorts. People were pressed up against the walls and squeezed into corners on the floor. Lorelei had her legs wrapped around the waist of some guy and half her face in his mouth. *Guess she got that figured out.* It seemed everyone had hooked up besides me and Martin.

In the dining room, small groups stood by the table, talking and eating. The painting that had hung above the fireplace was now on the floor with a shoe-sized hole in the middle of it.

In the kitchen, people were slumped on chairs surrounded by empty chip bags and platters. Conversation was at a low murmur. The sink was filled with empties and a liquor bottle tipped on its side dripped brown liquid down the counter.

Missy was sitting on Simon's lap, her head on his shoulder.

"Hey, Missy, have you seen Jessa?" I asked.

She raised her drooping eyes, blinked a few times, and then said, "She was with Mal, you know..." Lifting her hand as if it weighed a ton, she pointed to the ceiling. I followed the movement with my eyes and sighed. Last thing I wanted to do was barge in on her, but we were going to miss her 2:00 A.M. curfew if we didn't leave right now.

I made my way upstairs, stepping over a couple of girls propped up against one another. I stopped long enough to make sure they were asleep and not unconscious.

The hallway was dark now. Just one juddering lantern set on the floor at the end near the master bedroom. It went out as I stood there and I clicked my phone light on: 1:24 A.M.

I listened for any clues as to which bedroom was my best bet but the walls were thick. The second floor now smelled of new carpet and poo, and something else undefinable. Probably puke.

The doors were all closed. I knocked lightly on the first one. "Jessa?"

"Fuck off, Jessa," came a female voice I didn't recognize. No reply at the second door, so I eased it open. Gusty snores came from the bed. Holding my phone up high, I spied a large body, dark tousled head, face buried in a pillow, big feet hanging over the edge. *Drew?* He rolled over and farted. *Most likely Drew.* Was Suzie with him? I listened for a moment, hearing nothing but his heavy breathing, and left him to his dreams.

I checked the bathrooms. Vacant. The kids' room was also unoccupied. Which left the master suite. *Of course. Mal would never go for anything less than the best.*

I knocked on the door, then again more strongly. Silence. Jessa was nowhere else—she must be here. "Jessa?" I called, and kept knocking. I pressed my ear to the wood. *Was that a whimper?* My heart was hammering in my chest. I started to feel nauseous.

"Frankie, what's going on?" I turned and saw Martin at the end of the hallway. "What are you doing?" He approached and I noticed his lip was bleeding again.

"I think Jessa's in there with Mal. They might be passed out or something. The door's locked."

Thinking back, Jessa had seemed really inebriated. Maybe

she'd lost track of the number of drinks she'd had? "Can you force it open?"

Martin looked uncomfortable. "Well, you know, they're probably...we should wait a while, maybe?"

"She's got curfew. And I've been banging on the door. They would have yelled at me."

He tried the lock, ignoring my glare. "I already tried that," I said impatiently.

"Sorry," he said. "Automatic guy thing. You sure?"

"Yes!"

He set his feet and then ran at the door, putting all his weight behind his shoulder. The lock splintered and the door swung open with a groan.

Martin stood, panting and rubbing his arm as we took in the room.

Lanterns gleamed on the windowsill, candles flickered on the mantel. A cold breeze came through an open window. I could smell something alien mixed in with the jasmine scent of the candles. Rusty, like a bag of old nails. I caught sight of my reflection in the window, pale and crazied by the dancing shadows. A small decorative table was in pieces on the floor next to a heap of clothes.

But it wasn't.

It was Jessa, sprawled out as if she'd hit the ground hard.

The mirror was smashed and splinters of silver peppered the carpet. I fell to my knees—I didn't care if I cut myself—and reached for her slack hand. Her eyes were closed. Blood trickled down her forehead. Had she knocked herself out? I tapped her cold cheeks, noticing with relief that she was breathing. So slow and deep it was almost imperceptible.

"Jessa, wake up!"

Nothing.

I eased her into an upright position, bracing her body against mine. Her head lolled as if her bones had dissolved.

"Martin, she's not responding." I fumbled my phone one-handed. Tried to unlock it with clumsy, wooden fingers. "Martin, help me!"

Behind me, I heard him breathe in and out in short, quick gasps.

I turned my head. Martin was standing over by the bed. "Martin?" He stared at me, his mouth opening and closing mutely as if it were hinged like a ventriloquist's puppet. It was then I noticed the dark mass on the white sheets in the middle of the bed.

I laid Jessa gently down and stood up to get a better look.

It was Malcolm Bradley. One blue eye looked up at the ceiling, the other was a bloody wreck.

CARA

It was as if someone had kicked a wasp's nest. It didn't feel safe and my muscles were twitching, ready for a fight. I'd sent Toni out to look for Iggy and Shadow. She didn't find either of them, but as I was getting ready to head back inside they arrived from different directions—Iggy from the house and Shadow from back where the garden was—out of breath and sweaty. Her black jeans were filthy, dirt ground in at the knees, and a sleeve was torn. She was favouring her right foot. "You okay?" I asked.

"Yeah. Fine, I tripped on a pile of bricks," she mumbled. She didn't look fine, but I didn't have time for that right now.

"Let's split up the bulky stuff," I said. "Whatever gets us out of here fast." I checked to make sure Toni and Iggy were loading up.

The sound of something heavy hitting the floor echoed from inside the house and we all jumped. Were they throwing furniture around now?

"C'mon," I told them. "Let's move!" Iggy was grinning from ear to ear. She'd swiped a six-pack and it hung from her fingers by the plastic loops. I turned to quickly organizing our haul.

"Ooh, what's that?" Toni said, digging something sparkly out of the dirt by my foot. She pocketed it before I could see what it was.

Objects were scattered under the trees. I picked up a duffle bag Shadow must have unearthed and tossed in some random tools, a hammer, a pair of pliers, a long-handled screwdriver. I heaped boxes of nails and screws into a milk crate.

"Best way is to use those blankets like sacks," I said. "We can each carry one, drag it if it gets too heavy." I settled my bag onto my back, staggering a little under its weight, and gritted my teeth. All of this would make the winter a little bit easier.

"Once we're beyond the treeline, we can take a breather," I said, checking to see if the others were ready. Iggy draped the remaining thick blankets over the three of us before loading up. We must have looked like walking hills staggering over the craggy ground.

We were halfway home before we heard the keening wail of sirens. Gazing back towards the dim hulk of the house, lights coloured the night sky red and blue.

Out of habit we hit the ground. I landed right in a pothole, muddy water splashing into my mouth. I scrubbed my sleeve against my teeth, spitting out dirt. A few breathless minutes later we started moving again, crouched and slow. It felt like we were under the gaze of some huge, unblinking eyeball.

"Make for the treeline," I said. After a few hundred yards, we were hidden enough to rest up for a minute.

"Think it's about us?" Iggy said, taking the opportunity to drop her burden and shrug out her sore muscles. I did the same, groaning with relief as I stood upright. Shadow had already slipped ahead. I couldn't see or hear her.

"I don't think so," said Toni. "No one's sober enough to notice what they're missing yet."

"Another fight, maybe? This one more serious?" said Iggy. "They were whaling on each other," she added with a gleeful note.

I deepened my voice. "We should get a move on. That's a lot of sirens for a disturbance call."

"Who would have called in a noise complaint anyway? There's no one around here for miles," said Toni.

"I don't care about the whos, I care about the whys," I said, quickening my pace despite their whining.

The wind had picked up and a heavy rain started falling, soaking us in seconds. If I strained my ears, I could still hear the sirens mixing in with howl of the wind, but we were buffered here, hidden from view. At least I hoped so.

Half an hour later, there was a pink blush on the horizon and we were home.

I wanted to march right up to our front door, but I forced myself to follow the rules.

"It's when you relax your guard that they get you," Tick Tock had told me. "Always expect the worst."

Each time we approached our home through the trees, we took a slightly different path. This time I led us in a big circle along the creek and then up and over so we arrived at the back of the house.

"Fucking long way 'round," grumbled Iggy.

But there was a reason for this. This way we wouldn't wear a track directly to our front door. Instead, we mimicked deer trails.

I held my hand up to silence her and studied the building below. In the dawn light, it was little more than a collection of shadowy silhouettes, but I knew our home by heart. Had someone been poking around? Could there be anyone inside? From here it looked like what it was: an unfinished two-storey house. It was weather-tight but the siding hadn't been put on. The words *TYPAR* and *HOUSING WRAP* were printed on the thick material cocooning the side and rear walls. From the front, it looked almost perfect. Wood shingles up, doors and windows sealed with weather-stripping—the front door had even been painted a cheery blue like a robin's egg. We hardly ever entered that way, though. The rear entrance provided more cover, as it backed into the woodland they'd never had a chance to cut down.

"Can we go in already?" Toni said in an angry whisper. Like a cat, she hated to get wet.

My tongue was itching to remind her about the Maersk house. It was only a shipping container, a metal box, but we'd made it up so homey, with curtains dividing off the rooms and cushions we'd found on the street for furniture. But we hadn't been careful back then, and because of that we came home one night, exhausted and hungry, to discover that all our stuff was gone. Everything. That was the night I lost the only photo I had of my birth mother. And it's also the night I stopped thinking that good things could happen for people like us. We'd been in this new spot almost six months now and I aimed to keep it safe—even if it killed me.

"Please," said Iggy. She was so tired her eyelids were sagging. Shadow was quiet too but I could see her now, crouched with her bony knees near her ears, picking at her cuticles. It was a stress habit of hers; some days they were all raw and bleeding, strips of skin peeled away.

An owl hooted. I stood up, wincing as my spine protested. "Let's go."

"Thank freaking god," Toni muttered, pulling Iggy to her feet.

We dragged our wet blanket loads, too exhausted to try and lift them again. I'd come out tomorrow morning with a branch broom and get rid of the deep grooves we'd made in the dead leaves.

Once through the back door, I grabbed the flashlight and jammed the plank of wood we used as a lock against the doorknob. We dumped our burdens in the foyer and stepped into the kitchen. It looked just like all the other rooms in the house. Holes in the wall, bundles of capped wires and pipes where electrical and plumbing would have gone. Sheetrock and taping on the walls awaiting paint and tiles. Wood floors, linoleum, and carpeting laid; we'd removed the protective plastic covering from most of it.

Now that we were standing still, the cold set in. We spread the moving blankets out, hoping they'd dry a little bit. Toni and Iggy handed around whatever clothing they'd managed to steal. Pretty soon we were wearing oversized sweatshirts with athletic logos on them. I could still feel the damp move through my bones, taking up residence in my knuckles and knees, and we were all shivering uncontrollably.

"Let's get to bed," I said, setting my teeth to keep from biting my tongue in half. "We'll sort through everything in the morning."

Two rooms besides this one were downstairs. The big space Shadow and I slept in, bundled together on the carpeted floor, and a much smaller walled-off area where we stored food.

On the second level Iggy and Toni each had a room, but they usually cuddled up together. It was warmer up there under the roof, but I liked to sleep near the door so I could keep guard, and often I woke to find that Shadow had gone. She had trouble sleeping, so she'd roam the woods. Sometimes when I went to fill the buckets, I'd find her crouched on the rocks by the creek. I'd sit with her for a while in case it was one of the rare occasions when she wanted to talk. We'd been travelling together, surviving together, for almost two years now and I'd had to assemble all the pieces of her story from small details she'd let slip, questions she'd answered with more than a yes or no. There hadn't been many.

She'd mentioned her mother a couple of times and not in the best way. Her father, less than that. I figured that meant he was dead or had taken off. And she hadn't been in the system like me. After fifteen years with a seemingly unending series of foster parents who'd never kept me more than a few months, I'd aged out and been shipped off to a group home, one step away from being booted onto the street. There was this grey area between sixteen and nineteen when they didn't really know what to do with you. You weren't an adoptable kid but you weren't an adult either. I'd had the choice to stick with all the drama of the home, the constant fighting and the stealing, or leave and look after myself. I chose the latter.

Shadow was still seventeen but only a couple of months younger than me. I knew she'd dropped out of school, ended up on the streets. Other than that, I'd only had my imagination and her nightmares to help me fill in the gaps. Scary thing was, there was no end to the shit I could come up with. We all had our sad tales.

She was already in our corner, half-covered by a mound of blankets. Iggy trotted past me, licking stickiness from around her mouth.

"Don't eat all the cupcakes," I said.

"Hey, where's that cool leather jacket I snagged?"

"It's here somewhere," I said. "Worry about it tomorrow."

Toni appeared. I gestured to their blankets. "Time to crash. Take them up with you."

"Aye, aye, Mommy Dearest."

"Get!" I said, ignoring their giggles as they ran up the stairs.

I grabbed the sweatshirt I used as a pillow and rolled it up. Man, I missed pillows! Every morning I woke with my neck corkscrewed.

Shadow was already lying down, face towards the wall.

"Shadow? Are you sleeping?" I asked, slipping under the covers. Usually I kept my boots on—you never knew when you'd have to run—but tonight I'd eased them off, swearing at my stiff socks and the cheesy smell rising from them. I never noticed Shadow or the others smelling rank, so hopefully she wouldn't notice either. Her cold hand crept towards mine and I gripped it and brought it close to my heart. "What is it?"

"I just...those people remind me of my past. Stuff I don't want to think about."

"So don't. They've got nothing to do with our lives."

We huddled together for warmth, watching the rain fall in blurry sheets outside the plastic-hung front window.

Shadow's voice came quietly. "What if we set something in motion? They see us now."

"They won't come here. We're from two different worlds. Today they overlapped a little, but tomorrow they won't even remember we were there."

"What if...what we did gives them a reason?"

I felt my breath catch and I peered at her in alarm. I'd been careful not to draw attention to myself, but Toni and Iggy went crazy sometimes. I replayed the night.

"It was nuts in that house. They're not going to bother with us. Those high school kids were up to all kinds of mayhem. Probably someone had to have their stomach pumped," I said, trying to ease the fear in her voice. "That's why the ambulance showed up." I sweetened my tone. "They'll never find us here. We're safe."

And if we have to, we will run. All the way to ends of the earth.

Slowly she relaxed against me but her heart went on pounding for a long time. I could feel it under my palm, pulsing like a terrified mouse. When she finally fell asleep,

I watched her face in the light of the lantern I'd placed on the floor by our bed. I saw her eyelids spasm and her mouth twist through one of her bad dreams. All I could do was warm her with my body.

I remembered those thick pieces of lumber we'd been forced to leave and wondered when it would be safe to retrieve them. If I could, I'd build a fortress around us to keep the outside world out.

As it happened, it would be a while before we could return to that house.

MARTIN

Blood thudding in my head. A pain in my chest that sent cramping tendrils to my fingers. I couldn't process what I was looking at.

I kept waiting for Mal to leap up, pull the prosthetic from his face, laugh at my fear. But he stayed where he was, and there was no sign he was breathing. My body transformed to a lump of stone. Sounds came from a great distance, muddied and meaningless. Then Frankie's voice cut through the fog.

"Send an ambulance! And the police," she yelled into her phone. "The big showroom house outside town. Heartbreak Homes. What? No, I mean Heartwood." She continued with her name and age, her voice rising. Then, "He's not moving. And she won't wake up!"

I dragged my gaze away from Mal's face and focused on Frankie. She was back on the floor, cradling Jessa's limp form in her arms. Her phone lay by her side. I could hear a garbled woman's voice coming from the speaker. "I'm here," Frankie said, her fingers wrapped around Jessa's wrist. "I can't feel a pulse. I don't know what I'm doing. I forget how to do it!"

"Jessa! Is she...?" My feet felt nailed to the floor.

"She's breathing." Frankie was so pale her freckles stood out in stark relief. "Come on, come on, come on." She kept repeating it like a prayer. The 911 operator spoke: "Stay calm. The paramedics will be there in just a few minutes." Frankie turned her head to the right as if she were listening. A gust of crisp air and rain blew in from the open window, making me shiver and finally breaking the awful spell that had kept me immobile.

My hand reached out towards the sheets tumbled on the bed. I needed to cover Mal up. *He must be cold. He's just sleeping.*

"Don't touch anything!" Frankie yelled.

I pulled my hand back like it had been scalded and tried to gather my thoughts. Sounds from the party wafted upstairs. It seemed incomprehensible to me that people could still be celebrating. That they had no idea. I pushed the door closed and it felt like I was sealing us in a tomb.

"Where are they?" Frankie gestured towards her phone. "Ask how much longer."

I crouched down next to her. Jessa's eyelids flickered and I felt a rush of relief. "How soon?" I said into the phone after I'd identified myself too. "They're almost here," I relayed to Frankie.

Almost immediately, I heard the sirens. And then a roar of voices swelled from downstairs. I could imagine the frantic exodus as drunk teenagers stumbled to find their keys, their rides, their footing, and realized too late that the cops were here. None of them knew that this was something more serious than breaking and entering, underage drinking, and some recreational drug use.

Footsteps pounded up the stairs. A female voice said, "Get the tents up around the perimeter. This rain isn't doing us any favours. You three, wrangle those kids downstairs. Let's try to contain this. No one leaves." Four paramedics came in first, followed by a tall woman wearing blue pants and a floral blouse. She directed two of the paramedics towards the bed and the other two in our direction. Her strong-featured face melted as soon as she saw Frankie.

"Casey," said Frankie on a wavering exhalation, her mouth caving in. "I tried to wake her up. I'm sorry."

"Hush, Frankie, let me have a look."

It clicked all of a sudden in my brain. This officer was Jessa's mother. Not just a cop but the chief of police.

Casey crouched down and pressed two fingers to her daughter's neck. Her stricken expression didn't vanish but her face lost its mask-like rigidity. For a moment she stayed there, smoothing Jessa's hair away from her face. "Let's get out of the way of the paramedics," she said, drawing Frankie to her feet. "She's unconscious, but breathing. Do you know if she drank, if she took anything?"

"Just a beer. Why won't she wake up?"

"They'll stabilize her and get her to the hospital," she said. "They can run tests." Her voice was calm but her eyes betrayed her concern. "And how about you?" she continued. "Are you hurt?"

"I'm fine," Frankie said. "I'm good." Her voice caught on a sob.

Casey drew her in close for a hug and squeezed her hands before turning to me. "And you're Martin Weber?"

"Yes, ma'am." I noticed a small muscle jumping along her jawline.

"I'm Captain Dawson. Both of you need to go downstairs with Sergeant Whalen and answer a few questions. Give me a minute." She nodded at a tall, grim-looking cop with a salt-and-pepper crewcut who had appeared in the doorway. He took out a small notebook. "See if you can recruit some help from Campbellton and Dempsey Hollow PD," she said to him. "We've got to get everyone ID'ed immediately. Make sure the scene is as undisturbed as possible—although it might be too late for that."

"I'll liaise with Alvarez. He's SOCO-trained," Whalen said, jotting down notes.

Casey nodded. "Good. It'll take a day or two to get IDENT in from Burnley PD but get that started okay? Put a call in."

I knew from watching crime TV that they were calling for crime scene officers. Those people in white hazmat suits and masks. *Oh my god, this is an actual crime scene.* Not exactly the thrill ride I had envisioned.

"Will do, Chief."

"I'll make the big call," she said, her gaze sliding over to the bed. "Although it will be best to do it in person."

Turning her attention back to us, she continued in a softer voice. "Frankie, I promise it will all be fine but I need you both to go downstairs now. Officer Whalen will look after you."

Frankie seemed like she was about to protest, but before she could say a word, Whalen guided us firmly towards the door. "She'll be all right," I said to her as she cast one look back at Jessa. She frowned ferociously at me, eyes glittering with unshed tears, and I felt my throat tighten. I knew it was false comfort, but it was all I had.

Downstairs were more police officers and it was clear that the news had spread already. People were huddled in small pockets, many of them crying. I saw Drew, a cop's heavy hand holding him down in his seat. He caught sight of me and his face suffused with rage. Simon crouched against the wall staring dead ahead; Missy leaned against his shoulder, tears dripping down her face. And close by was Suzie, sitting with Anabel. Anabel was weeping but Suzie, dishevelled hair and bare arms tightly folded, looked like she'd shut down, her cheeks pale and lips pressed together. I wondered if she was in shock.

It was far colder in the room now. Wind gusted in from the open doors, and outside rain fell heavily. All that frenetic energy had dissipated and an uneasiness now thickened the air. Most people seemed dazed, as if they'd been clocked with a two-by-four. Snatches of conversation buzzed in my ears. I heard Mal's name coming from every corner of the room, a whisper that grew. A guy I recognized from a long-ago chemistry class grabbed my arm. "Is it true? Is it Mal? Is he dead?" He might as well have been speaking Russian. I couldn't make my mouth answer him. Shaking my head, I pulled free and followed the police officer's wide back.

"Come over here," Sergeant Whalen said. His face was impossible to read. I felt my stomach plummet, all the beers and sour cream and onion chips sloshing around in an unpleasant way.

Frankie and I sat on the floor. I could smell vomit. I really hoped I wasn't sitting in it.

"I'll need your IDs," Whalen said. His voice was brisk and unemotional, his eyes skipping all around the room like he was memorizing people's faces and filing them away.

I had no trouble imagining him playing bad cop in an interrogation room. Clumsily, I dug out my wallet, dropping my license and a bunch of other cards. Library. Pizza Palace VIP. An expired Splashworld summer pass. Whalen tapped his foot as I hastened to gather them up with fingers that were suddenly trembling. The man had the death stare nailed.

After Whalen had finished inputting the information in his notebook, he handed back our IDs.

"Can I call my grandparents?" Frankie asked. "To tell them what's happened?"

"Let them know you're okay. As witnesses, you'll have to come down to the station right away. You can call again from there and have them meet you once we're finished with our questions. Since you're both eighteen, they're not required to be present."

Whalen frowned in my direction. I felt like he could smell the alcohol oozing out of my pores. "Anyone you want to contact?"

Dad struggled with insomnia but I was pretty sure I'd be waking him up. He'd probably leap into action and that was the last thing I wanted. I pictured his slovenly appearance and although I was ashamed of my feelings, I said, "I'll call him when we get to the station."

I half-listened as Frankie stumbled through an uncomfortable conversation with her grandfather, whose furious tone was evident even if his words were not.

Belligerent voices rose from the corner. Drew was on his feet, chest inflated, shouting about his rights. Whalen muttered a curse and stalked over to help the other officers calm him down.

"What the hell happened up there?" I asked Frankie under my breath, one eye on Whalen.

She shook her head. "I don't know. Who would kill Mal, or hurt Jessa?! It had to be an intruder or..."

I finished her sentence. "Someone at the party?"

We stared at each other while those words sank in. I leaned back against the wall, needing the support. A few hours ago, I'd been thinking how isolated I'd been from everyone and their drama. Now I was right in the middle of it.

FRANKIE

As soon as we arrived at the station, Sergeant Whalen escorted me and Martin into individual rooms to give our official witness statements. When we were done, he led me to a hard bench in a drafty hallway. A clock on the wall ticked loudly. It was 4:05 in the morning and it felt like years had crept by.

"Wait here," he said, "while I talk to my associate. You can go ahead and call your guardians. We may well have further questions before you can leave and you may wish to have them present for support." He hesitated, his craggy face relaxing somewhat. "I'll send a female officer out to show you the facilities. And I'm sure we can rustle up some food and drink for you."

Forty minutes passed before my grandparents arrived. Time I'd spent agonizing over Jessa and wondering where Martin was. Were they still interviewing him? I'd scrolled through my phone but all the chatter on social media had just amped my anxiety up to an unbearable level. A young uniformed officer with a shiny black ponytail had shown me the water fountain and the bathroom, and given me some coffee and a packet of crumbly cookies I couldn't bring myself to eat, but otherwise I'd been on my own.

"Frances," my grandmother said, making me jump. She was wearing a scarf over her tightly braided hair, a coat, and a faded cotton shirt with the buttons done up the wrong way. My grandfather was in his work clothes, faded and smelling faintly of grease and oil. Even though he complained about the lack of business, he still spent every day down at his appliance repair shop.

They looked like they had fossilized over the last eight hours, hair greyer, wrinkles more pronounced. When I was about nine, I flirted with calling them Pop Pop and Grannie until Jessa told me not to bother. "This isn't Green Gables," she'd said. "No hearts of gold."

"You'd think that girl's mother would take the time to speak directly with us since she's in charge of all this," my grandfather fumed as if he'd been mortally insulted. I bit my tongue against the heated retort that rose to my lips. I knew the last time—probably the only time—he'd been in a police station was after he'd gotten the call about the car accident that killed my adolescent parents. He'd had to identify them.

"I'm sure Casey's still at the scene and Josh had to figure out what to do with the twins before heading over to the hospital," I said. Jessa's brothers were only eight years old.

My grandfather swung his slack-jowled head in my direction, his mouth a downturned horseshoe with all the luck running out. "Perhaps if Captain Dawson had paid more attention to her mothering duties, we wouldn't be here now."

I felt my temper rise. "That's exactly what she's doing. Trying to help Jessa." My voice cracked on Jessa's name and I tightened the grip on my fingers. I wouldn't cry in front of him.

It felt like a cinderblock was balanced on my chest.

I looked down at my hands and saw Jessa's: nails painted teal, cold to the touch; felt the soft yielding weight of her body against mine, her head strangely heavy for her neck. I needed to see her and hear her before I'd believe she was going to be all right. My brain pelted me with thoughts.

Has she regained consciousness? What about that wound on her forehead? What the hell happened in that room?

The memory of Mal's ruined face haunted me every time I closed my eyes.

Did someone try to kill her too or was she just in the wrong place at the wrong time? Who hated Mal that much? Did it have anything to do with the fight? Was it someone with an axe to grind?

I kept circling around the one thought I didn't want to have. *Could Martin have done this?* I knew he was holding a lot of anger, and he'd been there in the hallway when it happened, but was he capable of that kind of violence?

I was jarred out of my downward trajectory by a deep voice.

"Mr. and Mrs. Robson?" Sergeant Whalen said, returning at last.

"Frances is a Robson. We're Barclays," my grandfather said, widening the chasm between us. I wished desperately that I was with Jessa.

"Apologies," Whalen said abruptly, his eyes examining each of us in turn. I felt my cheeks redden. "You can accompany Frances if you like."

My grandfather grunted assent.

Whalen led us farther down the hall. "I'm sorry this is taking so long but our small force is a little stretched getting all these statements down. I have a few more questions." He gestured us past a couple of closed doors down a long hallway. "We'll need Frances to be available throughout the investigation. She's a key witness."

"Frankie," I said. Frances was the person my grandparents had hoped I would be. Not the person I was.

I felt a sense of impending doom as our footsteps echoed on the linoleum floor. Maybe Martin was being held. We were witnesses, but were we also suspects?

"Right in here," Whalen said, holding a door open. Most of the room was taken up by a wide metal desk and two chairs by the door. It was different from the one I'd been in before. His own office, I guessed, rather than just an interview room. We stood awkwardly until the grandparents sat down. I was unsure what to do with myself.

"Frankie?" The officer moved some file boxes and dragged a third chair from against the wall for me, taking his place on the other side of the desktop piled high with folders. The window sill held a sad wilted plant and a few framed photos. Jarringly, a cute kid with a gap-toothed smile, curly hair, and a wolf-eared headband, and Whalen almost unidentifiable in summer khakis, facial scruff, and a Hawaiian shirt.

"Okay, just a few more questions," he said, slipping on a pair of wire-rimmed glasses and drawing a sheaf of papers towards himself. He thumbed through them and then flipped open his notebook.

"Is that her statement?" my grandfather said.

Sergeant Whalen raised one hand for silence. "Yes," he said finally, rubbing his fingers over his forehead. "I do appreciate your patience."

Beside me, I felt my grandmother relax her posture, only to stiffen up again with the officer's next words: "I'm sure you appreciate the seriousness of this. This *is* officially a murder case." Whalen's eyes behind the thick lenses pinned me to my uncomfortable plastic chair. I moved uneasily and it creaked. He continued, "Malcolm Bradley was killed by a person unknown. He suffered a brain hemorrhage as the result of a deep puncture wound to his left orbital socket. When we arrived at the scene, following the ambulance, it was more a matter of crowd control than anything else. There were upwards of a hundred and seventy youth there. Many underage. Under the influence of alcohol. Drugs. Marijuana, but also pharmaceuticals."

Out of the corner of my eye I saw the ridges on my grandfather's face deepen. "Whose party was it?"

"It was an illegal party hosted by the victim, Malcolm Bradley. His father, the property owner, claims he was not aware of it. There's a lockbox and Malcolm must have discovered the code."

Grandad's shaggy eyebrows reared up like angry caterpillars. My grandmother uttered a squeak of outrage.

"We had to ID everyone there. Establish a means of follow-up communication and make sure every minor had a parent"—he seemed to sense my grandfather's irritation—"or guardian present before further questioning. Which brings us to now." I saw him glance up at the wall clock. It was 5:45 A.M. "From what we can tell, other than Jessa Renaud, only two people had direct contact with the victim close to the time of his death. That's you, Frankie, and Martin Weber." His fingers tapped the page in front of him.

"It's that Jessa or that Weber boy then," my grandfather proclaimed, back rigid, his big swollen fingers tightening and splaying on his knees. "His father's a drunk no-good."

"It wasn't Jessa," I said, leaning forward in my chair. "She was hurt by whoever this was."

Whalen pinched the bridge of his nose. "Jessa Renaud was unconscious at the scene. Bloodwork and tox screens aren't back from the lab yet but we're fairly certain she was drugged."

I inhaled so sharply I almost choked.

Shooting me an incisive look, Whalen continued. "It may take up to six weeks to get the results. We'll have to wait until she regains consciousness to see what she remembers, if anything." His eyes moved from the grandparents' angry glares to my strained expression and his voice lost a bit of its coldness.

"Martin Weber is still being interviewed. Frankie, you are not a suspect presently but I have to ask that you not leave town. We need to gather as much evidence as we can. You might have noticed something important, something that can help us to find out who did this."

"I'll try," I said.

He looked down at my statement. "Why don't we start with what was happening before you went upstairs to find Jessa? Any observations?"

Conscious of my grandparents' tangible disapproval, I said, "I don't know. It was so crowded. People were starting to get crazy. There was a fight."

Whalen flipped to a different page. "Andrew Marshall stated it was a group of young men goofing off. Malcolm, Glen Johnson, Martin Weber, some others." He glanced at me. His stormy eyes had darkened. There was an intense, watchful look about him that made my tongue stick to my teeth.

"I guess." I cast my mind back. "There was something going on with Mal. Him and Martin had a falling out." As soon as the words escaped, I wanted to snatch them back. It felt like a betrayal somehow. Whalen looked up. I couldn't read anything on his face. "Martin said that Mal started it."

"Was anyone specifically targeting Malcolm Bradley during the fight? Someone you might not have recognized?"

I shrugged. "It was a pile-up. You know, jocks. Guys. It got out of hand."

"Anything else? Someone behaving strangely that you might have noticed?"

People had been pretty much off their heads, but that wasn't something I wanted to share in front of my elderly relatives. "There were a lot of kids there who I didn't recognize. From other schools, I guess."

"No adults?"

I shook my head.

"We're talking to students at all the area high schools, but it'll take a few days."

"I took some pictures...of the crowds. People dancing and stuff."

"On your phone? I'll need you to surrender that to us then." He stared at me until I reluctantly nodded my head and handed it over. He bagged it, recorded a number on a ticket, and gave me the stub. "It'll be a few days before you get it back." It was a crap phone but I still felt like I'd lost a limb. He thumbed through some papers. "We're still going through social media. I'll have you sign off on everything in a moment." He made a note on my file. *My file.* It was thicker than I had expected.

My mouth was parched and I wished for some water.

He led me through more of my initial statement. "So after the fight, you sat outside with Martin. How did he seem?"

"Bruised. Roughed up. His lip was bleeding. He offered to drive me home."

My grandfather stiffened.

"I said thanks, but no."

Whalen clicked his pen. "Was he drunk? Under the influence of drugs?"

I shook my head. "No, a few beers I think. He was angry, but mostly..." I tried to find the words for how Martin had appeared to me. "... embarrassed by it all. He regretted coming to the party."

"And why was that? Had he been expecting trouble?"

I thought about what Martin had said. That maybe Mal had been trying to provoke him. Bait him. I shifted again uncomfortably, feeling like every squeal of the chair was broadcasting my reticence. My suspicions were half-baked at best. I chose my words carefully.

"Martin said that he felt ganged up on."

"By Mal Bradley?"

"And Drew, and the guys from the Razorbacks."

"The football team." Whalen scribbled a line. Saying it out loud did point fingers in Martin's direction, but that was impossible. Wasn't it?

Thankfully, he moved on. "And then you went to find Jessa?"

"Yes, I was worried she was going to miss her curfew."

My grandfather rumbled and shook off my grandmother's hand. "*You* should pay more attention to the rules of *my house*. You lied to us about your wheareabouts, you attended an illegal party with underage drinking, you—"

"Albert," my grandmother said. "Calm yourself."

"I'm eighteen," I said.

"And living under *my* roof." That was the trump card my grandfather always played when we had a disagreement. It made me want to go live under a bridge.

Whalen cleared his throat noisily. "Perhaps we can return to the matter at hand." My grandfather subsided but I could see the tension in his hands, knuckles lumpy as walnuts showing white under chapped skin

"Okay, so you're upstairs, Frankie," Whalen continued. "Did you meet anyone else going up or coming down?"

"No. And the hallway was empty."

"And upstairs? Was anyone in any of those other rooms?"

I tried to remember. During the night I'd wandered all over the house. There was that person standing in the darkness in the floral bedroom—but no, that had been earlier. Later it had been the snoring guy I'd taken to be Drew. And in the other bedroom, the girl who'd told me to fuck off. I relayed all this to Whalen, editing the curse words out for the grandparents' benefit.

"How long were you at the door of the master suite before Martin arrived?"

"A minute or so. I was knocking and yelling."

"Did you see him come up the stairs? Could he have been concealed elsewhere on the second floor?"

Once again I felt my stomach twist. Was he suggesting that Martin had something to do with it? Had they found evidence? His DNA? He'd had blood on him—was it possible that it wasn't all his?

"No. He was just there. But the door was locked. I am positive."

"And Martin's the one who forced the door?"

"Yes."

"And then?"

I told him how'd we'd gone in and I'd found Jessa on the floor unconscious and tried to revive her and then—"Martin called me over to the bed, and that's when we saw Malcolm."

"Did you touch him? Did Martin?"

"No!" The word shot out of my mouth. "I didn't. I don't think Martin did either. I stayed far away from the bed."

"Anything come to mind? Something unusual you might have noticed?"

I closed my eyes, thinking it might help me visualize the scene. I could smell the sickly scent of jasmine again, but all I could picture was Jessa, unconscious on the floor, blood trickling from the wound on her forehead. *Did she fall? Was she pushed?* I felt my throat tighten and gulped for air. My grandmother wordlessly handed me a bottle of water from her capacious handbag. "I don't think so," I said, embarrassed that I'd been less than observant.

"We've already had multiple reports of stolen items from the scene," Whalen continued. "Clothing, purses, that sort of thing. Do you know anything about that?"

I shook my head. "No." Could that be it? Someone tried to rob Mal and he fought back? I thought about the chunky gold Rolex he always wore. Had it still been on his wrist? I couldn't remember.

"Well, that's it then," my grandfather said, sounding like he'd cracked the case. "A robbery gone wrong. Did the boy have his wallet on him?"

"We're pursuing the lead, Mr. Barclay," Whalen replied in a tone that suggested he repeated that phrase often. "Give me a few minutes to review everything." We watched him shuffle paper. My grandfather checked his watch repetitively, and even theatrically held it to his ear to make sure it was still ticking.

Whalen's face was still relaxed. I risked another question.

"Have you found the weapon?" I asked, swallowing hard.

"I can't disclose that information to you, but with a homicide like this—most likely unplanned—there is always evidence."

Something clicked. My memory took me back to the room. That awful hole in Mal's face. The broken side table. Jessa. Candle flames leaping. The cold breeze ruffling the curtains.

"The window was open when we came in," I remembered, fighting against the tightness in my chest. "The killer, they must have got out that way."

He held my gaze as he added this to my statement and then pushed a sheaf of pages across the desk to me. "Can you look these over and sign at the bottom if it's accurate, please?"

My grandfather leaned in, reading over my shoulder. His breath, smelling of bitter coffee, made me feel sick.

"What happens now?" I asked.

"We investigate. Exhaust all possibilities." Whalen stood up, pointing to the business card on the desk in front of me. "My direct line. You think of anything else, you call me." He switched his attention to the grandparents, who had risen to their feet. My grandmother held her purse to her chest like a barricade but they both reluctantly shook his hand.

"Thank you for your time, Mr. and Mrs. Barclay. I'll be in touch, Frankie, once we've had a chance to review the material on your phone."

I tried to remember what I had photographed. My cheeks flamed. He'd find a lot of photos of girls I thought were fascinating or cute. Some extreme close-ups of Lorelei and her kissable mouth. And quite a few of Jessa and Mal. I thought again of Suzie implying I was in love with Jessa. Did other people believe that? Did it make me a suspect?

I glanced quickly at Whalen on the off chance I could read him but he'd returned to his chair and was writing furiously.

I followed my grandfather's long strides through the station, hoping to see Casey as he hurried us along. My grandmother almost had to break into a jog to keep up. I could guess what was roiling through his mind. This was literally all their worst nightmares come true. If a couple of girls ended up pregnant, it would be the trifecta. I needed an update and now I'd have to wait to use the landline to find out how Jessa was doing. We made our way swiftly toward the exit and I tried to prepare myself for the barn-burning sermon awaiting me.

"Frankie!" a voice came from the right. Martin sat on the bench I'd occupied earlier.

I started walking over to him but before I'd taken more than a couple of steps, my grandfather took me by the arm and pushed me behind him.

"She's got nothing to say to you."

"Haven't you done enough?" my grandmother added in a furious whisper.

Martin looked startled. "Are you okay, Frankie?"

I nodded over my shoulder as my grandfather marched me double-time out the door.

CARA

We had to hole up. Police were crawling over the hillside like beetles. So far, they hadn't made it all the way over here. My hope was that the heavy overnight rains had washed away any trace of us.

As soon as the sun came up, I was on my belly in the gluey mud, high up on a little ridge that gave me a 180-degree view of everything below. Although I'd kept my fears to myself, I knew that amount of police activity meant something serious had gone down. I could see the party house, the cleared ground surrounding it, the dirt road. A large area was taped off and tents erected. After a few hours of squinting, trying to figure out what the hunched-over figures in their reflective yellow raingear were looking for and what they had discovered, I found myself wishing for a pair of binoculars.

By day's end there were more cops. How far would they look? And what would they do if they found us? In my experience, the cops never cared that much about the homeless unless we were bothering other people. Mostly they told us to move on. And we did, setting up around another corner until the next pair of them forced us to leave.

But this was different.

Thieving was one thing; murder was another.

Two days after the party, Iggy had come back from a quick run into town to grab some gas station coffee. When I saw her, all hyped up and sweaty, I went off on her. I'd made it clear that we should stay put, drawing no unnecessary attention to ourselves until things quieted down, and she'd gone and snuck out. But I forgot all of that with the next words that came out of her mouth.

"Turns out some kid was murdered," she said, waving a newspaper in my face. "In the fancy house." She and Toni seemed more thrilled about it than anything else, but I got that sour feeling in my stomach that meant our luck had changed. Winter was coming and the burden of having to find someplace else to live, somewhere safe, scared the hell out of me. I'd relaxed into our little home. That was the problem. I'd let my guard down.

I peeled the front page out of Iggy's hand, sat down on the staircase to read the story, and felt the queasiness change to a lump of ice. It was dated yesterday, the day after the party. Below a headline that blared MURDER PROBE AFTER STAR ATHLETE FOUND DEAD, I read that an eighteen-year-old had been stabbed with an undisclosed weapon and died at the scene. A second victim was in hospital recovering. There were no suspects in custody yet. The murder victim's father, a prominent businessman and owner of the property, was demanding swift justice. I studied the yearbook photo they'd reprinted, the description of the boy. Shadow hovered, reading over my shoulder.

"What was the name of the guy who was killed?" Toni asked.

I scanned down. "Emerson...no...Malcolm Bradley," I said. "His friends called him Mal."

"Bradley," Shadow repeated. I shot her a look.

Iggy danced around, making stabbing motions with her hand along with the *ee-ee-ee* sound from *Psycho*. Shadow chewed her lip.

"Did any of you see him at the house?" I asked, keeping my tone light but watching Shadow. It was easy to tell this boy had come from a good family. He was rich. White. The police wouldn't sleep until they found out who had done this.

"Nah, they all look the same to me," Toni said. "You know, boys." Iggy guffawed.

Shadow glanced up briefly. "I'm going to get some water from the creek," she said.

"I already filled the buckets earlier," I called after her. Her response was the door slamming.

My eyes went to the last line again and I read it aloud. "'The Lincoln Police Department is asking that any persons who were present and have yet to be interviewed come forward.'" I felt a wave of panic. Tick Tock had been right about that warning shiver on the back of my neck: trouble was heading our way. I thought furiously. I couldn't let myself jump too far ahead—leaving Lincoln, hitting the road—but there were smaller steps I could take immediately. Steps to protect us.

Two minutes after I finished reading, I was on my feet. "Pack it up," I yelled. "Everything we took from that party."

If the cops did make it out this far, at least there'd be nothing to tie us to the scene of the crime.

Toni and Iggy immediately started complaining. I ignored the noise and kept barking instructions. Dealing with the two of them sometimes felt like banging my head against a wall, but I'd learned that as long as I refused to back down, eventually they'd bend. Sure enough, after some hard looks, under-the-breath bitching, and foot-dragging, they started making bundles of the smaller items.

"Not the food or the booze, right?" Iggy asked. I ran through the inventory quickly. If the police showed up here, what could they pin on us? Squatting for sure. Robbery. But there was no way to prove where a bunch of cupcakes came from. Or a couple bottles of hard liquor.

"The other stuff we were going to try and sell," I said. "Those metal ashtrays. The vases and clocks. And the bed-side lamp you took, Toni." I wasn't even sure why she'd snagged that. It was pink and frilly and we didn't have an electric hookup. When I'd asked, she'd said it reminded her of the one she'd had before she left home.

"We hauled all this crap here and now we gotta haul it out again?" said Toni.

"Where are we taking it?" asked Iggy, twisting her bangs up out of her eyes.

"We're going to stash it in the old well." It was set back in the trees. A mostly dry hole about ten feet deep with crumbling brick walls full of hand and toe holds. "Take only what we need."

"Shit," grumbled Toni. "It smells like rotten potatoes in there." She caressed the beaded tassels on her lamp.

"Only till all this hoopla dies down," I said. "Did Shadow come back?" She was like that. Disappearing. Reappearing.

They both shrugged. I felt a sting of fear. We all knew so little about Shadow's past; I worried this murder had brought some unknown trauma bubbling to the surface. I couldn't go down that rabbit hole yet. I needed time and space to think.

"Where will we sleep?" Iggy asked.

I steeled myself for the kickback I knew was coming but got the words out anyway.

"For the next couple of nights, we sleep outside. Near the treeline."

"We'll freeze!" Toni said.

"It's only until we see what's up. Shadow and I roughed it for months," I reminded them. "We've got those new blankets. Our sleeping bags. It's great sleeping under the stars."

They exchanged disbelieving looks. I felt my temper rise. Shadow and I had endured one winter by scrounging for cardboard boxes and bubble wrap and crashing under overpasses and bridges. They had no idea how easy they'd had it.

"Just do it!" Striving for patience I added, "It's only October." And then before they could get a word in, "Make sure there's nothing you want to keep in your room. Clear it out in case the cops bust down the door." I was hoping that if the cops did find this place, they'd think we'd left town.

Toni and Iggy exchanged looks.

"We're coming back though, right? This is our home," Toni said, stroking the drywall.

Lie or truth? It broke my heart, but I said, "Maybe not." For once Toni didn't zing me back with some smart comment.

She blinked at me, and then a quiver started in the corner of her mouth.

"Hey," I said, reaching out for her. "Maersk Crew for life, right?"

Iggy drew her close and Toni buried her face in Iggy's shoulder.

I mouthed, *You okay?*

Iggy glared at me. For a second she looked a lot older than seventeen. "We're tired of running all the time."

I didn't voice it, but I felt her words in every bone of my body. And it took everything I had to resist that wave of desperation.

The only cure I'd ever known for feeling helpless was moving my legs and finding one small thing I could control.

I went into the kitchen to check out our food situation. I couldn't help but remember the first time I'd lost my chosen family and the roof over my head.

Tick Tock and I had met at a punk-house party, though once I'd started sleeping there on a flea-infested couch, I realized there was always a party happening. At first it had felt exciting and free, like I'd found my tribe and we were rebels delivering a big middle finger to the normal, boring world and all the messed-up adults who lived in it. But the art and music started happening less and the faces grew unfamiliar as the parties got wilder, alcohol traded in for the mind-numbing obliteration of heroin. Tick Tock got arrested in a big police raid and I hit the road alone, until I found Shadow and the others. I hadn't heard word of him since, and often wondered if he was still locked up, and whether we'd ever cross paths again.

I looked around at the solid walls of our house, the barricades we'd put up to keep us safe, all the precautions we'd taken, and felt a sob begin to worm its way up my throat. I forced it down. If everything turned out the way I hoped, we'd move back in a couple of days.

Biting my cheek, I shook out a garbage bag and started sorting through what was left of the food and drink. A dozen packages of chips and cookies, a six-pack of beer and one of soda, ramen noodles and cans of beans, and a few bottles of hard liquor. I put the heavy stuff in a milk crate, balanced the bag of food on top, and heaved it over to the open back door.

Toni and Iggy staggered in with their loads. They'd bundled mine and Shadow's clothing and bedding up as well. "Thanks," I said. I could tell they'd both been crying.

"Shadow's outside," Iggy said, her voice thick with snot. "I saw her from the upstairs window."

"Give me a hand getting this through the door. We're almost ready to go." A leaf crunched and I looked up. "Shadow." Her grey eyes were rimmed in black, weariness showing in every line of her face. Was it her usual insomnia, or was there something else going on?

"You okay?"

"Yeah, don't worry about me."

But I did worry. If she was in trouble, I had to do something about it.

"You'd tell me though?" I squeezed her forearm until she looked at me in annoyance.

"Yes." Her eyes drilled into me and I believed her right up until she glanced to her left. Tick Tock had told me about tells. The way to figure out if someone was lying. And Shadow was lying about something.

She flashed me an impatient look. "Where are we going?"

Swallowing my worry, I said, "The woods there on the other side of the creek. Help me with this?"

I hefted some planks of wood and set them against the back door frame. Shadow rooted around in the tool bag and located a hammer and some nails.

I held two boards crosswise against the door and Shadow securely nailed them. It wouldn't keep anyone like us out, but it would stop any animals looking to hibernate for the winter.

From the outside, our beautiful home looked abandoned, unloved.

"You'd think no one would live here, eh?" Iggy said.

"Old dump," Toni said off-handedly, but her voice broke.

I picked up a couple of heavy milk crates and turned to go.

"Wait," Iggy said, tearing a beer off the plastic six-pack ring. She opened it and beer foamed out. "To our house," she said, raising the can high, tossing back a mouthful, and holding it out to Iggy. I put down my load. Iggy drank, and passed it to me.

"To our family. I would do anything for you," I said, before handing the remainder off to Shadow. For a moment she held my eyes with hers, and then she drank.

FRANKIE

I almost didn't grab the phone. The landline was for the grandparents' use exclusively—my grandmother's church group, the men my grandfather went fishing with—and neither of them were home. I was lounging half-asleep on my bed with Bumble curled into my side like a warm, squishy shrimp, taking comfort in her corn chip smell and gentle snoring.

Yesterday, school had stayed closed in light of what had happened and Tuesdays were a late start for me. My first class wasn't until eleven and I'd been flirting with calling in sick anyway. I'd checked out the latest news on my laptop and seen the throngs of reporters milling around the front entrance of Lincoln Academy. They reminded me of gulls waiting to pounce on the baby turtles making their way to the sea. Predators. Right now I couldn't even see the point of school and I knew it would be practically impossible to sit through my classes. The phone's shrill tone broke through my drowsy thoughts and I tripped over my feet as I rushed to answer it.

"Hello," I said breathlessly.

"Frankie, it's Casey. Jessa has been asking for you."

———

I TOOK MY BIKE. IT HAD ONLY THREE GEARS AND THREADBARE tires and was punishingly hard to pedal uphill but it was my only choice.

By the time I reached the hospital, my face was beet-red and my breathing sounded like rusty machinery. I locked my bike up and hurried in. Before I even joined the line in front of the reception desk, I noticed a familiar rumpled head bent over the free-coffee dispenser in the waiting area, sifting through packets of sweetener.

"Josh!"

Jessa's dad looked up and opened his arms wide. Any fear that they might somehow blame me for what happened evaporated. "Frankie. Casey said you were on the way."

"She woke up?" I said, my voice muffled by his shoulder. Josh gave epic hugs and he usually smelled of fresh-baked bread and maple syrup.

"Last night."

"Ohh." My breath came out in a shuddering gasp but I managed to keep a lid on my emotions.

"Let me take you to her."

"How is she?" I asked as I followed him down the hall, my hand engulfed by his.

"She's stable. They've stitched her up. She sprained both wrists, chipped a tooth. It was a pretty violent fall."

I remembered the smashed table. Jessa was shorter than me and maybe weighed a hundred and thirty pounds. If I'd been better at physics I'd have been able to figure out the force involved to achieve that kind of damage.

We arrived at room 214 and Josh paused. "I'll give you some time alone with her, but try not to get her worked up. She's a little shaky emotionally." He softened the words with another quick squeeze. "I'm so glad you're okay, Frankie. Thank you for looking after her."

I teared up. *But I didn't look after her, and now she's here.*

"Can I bring you back a coffee?" Josh said, indicating his cup. "Although I am reluctant to call it that."

I shook my head and he nodded and turned back down the hallway. I stared at the door, took a deep breath, and pushed it open.

My first thought was how small she looked tucked up in that bed. Her head was tilted away from me. I wasn't sure if she'd fallen back asleep.

"Knock knock," I said softly.

Jessa turned over slowly, and the tiny smile she gave me catapulted me to the side of the bed like we were attached by a rubber band. I stroked her arm, trying not to hurt her, and when she pinched the skin above my elbow I wanted to burst into tears. I examined her furtively. Both wrists were bandaged. The cut near her hairline was stitched neatly. Her mouth was swollen and a bruise bloomed on her forehead. But she looked the same fundamentally, only more tired. The most obvious difference was how she was holding herself. Carefully. Like she might break apart.

Her smile widened just a little bit and she patted the area next to her. "Stop staring at me," she said. "It's creeping me out and I'm getting enough of that from the parents."

"How are you, really?" I asked as I arranged myself without bumping her.

"Sore. Achy." She grimaced and I caught sight of her chipped front tooth. "Freaked out. I don't remember any of it. Mom and Dad filled me in a little but it's so awful. Mal. Part of me wishes I hadn't woken up."

"Oh, Jessa, no." I clutched her hands.

"I don't mean I wish I'd died. Just that I was...oblivious. Waking up to find out all this stuff is a lot. Mom didn't want to tell me much but Dad thought I'd imagine worse so she gave in to him." A twinkle appeared briefly in her eyes. "Some of it I overheard when they thought I was asleep."

"Like what?"

"That I was probably drugged."

"Yeah, Officer Whalen said something about that." I remembered how she'd written her name on her cup. "Who, though? You were so careful."

"Maybe I put my drink down somewhere. I don't know what would have happened if you hadn't come looking for me, Frankie." She snuggled in closer to me.

"You're safe now," I said, carefully insinuating an arm around her shoulder.

"When I try and think about it, my brain starts to hurt. But that might just be the head wound talking."

I stroked her shoulder gently. "What's the last thing you remember?"

"Going upstairs with Mal. We were just going to make out." She gave me a hard stare like she was challenging me to criticize her.

I made myself shrug. "You liked him."

Her face cleared. "I did. I really did."

We were both silent for a breath. "Why would someone kill him?" she asked, her voice raw.

I sighed. "I don't know."

Her fingers tightened around mine. There was something she wasn't telling me. I could see the fear in her dilated pupils.

"What is it, Jessa?"

"I'm scared, Frankie."

She looked around the room, then whispered in my ear. "What if they tried to kill me too? What if the only reason they didn't is because you interrupted them?"

MARTIN

The week passed in a blur of online memorials, editorials, and nightmares that woke me up gasping. It was weird. I could go half a day without thinking about Mal and then I'd be tying my shoelace or ringing up a sale and out of nowhere, I'd remember. *The room. The bed. His face.* And it would shock me every time.

Why would anyone do that to him?

The case was ongoing, but from what I could tell nothing new had materialized. The police had warned me not to leave town. I was a *person of interest*. A term that made me want to run as far as possible. The newspapers had already pushed the story onto the second page, despite everything Mal's dad, Emerson Bradley, had to say about it. And he had had plenty, firing off online threats to the editor that ripped a new hole in everyone from the mayor to the county police chief to his prime target, Captain Casey Dawson. She'd interviewed me three times down at the station in the last few days but I hadn't been able to add anything more to what I'd told Officer Alvarez. I'd racked my brain but I just couldn't figure it out. Where was the motive?

The rumour mill was running wild. I'd heard plenty of whispers in the hallways at Crestview. That it was a contract killing. A gang hit. A transient psychopath with an ice pick who escaped through a secret tunnel. All ludicrous, but still...I wondered.

Was it random? Premeditated? Was it a warning to someone else? Emerson Bradley, for instance? Surely he had enemies? And what about Jessa? Had she been a target too, or just an unfortunate bystander?

Call me naïve, but when Drew showed up at the Quik Stop on Sunday morning I had some vague hope we'd be able to hash things out, get back to being cool with each other and maybe figure out who had killed our friend. Things were slow in the early hours, when the only people who came through were buying a pack of cigarettes or gum or asking for spare change. I'd been reminiscing about the distant past—the days when the four of us had been a solid crew— and feeling all nostalgic.

I raised a hand in greeting and stepped outside the kiosk ready for a rueful grin and maybe a manly hug. That is until I caught a glimpse of the three Razorbacks in Drew's car and Drew's thunderous expression as he bore down on me. Before I knew it, he had me pressed up against the window, the full weight of his brawny forearm across my neck. When had he gotten so jacked? I remembered a rumour from a year back that some of the athletes at Lincoln were messing with steroids. Was that why he'd been so out of control recently? His alcohol-sodden breath hit me in a warm wave, his bloodshot eyes like puffy slits. He looked like he'd been up all night drinking. I attempted to push him off but he'd settled into it, locking his knees. I was nothing more than a blocking sled to him.

"Drew, what the fuck?" I managed to gasp. He relaxed his elbow a little. His face was red, veins poking out like twisted worms and he was breathing harder than I was. "Drew, listen to me—"

He shook his head violently, pushed down a little harder. A groan wheezed from my chest. "Why couldn't you just stay gone?" he said in a hoarse whisper. "None of this would have happened if it wasn't for you starting shit."

"C'mon man, let me go." I tried to twist away from under him but he leaned in even more. White dots danced in front of my eyes. I got one arm loose, and with everything I had, I hammered a close-fisted blow at his head. He backed off and I slithered out and ran to the kiosk door. If I could get inside I could throw the lock, and either wait them out or call the cops.

My fingers had just caught hold of the door handle when I was dragged backwards by my shirt. I gasped like a landed fish. Eyes watering, I heard a ripping noise as my collar tore loose. I managed one gulp of air before I was shoved to the ground. I tried to crawl to the wall but the other three guys were out of the car now. A volley of boots and fists struck my stomach and chest, shooting paralyzing arrows through my body. I twisted myself into a knot, hopelessly trying to protect my groin, until the pain became one big numbness and my vision tunnelled to black.

WHEN I OPENED MY EYES NEXT, ONLY ONE SEEMED TO BE focusing. I was lying on my side covered by scratchy sheets that smelled medicinal. Bright light streamed in through the window, and close by machines beeped steadily. I moved an arm to shield myself from the glare and realized that the left one was in a sling. Feeling like I might come apart, I rolled carefully over onto my back. The bed next to me was empty. A TV with the sound turned down played a talk show. A clatter surprised me and I craned my neck so I could see who was in the room.

The door had swung open and a short man in green scrubs wheeled in a cart. His hair was red, as was his carefully clipped goatee. He came around the side of the bed and I read his badge: *Erroll Moseley*.

"Good to see you awake, Martin," he said, putting a tray down on my bedside table. Toast, yogurt, orange juice. I worked my jaw. My teeth felt loose and my lip was split again. I could imagine how much that citrus would sting.

I tried to speak but my throat was bone-dry. As if he could read my mind, the nurse raised my bed, helped me to sit up, and poured me a glass of water. He popped a straw in and held it to my mouth. I leaned forward. Pain tore through my chest.

"Easy there, you've got two broken ribs," he said in response to my screech. "Some damage to your left eye but the retina's okay. It'll take some time to heal. You're looking at three weeks, all told." Whistling under his breath, he took my blood pressure and then applied a thermometer to my forehead.

Once he was done, I put my hand up and felt a bandage. I licked my lips and tried again to speak. This time a few words came out in a shredded whisper: "Anything else?" How the hell was I going to work? I could barely lie down.

"Bruises, contusions, mostly around your torso and neck. Might be painful to talk for a few days. Your shoulder is sprained; that's why it's in a sling. Doctor will be in to brief you on aftercare but you can go home tomorrow, probably early evening." He pointed to the call button by my bed. "I'm Erroll and I'm on all day."

I struggled to speak again. "How'd I get here?"

"Cops brought you in. Passing car saw what was going on. You're lucky. A lot of people don't like to get involved."

I winced. "And those other guys? The ones who jumped me?"

He shrugged. "I guess they took off. Who were they?"

"Used to be friends of mine."

Why did Drew attack me? What is he blaming me for?

He gave me a sad smile. "There was a police officer here earlier." He glanced at my chart. "Sergeant Alvarez. He'll return later for your statement."

I lay back. Great. I'd have to ID them all. I wondered if the police would consider witness protection. Relocate me to another town, give me a new name. It could be the solution to all my problems: LOCAL TEEN VANISHES. NO ONE NOTICES.

Another nurse, brown-skinned with tight curls, pushed the door open. "Martin," she said, "you have a visitor."

My dad looked worse than I felt, the bags under his eyes purpled and puffier than usual. His hands fidgeted in his jacket pockets like he was juggling marbles. When was the last time I'd really looked at him? Mostly we passed each other on our way to and from the bathroom. Every month he'd take a conference call with upper management but other than that he stayed in his bedroom office, working up spreadsheets and reports for investors here and abroad. *A glorified accountant*, he called himself.

I felt an acute twinge of embarassment. Couldn't he have combed his hair, put on a tie? How was he ever going to dig himself out of his hole if he didn't even try?

"Dad, I would have called," I croaked. "You didn't have to come down."

He stood silent in the doorway. Erroll made a couple of notes on the clipboard hanging off the end of my bed, saluted us, and pushed his cart out of the room, whistling as he went.

"How'd you find out?" I pressed him.

"Charlie Swanson called. The cops contacted him. Said you were assaulted." He frowned. "But it wasn't a robbery?"

Ahh. My boss, and owner of the Quik Stop, letting the cat out of the bag.

He advanced, though he seemed reluctant to close the distance. His constant fidgetting was making me antsy. "Did it have anything to do with what happened at the party?" I'd told him there had been a fight that got out of hand but had downplayed my role in it.

"Maybe there's something fundamentally wrong with this town and no one is admitting it," I said at last.

His face furrowed and he rushed forward suddenly. My abdominal muscles seized at the thought of him knocking my ribs, and I held up my hand defensively. We weren't a hugging family. More like a sit-together-and-glower-family.

He stopped short, scratching at the patchy grey-and-black bristle on his cheeks. The sandpaper sound made me wince. I indicated the chair nearby and he sat. I allowed my muscles to relax against my pillows.

"Did you recognize them?" he asked.

"Drew Marshall and a trio of jocks."

He blinked, bewildered. "Drew Marshall?" he said wonderingly. "From baseball camp?" For a year or two before my mother died, my dad had been head coach.

"Yeah, 'Swing-at-em Drew,'" I said, trying to find some humour. Anything to erase that confused, hurt look in his eyes.

"But why? Does he blame you for the fight?"

"I don't know. Maybe. Mal's death is hitting him hard. Drew appears to have lost all reason." I sat up a little, adjusting my pillows and clenching my teeth. I made a mental note to google it but I was pretty sure that irrational rage was a side effect of steroid abuse.

"Have the police taken your statement?"

"Not yet. Someone is coming by later."

"But you'll tell them who it was? Make sure he gets reported?" He worried at his fingers, twisting the wedding ring he'd never taken off. His anxiety was contagious.

"Yeah." *Even though I'll have to dodge him for the rest of my life.* I looked around the bright white room, trying to find something else to observe.

The television on the wall had switched to the news.

Emerson Bradley's face popped up, eyes like black holes and skin off-colour. "Dad," I said, "can you grab the remote?"

It was behind the water pitcher on the bedside table. His knuckles bumped against my water glass, almost tipping it over. I wondered suddenly if he was drunk. I sniffed but he just smelled of old sweat and coffee.

"Turn it up," I said. My dad grumbled under his breath but did as I asked.

The interview must have been taking place at one of Emerson Bradley's new construction sites. Behind him I glimpsed scaffolding, some people in yellow hard hats. Despite the Heartwood project having failed so spectacularly, he was still developing other properties. It seemed as if the stink of failure had not been able to permeate his tailored Italian suits.

"There's a killer loose in our community. The police are wasting time waiting on lab results when they should be hunting this violent animal down. I demand justice. Justice for Malcolm!" His voice was frenzied and he gesticulated spasmodically like he'd lost temporary control of his arms. The reporter interviewing him looked a little freaked out. Mr. Bradley grabbed the microphone from her and moved closer to the camera until his entire face filled the screen. "I'm offering one hundred thousand dollars for any information leading to the arrest of the person or persons responsible for killing my son!" The anger turned to a plea, his eyes welling up with tears. "Someone knows something, saw something! The time to come forward is now!" He burst into harsh sobs. The camera swivelled away as the reporter retrieved her mic, then zoomed in on Bradley's rapidly retreating back.

Grief Haunts Local Businessman, ran the text across the screen, followed by *Funeral scheduled tomorrow at 3:00 P.M. at the Eternal Grace Memorial Chapel.*

I collapsed against my pillows. *Tomorrow afternoon.* And here I was, stuck in the hospital.

A collage of familiar photos followed. Mal with his wrestling team and the championship trophy; Mal in his tux at the Junior Winter Formal with Suzie Jackson, pretty in pink, on his arm. The Heartwood Homes showroom home—first in its glory, then in the aftermath of the party looking like a tornado had hurled it into the stratosphere and then sent it plummeting to Earth. Bottles and trash strewn everywhere, furniture in stained heaps, broken glass and smashed picture frames. In the footage of the exterior, black-and-yellow police tape flapped. *Murder House*, flashed the text underneath.

"That place is poison," my dad said, spitting the words out like they were nails. "A monument to grief and despair."

My eyes skittered with fatigue. I couldn't remember the last time I'd heard so much emotion in his voice.

At some point I must have fallen asleep. I woke later in a haze, tongue glued to my palate, sore from my feet to my teeth. The TV was still on and showing breaking news. I hauled my protesting body upright and turned up the volume. Heartwood Homes was featured again but not because of Mal's murder.

Someone had tried to burn it to the ground.

FRANKIE

Mal's wake was packed. It seemed as if every Lincoln senior was crammed into the funeral home, along with most of their teachers and parents. Like ornate bookends, a contingent of men in dark suits flanked women in plain but costly couture. Emerson Bradley's business colleagues, I guessed. Folding chairs were filled by extended family and those who were important for reasons unknown; the rest of us huddled in groups or leaned against the wall. Organ music droned from speakers. A couple of older women had their noses buried in white handkerchiefs, shoulders quivering.

Snatches of conversation reached my ears. A lot of people were talking about the fire. According to the news, it had started in the middle of the night. No word yet on whether it was suspicious, but I'd be shocked if it wasn't. The timing seemed so unlikely.

My eyes found Emerson Bradley. He was pumping the hand of a short, grey-haired woman I recognized as the town mayor. He looked more angry than anything. Another woman, slim and brunette, hovered close at hand, clutching her designer purse, her face partially obscured by a half-veil attached to a round black hat.

I stood in the back, feeling like a fake. If not for Jessa, I'd never have come. I'd gotten a ride with her, but she was busy commiserating with all the people she knew who I didn't. I felt a faint stirring of unease. Martin wasn't here. He had to know it would look sketchy if he didn't show up at his former best friend's funeral. The rumours were already starting to swell. Had something happened to him? We'd checked in via email a couple of times but not recently. I decided I'd ask Jessa to drive by his house on our way home. That is, if this whole thing didn't exhaust her. She was newly out of the hospital but still at home. I tried to spend time with her *not* talking. Just being patient until she found her way back to herself.

I scanned the room for Drew but I couldn't see him either, which was shocking. What did it mean if he hadn't come?

People once believed a corpse would start bleeding if the person who'd wronged them was present. Sadly that was unlikely to happen, but maybe someone would involuntarily reveal their guilt in some expression or gesture. I was wondering if I could get away with taking a few sneaky photos when Lorelei slid in beside me. "Checking out suspects?" she whispered with a wicked grin.

I had the grace to blush. "How'd you know?"

"You were staring suspiciously. And you might not know it, but all your feelings show on your face." I ducked my head and she went on. "You think the killer might be here?"

"Yeah. I don't think they would be able to stay away. Either from remorse or—"

"Like a sort of sick thrill? My money is on Anabel and Missy acting in tandem."

I stifled a giggle. A man nearby frowned at me and I tried desperately not to laugh. Sometimes when I was nervous, I couldn't help myself.

"Although..." She jerked her head towards the thin chic woman I had noticed earlier.

"Who is that?" The woman hadn't moved from her position at Emerson Bradley's elbow, though I hadn't seen him speak to her. She was like a perfectly coiffed shadow. I wasn't the only one who couldn't stop staring at her. Suzie seemed equally curious.

"Mal's mother. Emerson's trophy wife, Celeste."

"What?!" I tried to see past the veil. She appeared young, maybe even college age.

"She lives in Paris apparently, so I suppose she can't be a suspect," Lorelei said wistfully. "But she's got that whole femme fatale thing down."

I leaned closer to her, telling myself to ignore the lemony scent of her hair. She was just a friend. She was basically straight. "Did you notice anything that night?"

She shrugged. "Plenty of testosterone on display, for sure. Lots of guys acting aggro. I saw arguments spring up everywhere. Even Mal and his best boy, Drew. Before the big fight blew up, in that room back behind the kitchen."

"The pantry?" I said, surprised.

"Yeah." Her eyes slanted away. "I was looking for a little privacy."

I remembered her straddling the guy on the sofa and said hurriedly, "Could you hear what it was about?"

"Some girl, I think. I didn't catch a name but the tone was clear, you know. Angry, like they were fighting over her."

My breath quickened. "Drew's not here."

And then felt deflated by Lorelei's next words.

"No, he is. I saw him on his way to the bathroom. He looked wrecked." She elbowed me and nodded towards the part of the crowd where all the seniors were assembled. "There he is now."

Wrecked was the right word. Drew seemed diminished somehow, his ruddy face wan and tear-streaked as he stumbled his way over to Suzie and the others. She leaned in close and said something that made his shoulders tighten and a red flush creep up his thick neck. He pulled a small silver flask from inside his jacket and took a quick swig. Suzie slapped at his arm.

"Grief and remorse can look pretty much the same," Lorelei said, giving me a meaningful look before she walked away.

"She sniffing around you again?" Jessa said, popping up. She was clearly miffed.

I slipped my hand into hers, gave her a quick hug. The pressure bandages on her wrists peeked out from the sleeves of her dress and I tucked them back in. "You sound so mama bear."

"I don't want you getting hurt. You deserve someone who gets how awesome you are. Not someone who hasn't figured it out yet."

"Right?! Long-suffering sigh, woe is me," I said dramatically. I leaned over to whisper, "Holding up okay?"

"Yeah, yeah, I took my anxiety meds—but not so fast: why'd you two have your heads together?"

I hesitated.

"I want to talk about it. Talk through it," she assured me. "Otherwise I'm just trapped inside my brain all the time. And it's dark in there."

"We were discussing suspects."

Jessa let out an audible breath. "Us too, but I doubt it's a psychopath in a clown mask. Can we sit? These shoes are pinching."

There were no free chairs, so we found a place on the floor in the corner.

I was probably the only one who could see beneath the carefully applied makeup she was wearing to mask the bruises. Having appeased myself, I squeezed her fingers. Her palm was moist.

"This is bizarre," she said, squeezing back. "All the chatter, the rumours. Kind of like having a spotlight shone on you. But not for something good. I'm so glad you're here."

"You are?" My eyes travelled over to where Suzie, Anabel, and Missy clustered in their fitted black sheaths like a murder of crows. Suzie had her arms wrapped tight around her torso, like she was afraid her insides might fall out.

"Yes, of course, silly. Missy and Anabel talk about it from a distance, in the third person. Like it's just some kind of gossip. It's weird." Jessa shrugged. "Maybe it's a defense mechanism. And Suzie has barely said anything. It think it's really hard for her to be here. She keeps zoning out. She said she's worried about Drew. He's been acting *erratic*."

I thought back to what Lorelei had said. Drew and Mal had argued that night, before the fight with Martin. *Was it about Suzie?* "Worried about him how?" I asked.

"She didn't say exactly. There's a lot of history between Drew and Mal, which isn't making it easier for her to process it. I suggested she get some professional help. I'm worried she's shutting down."

"Have you heard anything about the fire?" Jessa had already confessed she'd been listening at doors at home.

"An anonymous tip came in. They've found evidence to suggest arson. Apparently it was lucky they caught it before it spread too much. I think they're waiting until after the funeral to question Emerson Bradley. Since his company owns the property."

"Anything else?" I tried hard to keep the excitement out of my voice.

"They still haven't found the weapon. And the DNA results they were able to gather so far are 'inconclusive.' I heard Mom complaining about how long it's taking to get the results back from the lab. My tox screens still aren't in."

My heart was beating hard. Maybe the weapon was still hidden away up there. Maybe I could find it.

"Mom also mentioned something to Whalen about bringing in a suspect. Some ex-con who recently served time for armed robbery. Matty LeDuc. Suzie remembered he went to Lincoln, a couple of years ahead of us. He hung around with the jocks, sold weed."

I racked my brain. I couldn't place him. "Was he at the party?"

Jessa shrugged. "Suzie isn't sure. He's a total ghost online but she said she'd hunt down some old yearbooks in the library. Text us a picture so we can see if any of us recognize him. I can forward it to you."

I nodded. "Email not text. I still don't have my phone. Has anything come back to you?"

"I've been trying to remember, but no. I start therapy next week. Maybe that'll bring something to the surface." Her eyes filled with tears. "I feel so helpless. Like there's a target on my back and the sniper could be anyone."

It was my worst fear too. That Jessa could be in danger for knowledge her mind was still hiding from her. "You're safe here. You're safe at home."

"God, yes." Her voice broke on a laugh. "Dad hasn't been taking any outside meetings. He's home all day. I can't go anywhere alone except the bathroom and my bedroom. The twins wanted to sleep outside my door last night."

"They love you." I looked around the room. "You know his mother is here?"

"Yeah. Suzie pointed her out to me."

"It must be so hard to lose a kid," I said.

"You'd think, but I remember Mal saying she'd given him up years ago, basically as soon as he was born. It was a *business arrangement*."

Jessa stood up and smoothed the creases from her skirt. "Will you come with me to the viewing room?" She held her hand out with a weak smile and I remembered linking hands with her as we ran down steep hills so long ago, bold in the belief that neither of us would fall if we just held on.

"Of course." I noticed Emerson Bradley looking our way, marking our progress.

"Does he know who you are?" I asked.

"Officially, the girl who was with Mal in the room," she said. "I did offer my condolences. Suzie did too. It was awkward to say the least." Her voice wobbled. I drew her closer, tucking her into the hollow under my arm. She'd always fit there.

The viewing room was off to the side, a large poster of Mal in a suit and tie on an easel outside. A lilting piano instrumental wafted from within.

It was a claustrophobic space painted in a soft shade of grey with a thick burgundy carpet that deadened our footsteps. Jessa drew a deep breath and we walked through the archway. No one else was here.

Set on a stand against the far wall was a white coffin. Closed, I was grateful to see, and accented with brass hinges and handles. A mass of white flowers spilled overtop. All those fleshy flowers that smell almost artificial, like they've been doused in sweet oil. Large assortments were arranged in silver metal vases around the room and a dozen photos were displayed: Mal as a baby; a toddler with wispy blond hair; in his wrestling singlet, which I'd always thought made him look ridiculous; suntanned on the beach hoisting a beer. I couldn't stop thinking about the smell the perfume was supposed to cover up. The carpet was a pool of blood. In the bedroom where Mal had died, the dim light had made his blood look black. I felt a little sick and wondered how Jessa was handling it.

"Have you ever been to a funeral?" she asked. She was breathing quickly.

"Not really. Kind of," I said. "My parents'." I'd been too young to remember much. "It rained really hard and I thought the sky was crying."

Her mouth twisted. "Of course. Sorry." I gave her a reassuring nod. "I went to my Nana's wake," she said. "It wasn't like this, all clinical and quiet. People were sobbing in each other's arms. We were sharing our grief, receiving comfort from each other, not bottling it up inside and being all private about it. They're sitting out there eating stale cookies, having polite conversation." A tear rolled down her cheek and I watched helplessly. "I didn't even know him that well." She wiped her face with her coat sleeve. "He was a *what if.* I thought coming here would give me some kind of an ending. Peace. But it hasn't. In a way it's just magnified the wrongness of it all."

"We can leave right now. You don't have to do anything you don't want to do." I hated seeing the despair in her eyes.

"No! They'll just tiptoe around me. It makes me feel worse somehow, trapped by all this suspicion and gossip. Someone might want me dead. I can't live like that, Frankie."

Someone jostled my arm.

Drew.

His eyes seemed emptied out, passing over us as he staggered his way towards the front of the casket. "I'm sorry. I'm sorry," he mumbled. His broad back shielded us from whatever he was doing but I heard the sound of metal clasps being opened, the heavy groan of hinges.

I gasped. Was he going to climb into the coffin? Pull it down? I imagined Mal's body crashing to the floor.

"Drew," shrieked Jessa, "stop it!"

Screaming like a wounded bull, Mr. Bradley rushed in and forced Drew back against the wall. He anchored him there with a fistful of Drew's shirt. "How dare you!?" he yelled.

Drew coughed and spluttered, his fingers releasing something metal that glittered as it bounced across the carpet. "I wanted him to have my ring," he said.

I picked it up. It was the heavy championship ring the football players wore, a silver *L* and *A* against a green background. Releasing Drew, Mr. Bradley took it from me, turning it over in his palm.

"I need him to have it," Drew wailed. Mr. Bradley stared hard at him, blinked furiously, and then pulled him forward into a hug. After a few moments, Mr. Bradley stepped back, readjusting his rumpled shirt and jacket and smoothing his hair.

Crowded in the doorway I saw Suzie, Missy, and Anabel, all big-eyed and open-mouthed.

A woman dressed in a smart navy skirt and jacket giving off serious executive vibes forced herself past them. "Emerson," she called, "there's trouble. I've called the police already."

An uproar arose from outside and everyone—except Drew, who was now sitting on the ground, moaning—left to see what was going on. Jessa and I followed the crowd. I looked back briefly to see Suzie crouched next to Drew, her hands gripping his shoulders as if she could hold him up.

The limos were still parked along the street. The hearse awaited its journey to the Bradley family mausoleum at the cemetery up the hill. And across the street dozens of people had gathered, chanting and brandishing homemade signs. I read the hand-stencilled and spray-painted messages: *Affordable Housing. Eat The Rich. No Land Barons! Save Our Town!*

It was a weird mix of people. Some looked like business owners and soccer moms while others looked like they volunteered at the soup kitchen. A shocked murmur rose from the funeral attendees. A few of the men and women I'd noticed inside the chapel shouted pleas and criticisms back at the protestors. The minister, in his black robe and collar, waved his arms as if to shoo them away, but they ignored him. As soon as they spotted Emerson Bradley, their chants grew louder: "Not for sale! Not for sale!"

In the distance, sirens wailed.

CARA

Everything was falling apart.

All I had ever wanted was a home. For the ground to settle under my feet long enough for me to put down roots. Instead, for the last fourteen days, we'd been colder, wetter, and hungrier than ever. This morning I'd dragged myself out of the pile of rugs and leaves we'd slept in like hibernating animals only to find Iggy curled into a ball, arms shielding her face from the weak sun. The air was thick and heavy, threatening a thunderstorm, and a faint smell of burning wood lingered from the other night. Big fire, Shadow had said, but luckily the unrelenting wind had driven it away from us. Still, I'd stayed up watching for smoke and flames.

Iggy whimpered.

"What is it?" I asked Toni, who was stroking her head softly.

"Migraine. She's already puked twice."

I winced. Iggy had compared her headaches to an ice pick through the brain and they lasted for hours, sometimes days, messing with her vision and making her, in her own words, "want to die."

I went through our dwindling food pile and found a bottle of water and a packet of dry ramen noodles.

"It'll help if you can get her to eat something," I said, handing them over.

"She needs medicine!" Toni snapped. "She can't keep anything down."

"I know. I'm on it." I was mentally cataloguing the stuff we'd stolen from the house and stashed in the well. What I could sell easily; money for painkillers and something nutritious to eat. I slung my backpack over my shoulders.

Shadow sat up, rubbing her eyes. "Where are you going?"

I had a million thoughts running through my brain but I didn't want to share any of them. At least with Iggy sick, I could count on them sticking with her. "I'll be back soon. Stay here."

Shadow reached for me. I touched two fingers to her forehead, the closest thing to a kiss she'd allow. "I've got you."

———

AN HOUR LATER, AFTER A STEEP UPHILL CLIMB THAT TOOK ME in a long swoop around to the rear of the mansion, I lay on my belly on the hill, staring at the police tape flapping in the breeze, breathing in the charred air. The fire had started here. I thought back over the last few days, Shadow's comings and goings. Had she disappeared for any length of time? I couldn't be sure, caught up as I'd been in all my worries. I could see that a huge section of the roof had burned and was now draped with tarps and plastic sheeting. Rough planks covered the giant windows, the ground sparkling with broken glass. Had we left anything behind? Something that could lead the police to us? It had been so chaotic and we'd let down our guard. A dozen people could probably ID us. I thought about Shadow that night, filthy and distraught; her limp, which could have come from a fight or from jumping out of a window.

And I thought about what she'd said. Her fear that we'd been noticed. Had someone witnessed her doing something? The inflection of her voice when she'd repeated Mal's last name. *Familiarity*. That was what I'd heard. Like she knew him. And if she knew him, could she have killed him?

I'd consumed nothing but a little water, but that wasn't the only reason my mouth was dry. Had that boy hurt her? These people were nothing to me and Shadow meant everything. I loved her with all my heart. I had to protect her even if the worst thing was true.

I'd already climbed down into the well, picking through items that were quick sales or trades, and looking for anything that could link us to the murder. My backpack now contained a mantel clock, the small bedside lamp Toni had loved so much, some metal candlesticks, and a couple of cut crystal ashtrays. I'd see what I could get for them downtown. The tools we'd stolen would have been even better but I couldn't find them. *Must be back at the campsite*, I thought. Though I could have sworn I'd stowed that bag safely with the other stolen goods.

I'd kicked a ton of leaves into the well for good measure and finally, heart in my throat, I'd examined every knife in the fancy wooden block for blood. Turning each one over slowly, and heaving a sigh when I found they were all sharp and shiny, factory-fresh. I buried them in a hastily dug hole just in case.

Now I stood up cautiously and looked down the long dirt road, checking for sunlight bouncing off a windshield. Distantly, a dog barked. Lincoln sat in the hollow below and to the right was the thick fringe of trees that concealed our creekside camp. As far as I could tell, there were no cars parked along the edge or by the house. I wouldn't be going in through the front door anyway.

I calmed my breathing, hefted my backpack, and made my way down into what would have one day been the garden if they'd ever finished clearing the trees. They'd sunk the hole for the swimming pool but it was filled with dead leaves and rainwater, a scummy sheen glistening on top. Looking more closely I noticed a dead rat floating on the surface, yellow teeth snarling in a gruesome smile.

The Porta Potti smelled like death, the wood planks I'd wanted to come back for were swollen with rain and spotted with green slime, and the area where we'd stowed our loot held nothing but soggy cardboard and plastic wrap. I put my backpack down, pulled my special paperclips from my pocket, and knelt down to examine the heavy new padlock on the basement doors. Shadow had spent most of her time down there and I wanted to check it out before I looked for the easiest way into the main part of the house.

The wind picked up and the plastic sheeting flapped like the wings of a pterodactyl. The hair on the back of my neck stood up. I sharpened my ears, alert to every rustle, every unidentifiable noise. No birds sang. Tick Tock had taught me to listen for them. They warned of predators, of silent observers, of people coming. I listened so hard my ears filled with the sound of my own blood whooshing through my veins. *Just get inside, Cara, out of sight.*

Taming my trembling hands, I inserted the wires, holding one steady and twisting the other sharply. The hasp unlocked. I eased the narrow doors open, careful not to let them slam, and then slunk down a short flight of steps, landing on the concrete floor. After closing the doors behind me I flicked a lighter, sweeping it across the room quickly before it burned my thumb. The flame barely penetrated the dark corners, offering just a glimpse of heavy beams overhead and tangles of wires hung like nooses. I returned the lighter to my pocket and let my eyes adjust to the dim daylight coming through small dirty windows set low along two sides. The middle of the room was clear, tarp-draped building materials stacked against the walls. The concrete underfoot was dusty and tracked with prints circling and shooting off in all directions. There was an underlying odour of dampness mostly masked by the smell of burnt wood.

I hunted around, searching for anything Shadow might have left behind—her blue bandana, the braided leather cord she wore on her wrist. I kicked through rubble, sheetrock, bent nails and screws and found nothing. A small room contained a furnace and water heater and then the space opened up again. It was darker away from the windows and I flicked my lighter again. In the corner opposite was a plain wooden door. I opened it, revealing a cramped stairway.

I went up, feeling my way along the rail, until I reached another door which led to a small room containing the fuse box and electrical shut-offs, and just past it the pantry and a small bathroom. Across the dark hall was the kitchen. Had Shadow come this way and entered the house? Had that boy attacked her? Even if she had killed him, I had to believe she'd had a good reason.

My shoes echoed on the tiled floor. Unnerved by the doubling of my footsteps, I moved quickly to the carpeted area in the dining room. A creak came from upstairs, then a thump, as if something heavy had been dropped or a door had closed. I froze, staring up at the ceiling, tracking the noises with my eyes.

Everyone knows that criminals often return to the scene of the crime.

I crept forward, hardly breathing until I reached the bottom of the long, curving staircase. I held on to the railing looking up, poised to break and run. Slow, muffled footsteps echoed from the far end of the house. The soft click of a door latch. The shuffling squeak of shoes on wood flooring—the unmistakable sound of someone stealthily making their way in my direction.

Adrenaline thundering through my body, I bolted back through the kitchen, hurled the door open, and threw myself down the staircase into the basement.

FRANKIE

I bent over and tried to catch my breath. Bumble collapsed in a panting puddle, giving me a wounded look from under her bunched eyebrows.

"Forgive me," I said, scratching her behind her ears until her back leg started jumping. I looked around. So much had changed in two weeks.

The mansion's lower windows were boarded up. The front door was barricaded with thick plywood sheets and pasted with *No Trespassing* notices and *Warning! Danger!* signs. Half the roof was gone, the remaining rafters like splintered ribs wrapped in sheeting that had blown loose. Metal girders shored up the portico above the sagging porch. I wondered how safe the upper floor would be. Was the grand staircase still there?

My phone had finally been returned to me, and shining the light through a thin crack between wooden boards, I saw piles of burned furniture and tattered curtains, blackened carpets rolled and stacked against the walls. Mixed in with the smoky smells was something sharply chemical. Bumble and I made our way around to the side of the house that was barely fire-damaged. At least to my untrained eye. I looked for a tree and tied her leash to it. She raised her beige eyebrows at me.

"Yes, I'm going inside but not you, babycakes," I said, giving her a red rubber Kong to chew on and dropping a kiss on her juicy nose. "Stand guard." I had to admit that I had no real plan. I just had to do something. Jessa's despair and fear were tormenting me. She needed answers, and maybe they were still here in this house.

I smashed the small downstairs bathroom window with a rock and then cleared the debris from the edges with a piece of wood. Hoisting myself up on the sill, I jumped down onto the black-and-white-tiled floor. I stuck my head out. "Back in a few minutes. Be good," I told Bumble. With a sigh, she circled around on the fallen leaves, making herself a little hollow, and collapsed her head onto her front paws.

It was dim in the pantry, but once I'd stepped into the kitchen, the daylight spilling in through the big unbroken side windows made it easier to see. Heaps of garbage were piled against the walls, dozens of empty bottles lined the counters. It seemed the flames hadn't gotten this far.

Still, it smelled of campfires and something like rubbing alcohol. I moved into the high-ceilinged hallway and pulled up my photos from the party, scrolling back to the first, allowing my feet to take me to the sunken sitting room where the dancing had happened. An icy finger ran up the length of my spine. What was I walking into?

I tracked my eyes from my phone to my surroundings. How the room had looked then, how it looked now—as if a bomb had gone off. The walls were water-stained and damp, ceilings scorched, wallpaper hanging like strips of skin. Cheap paintings knocked loose by the firehoses, frames crumpled, glass shattered. There was the white sofa, no longer pristine, the expansive armchairs where Mal had held court, tipped over, exploding foam like innards. I clicked to a photo of Jessa balanced next to him, his hand snug on her waist, lips on the nape of her neck. I thought of her glowing with happiness, a little tipsy, excited and hopeful. What if that version of Jessa had died that night too?

I couldn't bear it. I scrolled to the next. Simon and Martin sat near one another in deep conversation. Suzie and her girls close by, with their matching shrunken jackets and carefully pinned messy updos, ranking everyone in the room. Drew caught chugging a beer, foam spattering his face, Adam's apple bulging from his sinewy neck.

Here was the window sill I'd sat on. The plastic calla lilies were gone, a layer of soot dusting every surface, scummy foam in ridges across the floor like salt on the beach. I looked closer. There were faint chalk marks on the carpet. Circles and rectangles outlining evidence that had been photographed, bagged up, removed. What had they found? Who did it point to? If there was a suspect in custody, wouldn't Mr. Bradley have stopped ranting? Were they still investigating Martin?

Even though Jessa had said they'd questioned Matty LeDuc and let him go, Suzie had sent her an old group yearbook photo that included him. Even as a freshman he was extremely tall, at least six-foot-four, looming over everyone else like a sasquatch, hair strawberry-red and lank. He'd have been spotted at the party for sure.

I kneeled down and felt the nubbly thick wool. Sections had been cut away, leaving bare rectangles and squares over wood flooring. In the photos people danced with their eyes closed, arms upraised, fists pumping the air, in a state of ecstasy (or on ecstasy). I could almost hear the echo of the bass. I scrolled past group shots of Jessa, Suzie, and the other girls, Jessa and Mal, Suzie pulling away from Drew, arched eyebrows bunched, her lipsticked mouth made ugly by whatever she was saying to him. I could see the marks where his fingers gripped her arm. What was the story there?

I kept sifting through images. A blur of motion when my hand had jerked. Those accidental photos that were sometimes the best ones. Colours washing into one another. And another that captured a wedge of an alcove and was deeply shadowed. Blending into the black was a glimmer of dark hair, deep-set eyes, pale skin like a flower petal on an inky puddle. Who was she? When I zoomed in, the photo exploded into pixels. I made a note to print them all out. Each photo told a little story. I felt that if I could lay them out like a giant puzzle, I'd discover the sequence of events that led to Mal's death.

Bumble barked outside. I stiffened, every sense on high alert. Would she bark again? Silence. I convinced myself it was a squirrel. Bumble's eternal frustration was that she was never sly enough to catch one.

The wind had gained strength, shuddering against the windows, whipping up the plastic wrapping. There was indistinct groaning and soft thumping as the house settled, each one like a giant's footstep.

I moved quickly into the dining room, checking my photos as I walked. Here, where the fight happened, the fire had raged stronger. I looked up, tracing the smudge marks left behind when the flames had climbed high. The furniture was in pieces, the large table smashed and scattered as if a tsunami had rushed in, leaving destruction in its wake.

Slowly testing each step, I moved up the stairs, my boots echoing. It was like being inside a hollow heart. A heavy thud came from above and I jumped, then kept deathly still. I waited, but heard nothing more. *Stop psyching yourself out, Frankie. It's only the wind. Just get to the master bedroom.*

I forced myself to keep going.

Once I got to the top, I saw it: a giant black hole. A huge section of the floor had collapsed. Balanced on some two-by-fours, I slowly edged closer and peered between the boards. I was just able to make out the diamond-tiled entryway. My phone buzzed in my pocket, startling me. With a squeal, the plank I was standing on swivelled, pitching me forward. I pinwheeled my arms frantically, crashing to my knees and biting my tongue. The board continued to swing out before it tilted and smashed onto the hallway.

I spat a salty clot of blood onto the floor, jerking my head away from the mess, and wiped my mouth. Nerves twitching, I quickly checked the secondary bedrooms.

In the first two, the floors were charred and likely unsafe; I wouldn't be able to proceed past the threshhold. Here was where Drew had been passed out—or faked it—in the bed with Suzie. Unless it was someone else?

In the kid's room, I remembered the mystery person standing in front of the mirror. The scaffolding outside cast black-barred shadows against the grimy walls, making me feel like an animal in a cage. The taint of smoke brought the tickle of a sneeze and I smothered it quickly, as if breaking the silence would signal something horrifying.

See, there's no one there. No one behind you. Just look around and get the hell out.

Outside, Bumble barked again. A volley this time. A warning.

My inner voice was screaming now: *This is too dangerous. You need to leave now.*

But I had one more room to check.

Breathing quickly, I ran to the master. The door was closed. It took precious seconds to force my hand to turn the knob. My limbs felt almost detached and fear had full rein now.

What if someone is standing there, just behind it? What if they leap out at me with a knife?

I pushed. The door swung back and hit the wall with a boom like thunder. Images flashed like lightning before my eyes. Jessa on the floor. Mal staring up at nothing. That mask of gore on his face.

I forced myself to look.

All the furnishings had been removed. The bed, carpet, and draperies, the broken mirror. I feverishly snapped a slew of panoramic shots, aware of how cold my hands were, how my whole body was shaking. Running to the window that had been the escape route, I zoomed in close to the gouges on the sill where the murderer had forced it open.

Most of the sill had also been removed by the police but the wood that remained in the frame was splintered, hacked at with some kind of tool, like the killer had been in a frenzy. *Desperate to get out.*

I remembered the window downstairs. It had been nailed shut. An idea in my brain sat up and waved its hands. They couldn't find a murder weapon. The assumption widely held was that it had been some kind of sharp knife. But someone had used a tool to force the window open. *Maybe the same tool used to kill Mal.* I remembered the stuff left by the builders. Hammers, pliers, pry bars, screwdrivers—all readily available. *But where is it now?*

I groaned. What had I thought was going to happen? Some eureka moment, where the murderer's face magically appeared to me in the window's reflection?

I pressed my face against the thick glass looking for my dog. There was the silver birch I had tied her to, the leash and bright red dog toy. No Bumble. At the same moment, I realized her barking had stopped.

MARTIN

I'd been home recuperating for a few days but I already wished I was back at the hospital. My bandaged ribs chafed and my strained shoulder protested whenever I moved, but my vision was clear and the swelling had subsided, my wounds scabbed over. When Charlie called and asked if I'd take an afternoon shift I'd jumped at the chance. My dad had lapsed back into his morose walking-dead routine, and after completing my classwork I'd still had too many empty hours to fill, which meant more time to think about Mal, his murder, and most of all, Drew.

After I spoke with Sergeant Alvarez in the hospital, they'd arrested Drew and his buddies on assault charges. Unfortunately for me, he'd been released within a few hours pending his day in court. "He'd be foolish to come after you again," the policeman had said. "But stay vigilant, okay?" I wasn't so sure Drew's brain had much to do with his actions. He'd turned into a hulking ball of rage, and maybe if I could figure out why, I'd know what happened that night up at Heartbreak Homes. Whether it was a murderous fury brought on by steroid abuse, some weird love triangle gone wrong that involved Suzie, or...could guilt bring on irrational anger? I knew Frankie suspected him. Had Simon noticed anything? Maybe Suzie had confided in Jessa?

I called Frankie, but it went straight to voicemail. "Hey, it's Martin. We need to talk about Drew. Call me back ASAP."

It felt good to have a focus other than my aches and pains, even if it was inventory. I checked the rack behind me that held the cigarettes and condoms, noting down quantities on my checklist. After that, I rearranged the bottles and packets of medicine next to the cash register and then fell back into my thoughts. What drove someone to murder? I wondered. *Money. Love. Hate. Revenge.* All great motives, but how could I make one fit?

Garth, the monosyllabic night guy, was late and, call me crazy, but I didn't want to be here again after dark. He was lantern-jawed and scruffy with jailhouse muscles and a spiderweb neck tattoo. *FUCK YOU* was spelled out on his knuckles and the fact that there was a bare knuckle on his left hand really bothered me. Couldn't he at least have added an exclamation point? I had to check myself. If I ever got him to open up, I'd probably discover that he lived with his grandmother, volunteered at the pet shelter, and played the cello.

The clock read 5:15. We were supposed to switch over at 5:00. A light rain started falling, exacerbating my bad mood. Now I'd get wet on the walk home too. My car, currently languishing outside my house, needed a fill-up that I couldn't afford until the next paycheque.

THE IRONY FILES: GAS STATION ATTENDANT CAN'T AFFORD GAS.

I scratched at the scab on my jaw. A flicker of movement outside caught my eye. My pulse accelerated, and my ribs shrieked as I tensed involuntarily. Let's just say that ever since Drew and his teammates jumped me, my fight-or-flight instinct had been in overdrive.

It was a girl. Over by the gas pumps. She caught me staring, shrank back a little. A vehicle pulled up under the canopy, and she was over by the driver's side window before they'd even stopped the engine. Illuminated by the overheads, I saw that she was young, punky, and blond, wearing a stylish leather jacket that she floated in like a kid playing dress-up. Even from a distance, it was easy to tell that she was hungry-skinny or meth-head-skinny and a little grimy too. I saw the driver drop a couple of coins into her outstretched hand, the girl's head bobbing as she thanked them.

The light shone on her face and I recognized her—it was Coffee Girl. She came in on occasion just to buy a cup of our nasty drip coffee and always asked for free refills. Charlie preferred for me to dissuade panhandlers but she was always cool, never aggressive.

She strolled away and the driver got out of their car at the pumps—an older woman, dressed like an antiquated school teacher in a wool cardigan, silk scarf, and clunky brown shoes. She stood perplexed in front of the machine and I could tell tell from her body language she was having trouble. I went outside and helped her figure out the electronic pre-pay system and then offered to pump the gas for her. When I was done, she pressed a ten-dollar bill into my hand. We're not supposed to accept tips, but I always did. Every little bit helped. She drove off and I turned back to the kiosk, just in time to see Coffee Girl slip out, stuffing something into her pocket. Our eyes locked.

"Hey!" I yelled, breaking into a jog. She bolted.

It hurt to run but I was operating solely off of adrenaline. I tapped my right pants pocket, felt the fat bunch of keys. At least she couldn't have gotten into the register. But I thought of all the other pricy stuff she could have taken. Cigarettes, burner phones, batteries. She dodged around the corner, put on some speed.

Each breath felt like a razor slicing my lungs but I pushed myself, ignoring the voice reminding me I had left the station unsupervised and should have called the police. GAS STATION CLERK COLLAPSES OVER PETTY BUBBLE GUM THEFT. I was being propelled by sheer obstinacy.

She cut across the kiddie park and darted onto the narrow road behind it. A delivery truck lumbered towards her, horn blaring, but she dodged between two cars, skidded, and almost wiped out. Slowly, steadily, I was gaining on her. She cast a quick look over her shoulder. I lunged forward and caught hold of her jacket sleeve. She cursed, snaking her shoulders, and slipped free of it like she was sloughing her skin. The sudden change in resistant force made me lose my balance and fall to my knees. Dancing backwards, she gave me two exuberant middle fingers and a cheeky grin and disappeared down the street. I was left clutching my ribs with one hand, and holding the jacket with the other.

Seconds later, I heard the screech of brakes and the unmistakable sound of impact. Jacket forgotten, I was on my feet again before I knew it, racing around the corner where a car straddled both lanes. A young guy sat immmobile in the driver seat, hands gripping the steering wheel. I ran up to him, tapped on the closed window. He rolled it down. "You okay?" I asked. His airbag hadn't deployed and there wasn't a mark on him.

"Yeah, I think so." His eyes widened. "I pulled out and she ran in front of me. Musta been in my blind spot."

People began appearing from nearby apartments and shops. I was almost afraid to look. Coffee Girl was lying in the middle of the road, one leg bent weirdly, blood pooling from a wound on the back of her head. Someone called 911. Someone else kneeled beside her, holding her hand, checking her vitals. She wasn't moving. It felt like I wasn't getting enough air. I couldn't stop staring at the blood, the way it spread like a red halo. I was right back there at the bedside standing over Mal.

I tore my eyes away and fixed my gaze on a nearby tree, fuzzing out the peripheral scene until my breathing calmed and I could look again. More people had gathered, drawn by the crowd. A police car showed up at the same time as the paramedics. One of the cops was Alvarez, the officer who'd taken my statement at the hospital. I avoided his eye, ducking behind a taller man. Would he think it was strange that I was here? I seemed to keep turning up at crime scenes. Thankfully, he didn't notice me in all the chaos.

I waited until the ambulance had pulled away and made my way back to the gas station. It wasn't until I stumbled upon the jacket lying in the road that I even remembered dropping it. Maybe her ID was in it?

I could tell it was expensive—motorcycle-style with white leather stripes stitched on the sleeves—and it didn't really jive with her street urchin–like appearance. Plus, it was obviously too big for her. I shook it out, caught a whiff of spicy cologne, and a memory clicked in my head. *It smells like Mal.* He had been wearing a jacket like this one at the party. Heart thudding, I checked the pockets. Some loose change and a fat handful of those tubes of painkillers we sold at the gas station. Ibuprofen. Was that all she'd taken? I didn't understand. They didn't even get you high. And they sold for a few bucks each.

I shook the coat again and heard something shift. Inside was another pocket, zippered, and within that was a prescription pill bottle. I took it out. It was empty. *Flunitrazepam*, read the label. Then I glanced down at the patient's name.

Emerson Bradley.

CARA

It was the sound of crying that drew me from my hiding place in the basement. Before that, a dog had been barking like crazy and I'd worried it was the cops doing another sweep. I'd crouched down in a cobwebbed corner watching for flashlight beams and listening for walkie-talkies. A hundred breaths later, I slipped out through the doors, carefully re-padlocking them, and quietly made my way around to the rear of the house.

A girl with fiery red hair was crouched over something on the ground, her face buried in her hands, shoulders quivering with the force of her wails. Nearby was a two-by-four and a tangle of black cloth. I cleared my throat and she jerked around, eyes narrowing fiercely behind wire-framed glasses. There was blood in the corner of her mouth and she held a large brown and black dog in her lap. It wasn't moving.

"Is it...dead?"

"Some asshole hit her with that." She gestured at the plank of wood. I noticed a smear of red on it. She swiped furiously at her runny nose with her forearm. "I can't get her to wake up." She stroked the dog's heavy head. There was a wet clump of fur above its shaggy eyebrows, thick blood matting the fur around its eyes.

I knelt down beside her. Even from my careful distance—the dog was solid muscle, with a big blunt nose—I could hear the deep sound of its breathing.

"Who would do something like that?"

"A killer."

Noting my startled expression, she relaxed her frown. "I came up here looking for clues. There were weird noises, but I kept convincing myself it was nothing. When I was upstairs I realized that Bumble...had stopped barking."

I swallowed hard, trying to figure out where I'd been when she was in the house. Had we just heard each other? But no, I'd been hiding down in the basement for a good twenty minutes before I heard her crying. There was a third person.

Her expression hardened again. "What are you doing here, anyway?"

Part of me wanted to get the hell out. None of this was my business, but even though this girl was trying to sound tough, I could hear the panic and pain in her voice.

I dug in my backpack and pulled out a bottle. "I have water to clean her up."

She took it and looked around, picking up the black cloth. It was wet and covered in leaf mould—a jean jacket, dirty and ragged. A flurry of roly-polies fell out of it and scuttled away. "Ugh." She tossed it aside with a look of disgust that quickly turned back to worry. "I think she was chewing on it."

Emptying her pockets, she turned up a bookstore flyer for some place called the Book Nookery, some lint, a cough drop.

I removed my bandana and handed it over. "Use this."

"Thank you." Her eyes welled up and her mouth trembled. For a moment it looked like she might throw her arms around me. For a moment I thought I might let her.

"No big," I said gruffly.

She was close enough that I could count every freckle dusting her cheeks. Our fingertips touched, sending a shiver up my spine. I yanked my hand away and it broke her gaze. Carefully she made a pad of my bandana and patted it gently around the wound.

"You were at the party," she said. "Orange Bandana, that's what I called you in my head." She flushed. "I'm Frankie." I recognized her too. That dyed hair like a sunset, the long, speckled swoop of her nose, black-framed glasses magnifying hazel eyes, the cute overalls.

"Cara." I thought about lying or dodging but truth was, I was too wrecked from lack of sleep to think of an alias.

"My friend Jessa was the girl who was found with Mal. She was injured in the attack," Frankie said, her eyes intent on me.

My mind whirled. I could see Shadow protecting herself but was she capable of this? I scrambled to break her gaze.

"I think she's coming to," I said. The dog's eyelids were flickering, pulling away from the gumminess.

She threw her arms around her pet. "Oh, Bumble!" The dog tried to stand, shaking her head as if she had a bee in her ear, then sat down again heavily with a groan that almost sounded embarrassed. I had a flashback to one of my foster dads trying to get out of his chair when he was drunk. Frankie peered into the dog's dark brown eyes, and Bumble licked her nose and whined a little.

"Not concussed," she muttered. "But she's not walking anywhere."

"Can you call anyone?"

"Jessa's at her therapy session. Who's got a car?" She hesitated, biting her lip, then fumbled her phone out, tapped a number. Listened and put it away again, muttering, "Martin is probably in no condition to drive anyway."

"Let me help you." I felt it in my bones; I couldn't just leave her.

Frankie looked surprised. "Really? She's not light."

"We'll get her down to the main road and you can call your friend again."

It was hard-going over the potholed track. Bumble didn't like being carried like a sack of potatoes and I got her back end. She kept twisting her head around to stare at me like she couldn't believe I was touching her butt.

"You never told me what you were doing up here," Frankie said.

"Same as you," I said. She seemed to accept it.

"Was it only you in the house?" I asked.

"Yeah. Why?"

"I heard someone else up there, sneaking around. I split when I realized they were coming down the stairs. I hid in the basement. There's a way down off the kitchen."

"Bumble slipped her leash," Frankie said. "Maybe she went after them?"

"They'd only come back if they left something. Evidence. Like the weapon." I was trying to feel her out. Find out whether she'd discovered something that might point to Shadow. "I checked all around. Nothing but wet leaves and trash. No knife."

"This might sound crazy," she paused, checking my expression, "but I'm pretty sure the weapon was a tool."

"Power saw? Hammer?" I said with a nervous laugh. Obviously the same idea had occurred to her. There were things besides knives you could use to stab someone.

Her face was deadly serious. "I'm thinking chisel, ice pick, screwdriver, needle-nose pliers."

My heart rate picked up. I had to ask Shadow what happened to that bag so we could get rid of it once and for all. Whether it was her or—*could she even hurt a dog?* I stopped myself from spiralling. I was ninety-five percent sure Shadow was back at the camp with Iggy and Toni. It was that five percent that stuck in my throat like a bone. With effort, I shook it loose. What it came down to was this: guilty or innocent, I would protect her. People went to jail all the time for crimes they didn't commit. Especially people like us. This would just even the score.

"If the killer has the weapon already, why would they be snooping around?" I asked.

"There must be something else. I mean, that's why they set the fire, right? To cover up evidence."

Bumble was squirming. Without my noticing, we'd reached the end of the dirt road.

"Let's put her down," Frankie said. We did so carefully.

Bumble sniffed the ground around her and her tail thumped once. Before I could remove my hand, she licked it.

"She likes you." Frankie made a kissy face and took her phone out. "Let's get you to the vet, Bumble Bee."

"I've got to go," I said. My legs were exhausted, but the fastest way was to go back up the hill and then cut across to the creek.

"Wait!" She plucked at my hoodie. "Thank you so much. Tell me how to get in touch with you. Maybe we can figure this out together?"

I mumbled something, backed away, and forced myself into a slow jog, ignoring Frankie as she called after me. I could feel her eyes boring into my back.

I had just made a really dumb mistake. She'd clocked me at the party. Now she knew my name.

MARTIN

As soon as I got home, I looked up Flunitrazepam on my computer. A number of pages came up immediately. "'Prescribed for acute insomnia,'" I read aloud, "'a central nervous system depressant ten times more potent than Vallium. It is not approved for medical use in North America, where it is also known as Rohypnol: the date-rape drug.'"

The date-rape drug? Jessa had been passed out when we found her. Had Mal roofied her? Why would he? I'd seen the way she'd hung on his arm. The tender glow in his eyes. Even his voice had taken on a different timbre when he talked to her.

I tilted back in my chair and retraced the night of the party. Early on, he'd just been the Mal I knew. A little cocky, sure, but nothing out of the usual. He was drinking more maybe, but not as much as Drew had been. It had almost felt like we were reconnecting and that had felt good. And then...what? Something had set him off. I clunked back down to earth. I needed to talk to someone who knew him better than I did.

It was getting late but I dialled Simon. He picked up immediately.

"Hey, bro, how's the healing coming along?" he said. Simon had stopped by with a six-pack of beer two days after I'd gotten out of the hospital. We'd had to drink them in an old spidery treehouse at the bottom of the yard. My dad was back in AA and I didn't want to trigger him, but man those beers tasted good, and it had been cool to hang out like old times. Simon had been the one to tell me about the memorial service and Drew's meltdown, the demonstrators out front baying for Emerson Bradley's blood.

"Still a little sore," I admitted, downplaying it. "You busy right now?"

"Nope. Missy's visiting her grandmother. I'm just playing video games. What's going on?"

"I want to talk to Drew. I'm thinking it would probably be better if you came along. For security." I said it casually, but I had no idea how Drew would react to seeing me. Still, I needed to talk to him about the fight at the party and what I'd found out, and maybe clear the air.

"No doubt," Simon said. "I'll be right over."

"I'm stepping out for a while," I told my dad, who was slouched in his armchair, newspaper beside him, staring at some football game on TV. If moss started to grow on him, I wouldn't be surprised. Late at night I'd hear him tapping on his keyboard or pacing up and down the hallway, his worn slippers slapping against the linoleum. He slept most of the day. I wondered if I should be opening windows so we weren't breathing our own stale carbon dioxide in an endless loop.

The bell rang. I opened the door and exited quickly, not wanting Simon to get a look inside. If I had to describe our new place, I'd say the design aesthetic was modelled on 1970s seedy motel, a hallowed time of handlebar mustaches, wide-leg jeans, and unfiltered cigarettes.

"Have a good night, Mr. Weber," Simon said, giving me a puzzled glance as I closed the front door. My dad barely lifted his head. I hadn't told any of my friends about how bad it had gotten.

Simon drove his Audi. I was grateful I didn't have to make excuses about the empty gas tank or the fact that driving made my taped ribs scream. I plugged my dying phone into Simon's charger, noticing I'd missed an earlier call from Frankie. I'd call her later. Maybe I'd have some new info by then.

"Are you sure about this?" Simon asked as the town fell away behind us.

"I have to know what happened that night," I said, ignoring the voice that was telling me to leave it alone. "I'm a suspect in his murder, Si. A *person of interest*. They haven't charged me yet but if they find even a shred of evidence, they will. I need Drew to shed some light on what really went down."

"Ditto, man, but Drew still likes me."

"That's why I asked you to come," I said, trying to inject some optimism into my tone. "You're my protection."

"Or a witness?"

"It won't come to that," I said, fervently turning the phrase into a prayer.

While we made our way through wider and lusher tree-lined streets, I filled Simon in on what had happened earlier.

"Is the girl going to be okay?" he asked.

"I called the hospital and they won't let me see her, but the nurse said she had a broken leg. The head injury is superficial."

"What did she look like? Did you recognize her?" he asked.

"She's small, maybe five foot, with a buzzed head, punk-ish. She buys coffee at the gas station sometimes. Spare changes near the off-ramp."

"You think she's a runaway? My mom is involved with the county shelters. Improving them. Making them safer."

"Maybe. I certainly don't think she has it easy."

"Did you report the robbery?"

"No. I put the pills back. It seemed like she'd been punished enough, you know?"

Simon tapped his fingers on the steering wheel. "Do you think she stole Mal's jacket from the party?"

"She must have. But I didn't see her there. Did you?" There'd been the girl with the dark spiky hair who'd stared me down but I only recalled seeing her that once. And alone.

Simon frowned. "There were a couple of punk girls in the kitchen when I was hanging with Missy. One could have been her. They were swiping booze and food." He shrugged. "Seemed pretty harmless to me. It wasn't like we were going to run out." He snapped his fingers. "One of them had a small tattoo near her ear. Bird, I think."

I thought back to all the times I'd seen Coffee Girl. She usually had her hood up, head ducked as she paid for her coffee. Did she have a tattoo? Maybe.

I told him about the pills I'd found with Emerson's name on them. And Frankie's concern that Jessa had been unusually drunk.

"You think Mal dosed Jessa?" He shook his head. "Not his M.O. He never had any trouble with the *ladeez*." He said this in such an over-the-top way, I could almost hear Mal's voice. He got serious. "You know, Missy told me he really liked Jessa. He was *courting* her. That was the word he used."

"I don't think he was completely happy," I said, trying to articulate a feeling I'd picked up on that night, something dark simmering beneath the surface of Mal's laid-back attitude. Anger, maybe. Or hurt.

"Yeah. He seemed on edge that last week. But he didn't talk to me about it either." Simon indicated the jacket. "You'll have to let the police know."

"I will. I just want to get Drew's side of things first."

We'd reached an area of town where the maple trees met overhead like a green rooftop, houses spaced far apart on huge landscaped lots. I'd worked on quite a few of them, planting hundreds of bulbs in the springtime and pruning lilac-lined avenues.

Drew lived in what I would have called a mansion if I hadn't seen Mal's house. Still, it boasted a six-car garage, manicured garden, circular drive, and front entrance bracketed by Grecian columns. Simon drove up to the front path, parking behind a gleaming red pickup.

"He's home," Simon said, gesturing to the vehicle.

I felt like Dead Man Walking as we took the broad steps to the door.

Teen Idiot Ambles into Bear Den.

The knocker was the shape of a closed hand. Instantly my ribs ached with the memory of Drew's fists slamming into my torso. Simon shot me a sympathetic look. "Ready?"

He knocked twice. From the depths of the house, we heard a crescendo of barks. With my luck they'd be Dobermans. I wondered how long it would take them to rip me to pieces, how long it would take my father to notice I never came home.

When Drew opened the door, his face switched from vaguely annoyed to furious in two seconds flat. I had to stifle a laugh. He was cradling two tiny Morkies in his arms. Bright-eyed, button-nosed furballs. Teacup-sized but loud.

"Why'd you bring this motherfucker to my house, Si?" Drew said. And then to me, jaw thrust out like a boxer's. "You want some more?"

There was no way I was going to let him intimidate me while he was hugging a couple of Totos.

"I don't see your back-up gorillas, Drew. Maybe it can be a fair fight this time?"

The dogs picked up on the general atmosphere and started growling like electric toothbrushes. Drew spluttered for a moment, his ears flushing pink.

"Get the hell out of here," he yelled.

"Fine," I said, "I'll just go straight to the police!"

"You threatening me?!"

Any second, Drew was going to realize he could put the dogs down and throw a punch at me, and there was no way I would able to stop him without cracking a few more bones.

Simon stepped forward, effectively blocking him. "Come on. This has to stop now." He looked at me. "Show him the jacket, Martin."

I unbundled it from the plastic bag I was carrying. "Recognize this?"

Drew gasped. "Where'd you get that?"

"How about we come inside and talk about it?" Simon said, throwing an arm around Drew's shoulders. For a moment Drew stiffened but then he reluctantly stepped inside.

I followed them both down a hallway to Drew's wing of the house. Drew put the dogs down and they instantly ran over and sniffed my shoes, feathery tails wagging like metronomes, before jumping onto the sectional sofa.

I slid onto the edge of the deep leather armchair closest to the door in case I had to make a run for it. Drew stayed on his feet, breathing loudly and glaring at me. He had this quirk when he was super pissed off—a little muscle by his jaw that twitched. Right now it was trampolining.

Simon sighed. "First of all," he said, "you've got to know that Martin had nothing to do with what happened to Mal."

Drew's lower lip jutted. "How do you know that? He was there. Shit got crazy. Mal died. Everyone says it was him."

"He's been brought in for questioning more than anybody, but the cops have nothing on him. Mal's dad is demanding an arrest. You *know* Martin couldn't have done this. If we don't figure out what really went down, he could end up taking the fall. His life will be over. Is that really what you want?"

Drew appeared to be thinking it over. I stayed quiet, knowing just the sound of my voice could rile him up.

"Fine," he said, sitting down next to his dogs. One of them promptly crawled into his lap. He dropped a kiss on its nose without thinking about it, blowing his tough-guy act. I kept my face as impassive as I could, but my stomach muscles unclenched. All of a sudden, I caught a glimpse of big old goofy Drew, the guy who ate paste until he was eight.

All my senses were buzzing. I leaned forward, hands on my knees, faking nonchalance. "What do you remember about the party, Drew?"

"I was drunk," he mumbled. "High. I spent most of the night following Suzie around like a fucking puppy but she was playing hard to get. I can't remember much."

"Did you black out, Drew?" I asked.

A shadow passed over his face. It looked a lot like pain and a little bit like fear. "I don't know. I remember stuff up to a point, but afterwards..." He made a helpless gesture with his hands. He looked at me and his eyes hardened. "I do know that everything was cool, and then you said something and it blew the whole vibe."

I kept my mouth zipped, much as I wanted to defend myself.

"You know things were weird before Martin even showed up," Simon said. "He didn't talk to me about it but I could tell Mal was struggling with something. Hiding something. Did he tell you?"

"He was really pissed when him and Suzie broke up. But that was months ago."

"She dumped him?" I said.

"Yeah. It came out of the blue. She never gave him a reason." He paused. "Right after that he started working for his dad."

I remembered Mal boasting about his job. "He said he was being groomed to take over the business."

Drew uttered a harsh laugh. "Yeah, that. Prince of the Bradley empire." He stood up suddenly, spilling the dogs off his lap. "I could use a drink." He turned to face me. I tensed, but all he said was, "Beer?" and made his way over to the full-sized refrigerator in the corner of the room. Simon and I both shook our heads. When he swung the stainless steel door open and grabbed a tallboy, I saw it was fully stocked.

He took a long swallow on his way back to the sofa. I noticed how swollen he was around the eyes. Like my father's eyes before he started going to AA.

"Mal hated his dad. He hated everything about that job. He didn't tell me what happened exactly, but there was something that just ended it for him."

"What about the corner office, the secretary?" I said. I thought back—there had been a bitterness in Mal's tone, like he was challenging me to call his bluff.

"He probably just said that to get you riled up. Mostly he made copies, filed stuff, sat in on meetings. He was just trying to make enough money to leave. To get out from under his dad's shadow."

I burst out, "But he flaunted it." *Rubbed it in my face.*

"Once he got an inside look at how it all worked, he changed his mind."

"I noticed that too. It didn't sit well with him," Simon said. "He started questioning things."

"That party was a big fuck you to his dad and everything he represented," Drew added. "I'll tell you something else. You know that graffiti all over town. Switching the *Heartwood* to *Heartbreak*? That was Mal."

We all leaned back, taking in those words. I felt deflated somehow. And sad. This whole time I'd thought Mal was above everything that affected the rest of us. That he had somehow escaped it.

Drew cleared his throat and turned to me. "He also told me that his dad despised yours. Like, really had it in for him."

I bristled. "What? Why? They barely know each other."

He shrugged. "Don't know the details but I'll tell you this: Emerson Bradley is *not* a guy you want to mess with. You know he's coming for you big time, right? Demanding the cops arrest you already. He'll just keep throwing cash around until he can make something stick."

I tried to make sense of the emotions flooding my brain. "We lost everything because of him," I said between gritted teeth.

"Exactly. That's the kind of man he is," said Drew, polishing off his beer. He went and peeled off another can. "So tell me about that," he said, pointing to the jacket.

Gathering my thoughts, I told him about the girl, the chase, grabbing Mal's coat off of her, the accident. "She's in the hospital now," I said. "Busted up leg and minor head injury."

"So, she killed Mal?" He leaned forward, eyes glinting. "Is that what you're thinking?"

"No. Simon's pretty sure she was in the kitchen with a buddy for the better part of an hour before we found him."

"Yup," Simon said. "They were staking out the snack table."

"Where were you, Drew?" I asked, feeling marginally more on top of it again.

Drew chugged his beer, drawing out the moment. "Downstairs. Playing quarters in the kitchen with the guys from the team."

Simon cleared his throat. "That was earlier, Drew."

The vein in Drew's jaw was jumping again. Was he lying? My thigh muscles cramped with the desire to run. It felt like we were baiting a bull.

He scowled. "I told you, I was drunk." He took a long pull from the can. "I guess I must have been upstairs then. With Suzie."

I followed up quickly with my next question. "There's this too," I said reaching into the jacket pocket and pulling out the pill bottle. "Know anything about it?" I tossed it to him.

He caught it and read the label. Before he even spoke, I could read it on his face. Guilt.

"Spill," said Simon.

"Mal took them off his dad. They're, you know, like roofies. But for insomnia. They're illegal here but Mr. Bradley picked them up in Australia or somewhere. He's been taking them for years but he's so exhausted most of the time he never remembers how many he's got left."

"Why did Mal have them? Did he drug Jessa?" I asked.

"Hey, listen, it wasn't like that," Drew said, sitting up. "First of all, he was only going to use a little bit. Like, half a pill or a quarter or something. He had it all figured out. Crush it up and slip it into her drink. Just enough to loosen her up." His voice trailed off.

"Jesus, Drew. Don't you see how wrong that is?" Simon said.

Drew flushed. His eyes slid from Simon to me, reading the condemnation in our faces. He cleared his throat noisily. "I do now. First it seemed kind of funny. But then, when the time came, he didn't put in half a pill. He put in, like, two or three, all that was left in the bottle. I wasn't down with that, but it was too late."

"You should have stopped him," I said.

"I'm telling you, I didn't know!" Drew raised his chin again but I maintained eye contact. "He didn't tell me until after," he admitted with a sigh. "We had an argument about it. And then the fight happened and it slipped my mind."

"Jessa ended up in the hospital," I said. "The whole thing really devastated her."

Drew rubbed his jaw. "Yeah, I don't get how that happened."

"For fuck's sake, Drew!" I had the insane urge to hurl myself at him and pummel him with one of his dogs.

His eyes opened wide. And now he stumbled over his words. "They weren't for *her*. He would never have drugged Jessa. He liked her. A lot."

Then who were the drugs for?

"I just thought it would chill her out a little. So she'd be nicer to me. It was supposed to be a prank."

Simon shook his head. "This is all kinds of fucked up, Drew."

"I know." Drew's voice got really quiet. "I would never have forced her, but he told me she was up for it."

"Who are you talking about?" I asked. Then it hit me—a heavy feeling in my chest like I'd swallowed a brick. *The lipstick on Drew's collar.*

Suzie.

FRANKIE

"What do you mean, someone hurt Bumble?" Jessa said. Her furious face filled my phone screen.

"She's going to be okay. Granddad drove us over to the vet's yesterday." Since I couldn't reach Martin, I'd been forced to call home. I'd told my grandfather she'd hurt herself chasing a rabbit into the woods, and he was annoyed but impressed she'd embarked on such a dog-like endeavour.

"She's not concussed and she doesn't have to wear the cone of shame because there's no way she can reach the bandage," I added. Bumble's legs were comically short. I texted Jessa a photo I'd taken that morning before school: Bumble lying on her back amid an assortment of snacks and the new stuffed giraffe she'd disemboweled in five minutes flat.

"Ohh, sweet. Can you bring her to see me?"

"She has to take it easy, but I can come by later. Just need to make a quick stop first," I promised, ending the call. I had Jessa's schoolwork to drop off and I needed to talk to her. Earlier, I'd used the *Lincoln Progress*'s high-speed printer to make copies of all my photos from that night. Mr. Harris, our teacher-advisor, was cool with senior staff dropping in, and after greeting me he'd remained buried in paperwork. I stowed the photos in my bag, making sure they stayed in order, dodged the few reporters still hanging out in front of the school, and then rode my bike to the outskirts of town.

Every instinct screamed at me not to head back to a scene of murder and arson, but I'd been wracking my brain about why anyone would try to knock my dog unconscious. She was a barker, but since this was typically accompanied by an abundance of tail-wagging, I couldn't imagine anyone being scared of her. But what about that scuzzy piece of black clothing I'd found near her? Was it a clue? Was that what the murderer had returned to the scene to retrieve? I wished now that I'd looked at it more closely, but my head had been full of sharp objects. Maybe Bumble had dug the garment out of a hiding place and then fought over it with whoever came to claim it. I swore under my breath. Bumble had probably thought it was all a game.

Whatever the reason, it was moot, because search as I might through all the detritus, I couldn't find it. Had Cara gone back and removed it? Just because she made my stomach flip didn't mean I knew anything about her. On the other hand, she'd helped with Bumble when she easily could have bailed on me, and lord knows my dog was not a light load. So that left the other person Cara had claimed was inside the house with us.

Wheeling my bike back down the deeply rutted track, I paused to pick a small bunch of wildflowers for Jessa. We hadn't hung out face to face since the memorial service. Her parents were keeping close tabs on her and although she didn't like to admit it to anyone, I knew she was still scared. Afraid of what she might remember, and what someone else was afraid she'd remember. What had gone down with Bumble yesterday just proved she was right. Someone was willing to hurt, maybe even kill again, to keep their secrets.

When I got to Jessa's pretty purple-and-red house with the wrap-around porch, there were three cars in the driveway. The family SUV, Jessa's Golf, and where Casey's patrol car was normally parked, a much newer cherry-red VW convertible with a cluster of glittery charms hanging from the rear-view mirror.

Normally I would have busted through the front door, hollering my hellos as I went, but maybe this was something to do with Josh's graphic design business? Or a visit from a family friend?

I took a surreptitious sniff at my armpits. Day three in my favourite overalls and I'd gotten dirtier than I thought. In the midst of worrying about Bumble, showering had completely slipped my mind. A sudden awkwardness made me hesitate before I stowed my bike, climbed the stairs, and finally rang the doorbell.

Josh came to the door. As usual, his dark brown hair was sticking straight up. I'd seen his head adorned with chunks of peanut butter and milky Cheerios back when the twins were younger, but he always had this mismatched, boneless quality that made him resemble a ragdoll pieced together by some inexperienced quilter. His smile was infectious, though, and turned his pink cheeks into apples.

"Frankie, honey!" he said, waving me in. He was wearing an apron and smelled of spicy sauce, warm dough, and cinnamon.

"Am I interrupting? I have some assignments for Jessa."

"Not at all, love. Come in, come in. We've missed you."

I slipped my shoes off in the hallway and started towards the stairs to Jessa's room.

"They're in there," he said, and pointed to the sitting room before heading back to the kitchen. "FYI, it's breakfast for dinner tonight if you can stay. Tacos with eggs and chorizo, pancakes, and cinnamon rolls. Let me know if they need more snacks."

They? I carefully stacked Jessa's homework at the bottom of the stairs and went in, hyper-aware that my nails were dirty and I stunk of smoke.

The sitting room was cozy and comfortable. Couches slipcovered in bright colours, ottomans big enough to belly-flop on, a bookshelf filled with the best kind of escapist literature, and a wood stove in the corner. It was my favourite room in the house—other than Jessa's bedroom.

Jessa sat tucked in a corner of the sofa, hair in two fat braids, feet in sheepskin slippers. Surrounding her like lions with a plump baby antelope were Suzie, Missy, and Anabel. Jessa looked relaxed and well rested, the shadows under her eyes faded. She stopped in mid-laugh at something Missy was saying.

Okay, maybe lionesses with a prize cub.

"Hey," I said, forcing a smile. Jessa patted the tiny space beside her, but to sit there would have entailed stepping over

Suzie and I didn't think I could control my feet—they were itching to connect with her skull. I sank down on an Egyptian pouf. It expelled air with a sigh, earning a titter from Anabel, and I wished Jessa and I were alone. She looked at me and raised her eyebrows. I raised mine in return, our way of communicating silently that we were both okay.

"Suzie was showing off her new car," Missy said, finally breaking the tension.

"New bribe, more like," Anabel said. "You dad tries so hard! I wish my parents would get divorced."

Jessa shushed her. She'd told me that Suzie's parents travelled all the time, shuttling her between their two mostly unoccupied houses.

Suzie gave her a withering look and turned her attention to me. I felt every iota of dirt and wondered if there were still dead leaves in my hair. It took all my willpower not to check. Instead, I examined each of them carefully. Could the person who'd hurt Bumble be sitting right here in this room? But they all looked fresh, hair styled and nails manicured.

"Frankie Robson," said Suzie. She always used my full name and it instantly made me feel like a child. "What have you been up to?" She lifted a finger to her cheek. "You've got some gunk there."

I groaned inwardly and swiped at my face with my sleeve. Out of the corner of my eye I saw Anabel mouth, *Farmer Frank.* One of the sweet nicknames they'd thought up.

Which reminded me, I was still holding the bouquet I'd picked, now sadly wilted, and I thrust it at Jessa.

"Oh," she said, reaching out and then looking for somewhere to put them. "Suzie and the girls brought me flowers too. You're all so sweet." She tucked them behind her ear.

Suzie smirked and although she didn't move her head, I traced her sight line to a beautiful honey-coloured earthenware vase spilling over with a riotous blend of purples, pinks, reds, and deep blue. It was like a celebration in a pot. I expected it to break out in song.

"So, what have you been talking about?" I said, aiming for breezy and falling a few miles short.

"This and that," Suzie said, bored of me already.

Missy leaned in conspiratorially. "We were talking about Mal."

I glanced at Jessa. Her fingers were knotted in a shawl Josh had knitted. Autumn colours that made me think of pumpkin patches and hay rides and apple cider donuts. Suddenly I wished for quiet days like that. She met my eyes and managed a tiny smile. "About that night," she said.

"Have you remembered something?" I asked.

Suzie and the bots leaned forward like rubberneckers at the scene of an accident.

"No," Jessa said. "I remember going upstairs with Mal, but after that, nothing. Some key witness I turned out to be."

"The lab results still haven't come in?" I asked.

"Mom says another week or two."

"We've been doing some detective work though," said Anabel.

"You have?" I was surprised. I didn't think Anabel and Missy thought about much. I figured they were ornamental. Like a nice purse or necklace to accessorize Suzie.

"Yeah, asking around," said Missy. "Simon says there was a pretty strong rivalry between Lincoln, Campbellton, and Dempsey Hollow."

"You think this was over...sports?" I said.

"Well, *Simon says*," said Suzie with enough sarcasm to butter a piece of toast.

Missy flushed deeply. I felt sorry for her and decided to lob one back.

"What's Drew's opinion?" I asked Suzie. "He must have suspicions. Or ideas."

Her eyes glinted, nose rising in challenge. "He's got some."

"Any idea what he was up to yesterday afternoon?" I asked. He'd attacked Martin. I'd seen him smash opponents on the football field. I could imagine him clubbing my dog. My fists clenched. I met Suzie's gaze. I was determined not to look away first.

"At home in his weight room probably," she said. "He's suspended from the team."

"He's been loaded most days," Anabel said. "Since it all went down."

Suzie flashed her laser eyes at her and Anabel squeaked.

"He's still convinced it's Martin," Suzie continued. "Everyone knows Martin blamed Mal for the shitshow that is his life now."

I felt myself flush. Even though I'd had some of the same thoughts, I wanted to stick up for him. "I'm pretty sure Martin has moved on," I said. "Literally."

"The police don't seem to think so."

"Drew's a doofus," said Anabel. "He's grasping at straws." I high-fived her in my mind and then she continued, "It couldn't be anyone we grew up with."

"That's not true," said Jessa. "That's actually the most likely solution." It was good to hear the calmness in her voice. "There's a theory called Occam's razor, which says that the most logical answer is likely the right one. People are usually murdered by someone they know."

"Well, what about Matty LeDuc?" Anabel said.

"Oh yeah! He was on the wrestling team when Mal first joined in freshman year," Missy chimed in. "They must have overlapped."

"Matty got kicked out of school for dealing," Suzie said.

"They questioned him but they had to let him go," said Jessa.

"And no one saw him at the party anyway," I reminded them.

A glum silence ensued. I felt like I'd just told a bunch of kindergartners Santa doesn't exist.

"It was probably some weirdo then," said Anabel. "One of those kids who hang out behind the school by the dumpsters. They're always cat-calling from under their hoodies. Like they hate us."

Us.

There was another exchange of looks as they clearly remembered that I was not *us*.

I stood up. No way was I hanging around for this. "Those kids binge art films and smoke pretty French cigarettes. They're not hurting anybody."

"Mom said your photos from the party were really useful, but it's taking time to sort them all out," Jessa said, giving me a pleading look. I sat down again, feeling childish and annoyed. "There were so many!"

They all stared at me. "Stalker much?" Missy muttered.

Jessa frowned and Missy murmured an apology. Still, my face got hotter. I could feel the printouts burning a hole through my bag.

"There were, like, almost two hundred kids there," said Anabel. "From how many different schools? Four? Five?"

"Lincoln. Campbellton. Crestview. That one in Dempsey Hollow. Maybe even United?" Missy said, counting them off on her manicured fingers. "That's nuts."

"Wasn't there a serial killer in Dempsey Hollow a couple of years ago?" Anabel said with a theatrical shiver. "Maybe they came back?"

"She died. Drowned, I think," Jessa said.

"It probably won't ever be solved," Suzie said, dangling her fingers over a bowl of Josh's homemade potato chips. She inspected them like she worked for the FDA before carefully choosing one.

"It's my mom's reputation on the line. She feels personally invested," Jessa said, a spark of anger in her voice. "She would be devastated if the case remained open." I heard the words she wasn't saying. Her fear that the killer might want her dead too.

"Where were you?" I asked Suzie, determined to wipe the smirk off her face. "When Mal was killed?" Anabel and Missy exchanged shocked looks.

Suzie barked a short laugh and rubbed at her wrist. "Ooh, who's playing detective now? I was with Drew. Not that it's any of your business."

"The whole time?" Had she been in the bed with him upstairs? I couldn't know for sure since it had been dark and Drew was a hulk. I had to admit I wasn't even sure it had been Drew in the first place. It was more like an impression of Drew. Had I seen him downstairs beforehand?

She shrugged. "Yeah. Or with my girls."

"We were all interviewed by the police," Anabel said. "I heard they even asked some people to come back in."

"Like who?" I asked. Maybe I'd get a fresh lead.

"Anyone who had priors. Luke has a DUI," said Missy. "And those sophomore girls who stole their mothers' jewelry."

Anabel rolled her eyes so hard I thought they'd fall out of her head, and the girls all snickered.

"I know they got a ton of calls because of the reward money," Jessa interrupted. "None of those went anywhere and it was actually a huge waste of police time and resources." It made my heart thrill to hear her criticize them.

"It's obvious. Maybe you just don't want to admit it," Suzie said to me. "They've interviewed your *friend* Martin a bunch of times. Emerson Bradley brings him up every time he does a press conference. Not by name, of course, but everyone knows that's who he's talking about."

I stared at her dumbly. It wasn't like the thought hadn't crossed my mind, but hearing it come out of her mouth made it sound ugly.

"They didn't hold him. They didn't charge him," Jessa pointed out.

"Well then, who else was there?" said Missy.

"Why don't you show us the pictures you took?" Suzie said.

I didn't want their fingers all over the prints, so I handed my phone to Jessa and they hunched over it, scrolling through all the crowd shots.

"I saw this girl with the shaved head," Missy said pointing her out. "Actually, there were a few of them all together. *Punks.* Shoving beers in backpacks. Stealing. The older one looked like she could kill someone. Short but thick with a bandana over her hair."

With a jolt, I realized she was talking about Cara. I thought of the kindness in her eyes.

Suzie relaxed into the couch. "There you go. I remember them now! Four weird girls. Mal might have caught them stealing from us."

"Was he carrying a ton of cash on him?" I asked.

Anabel shrugged. "He usually had a roll, plus credit cards. That gigantic Rolex his dad gave him."

I remembered Whalen saying that a number of items had been stolen. *Was that really Cara and her friends?*

"I heard the police are looking for them," Suzie said.

I looked at Jessa for confirmation.

She nodded her head. "I overheard Mom say yesterday they're putting out an alert for a group of girls who have yet to be identified."

CARA

After leaving Frankie, I'd looped around through the trees where she couldn't see me and cut back down towards town. I was torn between wanting to talk to Shadow as soon as possible and the need for medicine and something more substantial than uncooked ramen for us to eat. We couldn't chance a fire. Telling myself it would only tack on an hour or so, I'd headed straight for the dumpster outside the Portuguese bakery. Right at the bottom, I'd struck gold in the form of a tightly tied plastic bag. The rolls were rock hard and tinged with green but we could soak them in water. And I'd lucked out at the pharmacy. The teenage boy behind the counter was distracted by a customer just long enough for me to palm a bottle of aspirin. It was later than I'd thought, the sun already sinking behind the hills by the time I got back up to the woods. The cold air nipped at my face and hands.

I trilled as I approached the campsite so they'd know it was me. No response. After whistling again, I froze in the shadow of a pine, scanning the ground for clues, trying to hear above my heartbeat. The birds were silent. A dry leaf floated down, making a sound like dry chapped skin when it caught briefly in a branch. I kept myself so still I heard it land.

Had the police found them? Had they hit the road, fed up with the cold nights, the lack of food?

As quietly as I could, I made my way over to the small hollow under the ferns where we'd stashed our dwindling supplies. A few bottles of creek water, the bucket, a couple of cans of the tough red beans no one liked. My pulse slowed with relief. They hadn't left me. So where were they?

I bent again, shoving the rugs aside hoping to find the tool bag, but it wasn't there. Not here, not at the well. That meant Shadow had moved it. And why would she do that unless she was keeping a secret?

Finally, I discovered Iggy huddled in her sleeping bag under some bushes, mounds of leaves piled around her like she was burrowing. Her face pale, eyes purpled with pain, dead to the world. She was breathing deeply and steadily. I laid my palm against her clammy forehead, careful not to wake her. I smelled something sharp and checked the surroundings. She'd puked again. I kicked some leaves over the mess, made sure she was well covered, and then grabbed another blanket and returned to the cold firepit. I wrapped myself in the stinky folds and watched the sun set in a blaze of red and pink that reminded me achingly of Frankie's hair.

Where are they? I switched back and forth from fury to gut-curdling worry. The bats emerged, diving and swooping after bugs.

It wasn't until she said my name that I realized Shadow was there. She stood at the west side of the clearing, shrouded by trees, looking as if she were part of the landscape.

"Where were you, Cara?" It was barely more than a whisper. "You've been gone hours."

I felt guilty. Could she tell where I'd been? What I was thinking right now?

"I went out. Checked on some things, you know. Looked for food. Then I—" Frankie's words buzzed in my brain. What if Frankie was right, that Mal had been killed with a tool of some kind? A weapon the killer had taken with them. "I lost track of time," I said. "Here," I pulled the plastic bag of rolls out of my backpack. "They're a bit stale." That was the understatement of the year. You could use them to hammer rocks.

She drew a little closer, still favouring her left foot. Maybe she'd broken a small bone that night and it wasn't ever going to heal properly. But if that were true, she couldn't have been able to walk all the way over to the mansion earlier. She hadn't hurt that dog.

I softened my voice. "You know you can tell me anything. I won't judge."

Something flashed across her face. Anger. "What's that supposed to mean?"

"Just that we're family. Family sticks together no matter what."

"You're the one who keeps leaving. Who's got secrets," she said. "The past is the past. Leave it there."

"Shadow," I said desperately, "if you hid that bag of tools, tell me."

For a moment she looked shocked, and then she turned away, shuttering her eyes, and crouched down, hugging her knees to her chest. It felt like an uncrossable distance and it filled me with panic. She'd been so strange ever since the party. I hadn't seen her for most of that night. She could have hurt herself jumping out of that window. *Could she kill someone? Maybe if he'd laid hands on her. But he'd been with some girl, right? In bed?*

A low moan distracted me, a series of dry heaves.

"Iggy!" I ran over to her, propping her up with my arm. She threw up a thin trickle of bile. "I've got pain meds. In my backpack," I told Shadow. She found the bottle. "Give her four." I helped Iggy swallow them and as much water as I could get her to drink. She crawled back under her rug.

"Toni hasn't come back either," Shadow said, still sounding mad.

I straightened up. "Come back from where?"

"I don't know. Town? I figured you'd run into her."

My mouth felt suddenly dry. "When did she leave?"

"A couple of hours ago."

"Listen, don't say anything to Iggy, okay?"

———

SHADOW EVENTUALLY FELL INTO ONE OF HER RESTLESS SLEEPS, but I stayed up all night, half dozing, half wakeful, checking on Iggy every hour or two, listening for the crunch of leaves, the snap of a branch that would tell me Toni was coming home.

By the time the sun rose again, I was freezing and cramped, one arm trapped under Shadow's body, and there was still no sign of Toni. None of us had ever stayed away so long. It was a rule. There was safety in numbers and safety in the camp. Out there on the streets, we were all vulnerable, and never more so than when we were alone in the dark.

I slid free, leaving Shadow under the blankets. Iggy crawled out of her nest, rubbing sleep from her eyes, picking leaves from her clothes, and squinting in the daylight. Her black hair was sweat-stiff, sticking out like porcupine quills.

"Is it morning?" she said. "Goddamn, it's bright."

She was shaky on her feet and I helped her sit back down. I'd sprinkled a few of the the rolls with water and sealed them up in a smaller plastic bag last night. Now they were soggy in parts but we'd eaten worse. She nibbled at one.

"You okay?" I asked, pitching my voice low so as not to wake Shadow.

"Kind of sick and out of it, but the headache is gone and my eyes work again," Iggy said.

I poured her some water from the bucket. She drank it down thirstily and I got her another.

"Have you seen that bag of tools we took from the party house?"

She gave me a weird look. "I don't know, Mom. Isn't it with the rest of the stuff?"

"Listen, I'm going out for a while. When Shadow wakes up, I want you two to stick around here today. I'll be back as soon as I can." I pressed her arm. "You hear me, Iggy? You stay put, and make sure she does too." I left before she could start to argue. Before she could ask me what the hell was going on.

FRANKIE

Straightening my spine, I marched up the steps and pushed open the police station door. I'd stopped briefly at home to drop off my school bag and let Bumble out for a pee break before biking downtown. It had started drizzling, a chilly rain that felt like slugs crawling down my back.

The waiting room was empty, which calmed me slightly. I scanned the wanted and missing posters but saw no artist's sketch of Cara or her friends. Maybe Suzie was just talking out of her ass; she always wanted to be first with the news. But Jessa *had* confirmed it.

I walked up to the officer behind the counter. I hadn't seen him before. He was young with a severe crewcut and angry ears; it looked like he'd lost a fight with a hedge trimmer. He was shuffling papers, but he looked up briefly after I tapped on the counter. He blinked, watery blue eyes with invisible lashes. I was relieved not to be facing Sergeant Whalen of the Piercing Gaze.

"Is Captain Dawson here?"

He barely raised his head. "Do you have an appointment?"

"No, but she knows me."

Now the stare, half disbelieving, half calculating.

"And you are?"

"Frankie...Frances Robson," I said.

I could almost see the gears turning as he figured out who I was.

He swept the files to the side, clearing a path to the desk phone. His hand hovered. "What's it in regards to?"

Feeling all detectivish, I said, "The Mal Bradley case."

———

CASEY LOOKED TIRED, THE TWINKLE IN HER DEEP BROWN EYES dulled, although she did summon a smile for me as she led me down the hallway to her office.

"Not that it's not good to see you, Frankie," she said, motioning to a chair and taking her place behind her desk, "but things are a little chaotic here. We've had to bring in support officers from other districts. Some of them are barely out of training."

She peered at me from behind a pile of papers, dirty coffee mugs, and more than a few greasy fast-food wrappers. Josh would have had a conniption. "What can I do for you?"

"Jessa said..." I stopped, trying to think of how best to word it. "She said you're looking for some girls who were at the party."

Casey leaned forward. "Go on."

"I think I know one of them. A little."

She fished out a pen and notepad. "Name? Address?"

"I only know her first name. Cara. And I'm pretty sure she lives in town but I don't know where." I was beginning to think this was a mistake. And Casey's strained expression didn't make me feel any better.

"Frankie," she said gently, "if you have information that can help us with the case, you need to let me know."

"It's not that. I want to help."

"Okay then. What school does she go to?"

I shook my head. "I don't know, sorry. Maybe Crestview?" *I should have asked Martin if he knew her.* "She was at the party with those two other girls. I haven't met them though. Only her. I don't think…I mean, she didn't feel like a violent person, you know?"

Casey sighed. "Be that as it may, we're looking for a murderer, and they don't always willingly reveal themselves."

I flushed and she muttered, "Sorry. Long days. It was your photos that brought those girls to our attention. So thanks for that." She tapped her keyboard and then turned her computer screen to face me. I was looking at a collage of some of my crowd shots. "Can you point her out?"

I found Cara, her bandana low on her brow, an island in a sea of dancers. "That's her."

She reclined in her chair and rubbed her palms over her face. "Why don't you tell me how you know her?"

Shit. Lying was unthinkable. I stared at a spot on the wall past Casey's left shoulder. "I met her yesterday." *Deep breath.* "I was up at the house."

Her chair creaked as she leaned forward again. "Please tell me you don't mean the Heartwood house?"

I nodded, eyes fixed on an old nail sticking out of the plaster. "I thought maybe, if I retraced my steps, I might notice something, remember something from that night."

"It's not safe, Frankie! The structure is unsound. What were you thinking?"

"I wanted to help and—"

She sighed. "I know you want to help Jessa. You're a good friend. But you have to trust that Josh and I are looking after her. She's getting the help she needs and it will just take time."

I nodded, ignoring every instinct to blurt out how scared Jessa was.

Casey's voice hardened. "Be that as it may, you can't go stomping around a crime scene. It's illegal trespassing." She took a beat. "Is it possible this Cara was there because of the reward money?"

I hadn't really thought about it until now. But it all made sense.

"Maybe. She said she heard someone else there. A third person creeping around. They attacked Bumble."

"Is Bumble okay?"

"Yes, she's fine." I thought of her licking Cara. She wouldn't have done that if Cara had been the one to attack her. She still hadn't forgiven my grandfather for accidentally stepping on her paw when I first got her.

"Good. That's good." She massaged her temples. "This third person, though. Did you see them?"

"No, but I had a feeling like I was...being watched the whole time."

"You need to promise me you won't go up there again, Frankie."

Her voice forced me to meet her eyes, and then she held my gaze until I mumbled out a "Yes, ma'am." It felt like an invisible rod had fixed me in place. I couldn't turn my head, I couldn't lift a finger as long as she was looking at me. And I knew I couldn't break my promise.

Thankfully, the phone on her desk buzzed and she broke eye contact. In a slightly more relaxed voice she said, "I have to answer this. If you see Cara again, please let her know we need to talk to her and her friends as soon as possible. I'll alert my patrol officers to keep their eyes open. And close the door behind you."

She spoke into the receiver: "Oh good, Alvarez. I know we can't spare anyone, but can you send an officer up to the Heartwood Homes site? A quick check to make sure everything is secure? I'm thinking Talbot. He's been pushing papers around the front desk for the last two days. Maybe the fresh air will wake him up." A pause. "Do you have something for me?" and the creak of her chair as she shifted position. I tried to linger, but she waved me away and I exited her office, feeling like I'd been judged and found wanting. The dual power of her momness and police chiefness had been overwhelming.

The baby cop at the counter watched my slow progress out the door with something approaching sympathy. I wondered if he was Talbot.

Outside, dusk had fallen. I checked my phone: 6:33. Late for dinner. The only thing worse than my grandmother's stringy beef goulash was her warmed-over beef goulash. Right as I pulled my bike from the rack, I felt a fat drop hit my cheek, then another and another as they picked up speed. I groaned out loud.

"Frankie," came a familiar voice behind me. "What are you doing here?"

I turned around. Martin.

"You look rough. Everything okay?" he asked.

We stepped back under the eaves and I made an effort to collect myself. Suzie's words echoed in my brain. How many times had the police interviewed him? Maybe I wasn't cut out to be a detective. I couldn't detach my emotions from my logical brain. Could this smiling individual with wet bangs falling into his eyes and hightops scribbled over and mended with duct tape be the person who'd clubbed my dog and murdered his childhood friend?

"I was talking to Casey, you know, Captain Dawson. Jessa's mom."

"Oh, right. I keep forgetting about the family connection. That must be uncomfortable." He laughed nervously. "Was it about Mal?"

"Kind of. You? Did they make you come back in again?"

He grimaced. "I actually came in *voluntarily* this time."

"Oh." Despite the cold rain, I felt my cheeks heat up. How stupid of me not to realize he'd heard all the rumours floating around. *It must be making his life unbearable.*

"I was talking with Sergeant Alvarez," he said.

I figured that was the call that came through when I was leaving Casey's office. *Put a checkmark in the Not the Murderer* column, I thought. But then again, it was common knowledge that a lot of criminals get a kick out of *helping* the police, joining search parties and discovering clues. *Checkmark in the Maybe a Murderer* column.

The rain started coming down harder.

He was shifting from foot to foot, clearly nervous.

"So...have you discovered something?" I asked.

"Yeah, actually, I need to talk to you about it. It's important. I'll drive you home," he said. "My dad let me borrow his car. It's slightly more reliable than my bucket."

I hesitated. I certainly didn't want to get any wetter and I was super late, but jumping into the car with a possible killer? I felt for my phone. It was in my jacket pocket, easily within reach. We were standing outside a police station, for Pete's sake. And I was pretty sure he was hurting. Each movement seemed to cause him pain. Still, every thriller movie I'd ever watched screamed, *Don't do it!*

"It's got to do with Jessa," he said.

"I can spare thirty minutes," I said. "And then drop me off at the corner."

MARTIN

I stowed Frankie's bike in the back, being careful not to jar my torso. Even so, beads of sweat pooled on my skin. She got in cautiously, giving me time to shove an ancient take-out container and several coffee cups off her seat. Dad barely drove anywhere these days. The upholstery smelled like stale fast-food grease and mouse droppings. But that wasn't the only heaviness in the air. Clearly, Frankie had heard the rumours about me. Her face was ridiculously easy to read.

I turned the car on for the heat but left it in park, cranking my window open a little to defog and wincing as pain ricocheted through my ribs. I'd take her home, but maybe she'd relax a little if we just stayed here for a few minutes. In full view of a building full of cops who were already gunning for me.

"There's water in the back if you can reach it," I said. She dug out two bottles and handed one to me.

"So, what's the scoop?" she asked, wiping the rain droplets from her face and glasses with her coat sleeve. "You said it's about Jessa?"

"Indirectly," I corrected. I told her about Coffee Girl, Mal's jacket, the pill bottle, and visiting Drew.

"So, Mal drugged her," Frankie said between clenched teeth. "And Drew knew about it."

"Yeah, but he says it was a mistake."

"*That's* his excuse?!" Frankie scoffed. She was silent for a moment, the only sound the windshield wipers fruitlessly battling the rain. "So what happens now?"

"I handed everything over to the police. Alvarez sent an officer straight over to the hospital to talk to the girl while I was still sitting in his office."

She settled back into her seat. "You didn't know her?"

"Other than the gas station? I've seen her around downtown. You know, panhandling and stuff. Runaway maybe?"

She gnawed on her thumb.

"It can't be random, the thefts, the jacket. I'm betting she was at the party. Simon said he noticed some punk girls, and I definitely saw one in the kitchen, stealing some food."

Frankie pulled out her phone, fingers furiously tapping and swiping until she shoved the screen under my nose. It was a crowd photo, but she'd zoomed in on three girls hovering at different spots around the snack table. There she was, Coffee Girl. Plus another girl, small like her, with spiked black hair, and a third with a brown buzz cut and an orange bandana worn low over her forehead. They were standing apart but there was a clear relationship between them.

"That's her," I said, pointing. She did have a small tattoo, just under her ear.

Frankie's finger tapped the girl with the bandana. "And that's Cara."

"Cara?"

"Yeah...this girl I met yesterday, and the reason I came to talk to Casey." Frankie squirmed uncomfortably. "Suzie Jackson told me that the cops were looking for these punk girls from the party. I wasn't able to help Casey out much. Cara didn't mention where she lived or anything. I have no idea if she's even from here."

"Impressions?"

"I don't know? She helped me after Bumble was attacked."

She noted my shocked look. "She's okay now. I'm spoiling her rotten. But Cara? I'm thinking, not a psychopath."

"Yeah, my girl too. She thanks people after she asks them for money. I get the feeling she's just struggling to survive, you know?"

"Struggle can make people desperate."

"There were tons of things she could have stolen from the kiosk but she only went for the painkillers."

"Did Alvarez say what'll happen to her?"

"She probably won't be charged with theft since no one saw her actually steal the jacket. And from what the other officer said, she's a minor. They're trying to track down her family."

Frankie was staring out the window, chewing on her bottom lip. "Suzie figures those girls killed Mal because they were robbing him and he resisted."

"If that was the case then why was she panhandling?"

"Maybe they stole stuff, not cash? It would take some time to turn goods into money. But Cara was up at Heartbreak looking for clues, so doesn't that point to innocence?" She clutched her hair. "This is all hurting my head."

For a couple of minutes, we listened to the drumbeat of rain on the roof.

Frankie turned to me with a suddenness that made me tense against the back of my seat. "How did Drew rationalize the roofies? Or is that something 'the guys' resort to often?"

Martin winced. "Drew swears it was a prank that went wrong. The dose was supposed to be tiny. I think Mal probably did it to humiliate Suzie. He was hurt by the breakup. And Drew went along with it because he thought it might make her relax and be, you know, more willing."

"Like that makes it any better?" she said. "Your friends are foul."

"I wouldn't exactly call them my *friends*, but I totally agree with you. Simon and I ripped him a new one."

Her eyebrows knotted. "It still points to something fundamentally wrong with Drew, though. He's lacking a moral compass. It sounds like he's obsessed with Suzie. And was probably jealous of Mal. Maybe it was his idea to dope Suzie and rid her of her inhibitions. He's been trying to get with her for forever. And the topper, he killed Mal to make way for himself. Like some crazed love triangle."

She seemed so excited about this theory I felt bad casting doubt. "Mal wasn't in his way. Drew said he and Suzie hooked up at the party. Her lipstick prints were all over his neck and collar."

"Yeah," she said slowly. "Suzie said the same. I guess they alibi each other."

"So he *was* upstairs with her?" I filed that information for later.

"I mean, I guess. It's not like I went in and pulled the sheets back." She stared out the window at the police station. "What are the cops doing with this new information?"

"They're re-interviewing Drew. And Mr. Bradley. And receiving the jacket and the pill bottle into evidence. But since Suzie was fine, it's kind of a dead end."

Frankie tapped her lip. "It can't be a coincidence. Suzie wasn't passed out that night; Jessa was." She sat up and pulled out her phone again. She started scrolling, muttering under her breath. "Dammit!" she said. "I should have paid more attention."

In answer to my bewildered expression, she handed over her phone. It was a photo of Jessa, surrounded by a mob of dancing people. She was smiling, eyes half-closed, apparently downing a beer. "What am I looking at?" I asked.

She grabbed the phone and enlarged the photo. On the side of the red Solo cup Jessa was holding was a name written in black Sharpie.

Suzie.

"Jessa drank out of the wrong cup?"

Frankie pounded my leg in excitement and I tried not to yelp. "I'll bet you Mal dosed that cup and then Jessa drank out of it by mistake. She said she wasn't drinking much, but she seemed so wasted all of a sudden."

"Do you think the police can prove the drugs in Jessa's system were the same ones?"

"Probably. But when I saw her yesterday, she said the lab results still haven't come back."

We both sat in silence for a while, watching the wind pick up, the tree I was parked next to losing the last of its leaves. Sheets of rain sluiced against the glass.

"I don't know what to do with all of this," Frankie said at last. "I mean, Jessa needs to know that Mal didn't purposefully drug her. But does it make anything better? I mean, he's still a bastard." She chewed on a fingernail. "*Was*," she corrected herself. "I keep forgetting he's dead."

"I know. Me too." I braced myself to ask the next question. "Should we tell Suzie?"

"I don't know. Ethically, I think we have to."

A thought occurred to me. "What if Suzie knew about the dosed beer?"

"And still let Jessa drink out of it?" Frankie groaned. "Maybe this is all kinds of fucked up."

"Can you email me the photos from the party?"

"Sure, but the cops already—"

"I know they have them, but we have the inside scoop, right? We might notice things that are off. Odd interactions. Facial expressions. Masks lifted."

"It sounds like you're writing an article."

"Maybe," I said, musing over the idea. I missed digging into a story, even though this was way more serious than investigating locker-room vandalism or why the vending machines no longer had potato chips.

Frankie gave me a strange look, partly apprehensive, partly quizzical. "Suzie's positive you did it."

I choked on a laugh. "What? Really?"

"You find that funny?"

"Honestly, I'm surprised she admits to knowing me. Listen, she's not my favourite person but if we want to find out the truth, we have to talk to her. They dated for a long time. And she's close to Drew. Maybe she can give us some insight into their characters. Telling her about the roofies just might make her mad enough to spill the beans."

CARA

I'd gone to all our regular spots, explored the obvious places and our secret haunts. I was tired and hungry and so thirsty I could have drunk a river. I slipped my hood on. Just to make things worse it had started to rain, a fine drizzle that hung in the air but somehow managed to sink into my bones.

I sat at one of the picnic tables outside Cheesy Joe's Pizza Palace. I inspected a half-empty soda can for cigarette butts before downing it, savouring the sweetness. The jolt of sugar gave me some energy but I knew it wouldn't last. What I needed—what we all needed—was a good meal, preferably a hot one, although I knew how unlikely that was.

This outside area was deserted now, but in the summer we'd loitered here, swooped in on the leftovers before the seagulls and crows could get them. It was mostly kids working and they didn't quite know how to deal with us. If one of the doofuses dreaming of a management position tried to get all bossy, we'd mean mug them until they backed off.

Through the windows I could see people chowing down. The smell of tangy sauce, oozing cheese, and baking crust made me light-headed. Maybe someone would come out with a takeaway box, see me, and hand it over with a smile and a kind word. Maybe. But I doubted it. I knew that most people wouldn't see me at all. And if they did, they'd keep their distance as if I were contagious.

Where could Toni be?

I'd already visited the dumpsters around the back of the grocery store, thinking she might have fallen in and gotten trapped, but they were locked up tight. The park with the pond. The half-pipes at the skate park. I was grasping at straws by this point. No sign of her either by the onramp to the highway—the best panhandling spot in town because the cars had to slow down at the metred lights—or at the bakery outlet.

I did spy a police car slowly cruising, so I ducked through the bushes and came out on the other side of the road before making my way to the pizza parlour. Could Toni have been picked up? Technically, panhandling was a crime, but most cops let you go with a warning.

Some people came out of Joe's, laughing and joking around. Their voices got super quiet when they saw me huddled on the table. I caught glances, heard low murmurs. I was a reminder that society wasn't perfect. That not everyone had found their purpose or stayed on track. They hated that.

Bad things happened to kids all the time. Their parents beat them, or didn't want them. Or liked to touch them. Or pushed them into the street. Or had no time. Or were kids themselves. Iggy had an uncle with roaming hands and a cruel streak. Toni had a mom who loved booze and drugs more than she loved her own daughter. Shadow had been thrown out of her home for reasons I could only imagine. Me? I'd lost my chance before I was even old enough to say *mama*.

I made eye contact with one of the emerging customers, a woman with sleek hair, yoga pants, expensive sneakers, and a face full of judgment. I looked away first.

A few minutes later, a burly guy wearing an apron stained with red splotches came out of the restaurant. I was sure he must eat at work regularly because his face was purple and sweaty and his shirt was straining at the buttons over his round belly.

"Hey, you!" he hollered.

I took my time raising my head, and then I slowly looked over my shoulder at nothing before saying, "Who, me?" just to get a rise out of him. This kind of harassment made me so tired.

"Yeah, you. One of our customers called and said you cursed her out, spat at her feet."

"What?" Now I was mad. "I never did anything."

"Well, anyways, this is private property and you've been hanging around here long enough." His lip curled. "You casing the joint?"

A red veil rose over my vision. I wanted to hit something and it might as well be him. "It's not a crime to sit!" I yelled, flexing my fists.

He pulled his phone out. "I'm calling the police," he said.

"For what? I haven't done anything!"

"Private property. Your call: stay or go—now."

I figured he was faking it but no, he'd switched to speaker and I heard a voice say, "*Lincoln PD, how may I help you?*"

Backing away, I caught snatches of his words. "Customer complaint...trespassing...medium-height...short brown hair, black clothing, dirty-looking."

Shit. I jumped down, dragging my hood further over my head even though it was too late to hide. The man watched me until I turned the corner, his arms folded across his barrel chest like he was some kind of superhero. He'd spoken of me as if I were less than human. I decided once the heat was off, I'd come back and peg a rock through his front window.

I ran, taking side streets away from the downtown core, until a cramp in my side doubled me up and I had to lean against a darkened storefront. Closed up for the night or maybe for good. The windows were so filthy I couldn't even see through them. I was tired of people and their holier-than-thou attitudes but I couldn't go back without Toni or at least some answers. Iggy would go crazy. And Shadow. I didn't think she could take one more thing before breaking into a thousand pieces.

The *boop boop* of a nearby police car raised my head. They were stopped at the four-way intersection. As I watched, they turned in my direction. Quickly, I melted into the shadows.

MARTIN

I'd taken a short 7:00 to 10:00 P.M. shift and for once, Garth had showed up on time. Even though I was bone-tired, as I pulled up to my driveway I wished I was anywhere but here. The house looked derelict through the sheet of rain. Devoid of life. Blinds drawn, porch in darkness. The neighbouring houses were dark too, although I knew that the closest one stood empty and the man across the street worked nights.

I parked, left the car idling, and got out to haul the garage door up on its stiff chain.

The highbeams picked up scattered shards of white that crunched under my shoes like small bones. I snapped on the outside lights. Dozens of eggshells were scattered across the driveway, mixing yolk and rainwater into a slimy paint, the empty cartons a soggy heap on the weed strip we called a lawn. I looked to where my wagon was parked along the curb and I saw that my rear window and hood were smeared with the same viscous yellow matter. It had collected in clumpy puddles along the base of the windshield. The faint stink of sulphur crept into my nostrils. The eggs had been rotten.

Turning my collar up in a futile attempt to stop the rain, I walked out onto the road, looking up and down. "Oh shit."

To add insult to injury, my car was now sitting on four flats, like an old dog that had given up the ghost. I noticed the asphalt marred with fresh burned rubber from someone turning donuts and a pyramid of crushed beer cans by our mailbox.

I stowed Dad's car, hitched the padlock through the hasp at the bottom of the garage door—although we had never bothered to lock it before—and let myself inside the house.

After securing the deadbolt I called out, "Dad? Are you here? Are you okay?" I flicked the lights on. And then I saw him.

"Why are you sitting in the dark?"

"Are they gone?" he asked, blinking in the glare. He held my old baseball bat across his lap.

I felt a wave of anger. "Did you call the police?"

"No—I was sleeping and then..." His speech was slurred. "Why not?"

"By the time I got to the window, they were halfway down the block."

My heart sank. "Who was it?"

"Couldn't see them or catch the license plate, but it was one of those big fancy pickup trucks."

A picture rose in my mind of Drew reducing cans to metal discs by slamming them against his forehead. It was one of his party tricks. "Was it red?"

"Maybe. Hard to tell with the rain. Should we call the police?"

I sighed and lay down on the couch. "They egged my car, slashed my tires. Is that even a misdemeanour?"

He put the bat down with a trembling hand.

What if I did call the cops, follow up on my gut instinct that it was Drew? We couldn't ID him formally. He'd get a warning or a ticket at best. Still, I thought I'd reached a kind of peace with him. What had gotten him all riled up again? Did he regret coming clean about the pills? Or was he mad that because of me, he'd had to talk to the cops again? Was this garden-variety bullying, or intimidation? Was there someone behind him pulling the strings? *Emerson Bradley?*

I kicked the wall. A dent appeared, the drywall behind the faded wallpaper crumbling away. My father was staring at me and I realized I'd been muttering under my breath. Something was nagging at me but I couldn't quite catch it.

"Have you eaten?" he asked, sounding concerned. He stumbled getting to his feet, catching the back of the chair to steady himself.

"Dad!" I hurried over to help him, spying the empty whiskey bottle tucked in beside the seat. "You're drunk." I couldn't keep the condemnation out of my voice.

He shrank a little more.

"Let me make us some coffee," I said, bottling up my frustration. I busied myself at the counter, putting dishes caked with congealed mac and cheese into the sink to soak, boiling the water.

"I'll call my sponsor in the morning," my father said. "Promise."

"Do you want to go to a meeting right now?"

"Tomorrow." There was such a wealth of sadness in his voice. Of disgust and disappointment. I almost couldn't stand to breathe the same air. I got the cups down, bashing them around and almost breaking one. What kind of a son was I? This was a sickness. He needed help, not criticism.

Once the coffee had steeped I took it over, set it in front of him, and sat back down. We both fell into silence. It was as if we'd forgotten how to talk to each other. I considered going to bed, but I wasn't tired anymore. Instead an energy pulsed through my body, generating a maelstrom of thoughts. Everything I had learned today and all the swirling questions.

Dad wrapped his hands around his mug, took a cautious sip. I'd made it extra strong. He seemed like a husk sitting there. Cowed. What could he possibly have done to enrage Emerson Bradley? I felt a pulse of irritation, followed immediately by shame. Drawing in a deep breath, I went for it.

"Dad, when I saw Drew, he told me that Mal's dad hates you. I need to know why."

His hands fumbled. The mug hit the edge of the table and broke, dark brown liquid soaking into the carpet. He buried his head in his hands, shoulders heaving.

"Dad," I said, crossing the floor and kneeling by his side.

His head bowed as if a great weight was driving him into the ground and he started sobbing. "I wanted to keep you out of it," he said, voice thick with tears and booze.

And that nagging thought leapt to the forefront of my brain. When I walked in he'd been holding a baseball bat. He didn't think this was a prank aimed at me. He'd needed to protect himself.

"C'mon, Dad, let me get you to bed. We can talk about it all tomorrow."

As I led him down the hall, all I was conscious of was a deep sadness. Once he'd collapsed heavily on the edge of the bed, I slipped his shoes off, eased him down, and drew the blankets up to his chin. I grabbed him a glass of water and some aspirin and left them within reach, then made to go, but his next words turned me back around.

"I blame myself for all of it."

My heart sank. "Dad..." But something had been flickering at the back of my brain, and I had to ask. "Dad, did you start the fire at Heartwood Homes?"

"What? No! How could you think that?" His shock seemed genuine. I felt my stomach settle a little. He reached out, clumsily seeking my hands.

"Martin," he slurred, blinking bleary eyes. "I swear it'll all be okay. Just promise me one thing."

I nodded. "Of course, Dad. What is it?"

"You'll stay away from Emerson Bradley."

FRANKIE

I hadn't slept much at all since my conversation with Martin. Luckily Sunday was a slow day at the Book Nookery and we didn't open until eleven, most of our regulars coming in after lunch or church. Once I'd turned on the lights, flipped the sign to open, turned the heat up, and counted the cash float, I called Jessa. It went to her voicemail. I switched over to text. *See you after work! Solo? It's important xo.* I still hadn't figured out how I was going to tell her that Mal hadn't roofied her on purpose but *had* been planning to roofie his ex. I didn't want to cause her any more pain, but she deserved the truth.

I put on some jangly guitar pop and sat with my chemistry textbook. It was the last of my midterms next week and let's just say I was no Marie Curie. I closed it with a thud. My mind just kept ticking from Mal to Cara to Drew to Jessa to Martin and back again. Over and over. So many conundrums. I tried to lose myself in busy work—dusting the shelves, vacuuming grit off the carpet, and even cleaning the bathroom, but my thoughts just kept tapping. Now I sat in the armchair by the window with Higgins, the bookstore cat, purring on my lap. He was a massive tortoiseshell tabby with extra digits on his front paws. Polydactylism. It made him a little clumsy. He was always jumping up on shelves and falling off and he walked like he had cushions taped to his feet.

I picked up the stack of photos I'd printed out and sighed. I'd already spent hours going over them. Using a loupe to focus in on people's faces, hoping to catch someone with their emotions exposed. "Who's the murderer, kitty cat?" He meowled and pawed the top photo. It was one of Cara and her friends. My spirits fell. "I sincerely hope not, Higgins."

Cara looked stern, almost big-sisterly, with her thick eyebrows bunched and a reluctant smile tugging her lips upward. I traced my forefinger over her tough-sweet face, over her generous mouth. All three of them were pressed together, arms interlaced, heads touching. I peered more closely. The blond's tattoo was visible in this shot. Not a bird but a dragonfly. What really shone was the affection between them all. A few feet away Jessa, Missy, and Anabel clustered together, bejewelled, white teeth, perfect hair. The contrast between the two groups was so apparent. The punk girls were rugged, hardened, a little dirty. The three others looked...well, loved. Where did I fall? I wondered, glancing out the front window. Somewhere in the middle?

That's when I saw her. She was looking down, hands shoved in the pockets of her black jeans, hood obscuring her face, but I had no trouble recognizing her. It was something about the way she carried herself. I'd noticed it at the party and outside by the mansion. Compact, no unnecessary movement, and strong. Fluid as a cat that was *not* polydactyl. She was pacing like someone in a waiting room hoping for good news, or more likely dreading bad news. Back and forth. Back and forth. For an instant I was a little stunned. I had so many questions for her and now here she was.

I knocked on the window. When Cara looked in my direction, I held Higgins up and waved. She came in furtively, looking around before she made eye contact. Those caramel eyes made my heart race, but I focused on the task before me. I needed to know if she was involved in Mal's murder.

"Is it okay?" she said from the doorway.

"Only me here. And Higgins," I said, hefting the cat up again, blatantly using his cuteness to entice her.

She stepped onto the doormat but no closer, so I went to her.

"Won't Bumble be jealous?" Cara asked, reaching out to stroke his thick fur. His motor started right up.

"What she doesn't know..." I said, putting him down. I joked about it, but to tell the truth Bumble hated sniffing Higgins on me. She'd probably sulk in her dog bed when I got home.

"How is she?"

"Good. Almost back to normal."

"I forgot you worked here," she said, tugging on her short bangs. They flipped up at the ends. There were new lines of worry around her eyes, and I could smell the damp coming off her. Her clothes were soaked, her shoes caked with red mud. "No, that's a lie," she said with an embarrassed look. "I saw the bookmark when we were up at the house. Made a guess when I saw the sign. I didn't know where else to go."

My heart melted a little. "I'm glad you came. Let's get you warm." My questions could wait a second. The bad news could wait, too. "Here," I said, grabbing one of her icy hands and leading her to the armchair. "This is the coziest spot." The heating vent was tucked in along the front bay window. I scooped Higgins up and plopped him on her knees. He was better than any water bottle.

"I don't know," she said, glancing through the window. "I should probably get back out there." Her voice shook with cold. "I'll get dirt on your floor."

"Relax, get warm. Let me make us some tea," I said.

In the back on the way to the bathroom, we had a narrow hallway fitted out like a galley kitchen with a long table and shelves overhead, and hooks for our coats and bags. I filled the electric kettle and found two clean mugs. Once the tea had brewed, I brought it out to her. She had her nose buried in Higgins's neck as he meticulously licked his gigantic paws. She'd removed her shoes and pulled her legs up underneath herself. She looked so defenceless tucked into the armchair it was shocking to me. In my mind she was this force of nature, but at this moment she appeared to be very alone and more than a little afraid.

I set the mugs down on the small table and went to the front desk to dig out a leftover muffin and apple from my lunch. When she saw the food, she tracked it with her eyes. I swear I'd seen the exact same expression on Bumble's face whenever I ate a peanut butter sandwich.

"Here." I handed it over.

"You're not hungry?"

"No." Watching her made me feel like I didn't know what hunger was. It was clear to me now that she was homeless. I felt stupid I hadn't figured it out before.

She ate half the muffin in a huge gulp, then looked embarrassed.

"Good, right?" I gave her a tiny smile and then purposefully directed my eyes elsewhere. I could hear her eating. Small, quick bites, sighs of pleasure. She was obviously starving. The apple she slid into a ragged backpack and I wished I had more to give her.

I balanced on the windowsill next to her and breathed in the spicy scent of the tea, looking out at the rainy sidewalk and the cars streaming past.

"Cara, I need to tell you something," I said.

Her eyes grew bigger as I told her about the girl who'd been hit by the car. I shuffled the pile of photos on the side table. Showed her the one of Martin's Coffee Girl. "Is this her?"

She drew in a ragged breath. "Yes, that's Toni." Next she pointed to the dark-haired one nuzzling Toni's neck. "And that's Iggy. I thought maybe Toni had split, but I should've known she'd never leave Iggy behind."

I found her hand, enfolded it in mine. "She's going to be okay. She's in the hospital. Broken leg."

"Dammit!" Her eyes looked wild. "There's no way I can get to her there."

I could feel the tension carved into every muscle in her body, but I had to tell her everything.

"The police have interrogated her. She was wearing a

jacket that belonged to Mal. They know you were all at the party. And they need to question you."

Her hands were trembling.

"It's not that bad, I promise."

She choked. A weird noise I realized was a sob quickly stifled. It was the most awful sound I had ever heard. Like something inside her had ripped loose.

"Cara." I knelt in front of her, took her raw hands in mine and blew on them. "Why were you at the party?"

She took a moment to gather herself before she spoke. "We were squatting up at one of the other houses on the development. We came down to see if there was anything we could use." She spoke into her shoulder, avoiding my gaze. "Mostly food and supplies. Anything that the builders abandoned. Shadow was grabbing that stuff out of the basement."

"Shadow? Is she in these pictures?"

"No. She stayed outside. She didn't come in. She doesn't like being around people much."

"There are four of you?" For some reason this extra girl set off an alarm bell in my mind but I didn't know why. "And you took building equipment? Tools?"

"Yeah, but I've looked everywhere for the bag. I couldn't find the tools."

"Did any of you know anyone at the party?" I flipped through the photos, looking for the crowd scenes. "Can you look at these?"

She scanned them closely and then shook her head.

"We're not even from Lincoln. We've only been squatting here since the spring. Are you going to turn us in?" She was still shivering.

"No! I swear, you are safe with me." I ran over to the children's area and grabbed a fleecy throw. Draping it over Cara's shoulders, I squeezed in next to her and Higgins. The armchair could barely accommodate Higgins when he was in a particularly fluffy mood, but somehow we fit. It felt natural to slip my arm around her back and hug her to me.

"Where are you living now?" I asked.

"In the woods. But the nights are getting colder. There's an abandoned car in a quarry nearby. I thought about moving us all there, but I'm not sure."

"Aren't there...services?" I said. "Places to go until you get back on your feet?"

"Not enough," she said. The pitying look she gave me made me feel deeply ashamed. "And the shelters, they're a scary place if you're young and female. That's why we banded together, we decided it was safer to make it on our own." She nuzzled into Higgins's neck again for a moment. "They'll put Toni back into the system. Iggy is going to freak out when I tell her. We should have left town, like Shadow said. It's like I can't keep us together anymore no matter how hard I try."

I remember the article I'd read the other day. "The newspaper said she'd go to a youth home in the next day or so."

"Did they say which one? What if they ship her out of the county?"

"No. But when you go to the station, they can probably tell you."

"I can't do that." Her voice rose in frustration.

"I know the police captain. She's my friend Jessa's mother."

She stared at me. "You don't get it, do you? It's not the same for us. Cops aren't there to serve and protect us."

"I'll vouch for you. I'll go with you." I tried to capture her hands and she tore them away.

"Will you?" Her voice was quiet and monotone. I didn't know what to say. She got up and let Higgins down gently on the floor, giving him one last pat.

"Yes," I said, rising too. "Don't you see that the more you avoid this, the guiltier you look?"

Her eyes went wide and blank and then she shrugged her shoulders. "I can't worry about that now. I need to get Toni back and we can move on." She grabbed her backpack off the floor.

"Wait, please." I ran to the kitchen, calling back to her. "Let me help you." My wallet was in my coat. Surely I had a few bucks. Before I could locate my money I heard the bell tinkle and then the door slam.

She was gone. All that was left of her was a warm spot on the chair and a smear of reddish mud on the carpet.

It wasn't until I packed up to go home that I realized she'd stolen all the photos of herself and her friends.

MARTIN

The Dead End Coffee House might have resembled Satan's playroom, but it served the best coffee and it was also neutral territory on a cul-de-sac in the industrial part of town.

I was pretty sure Suzie Jackson had never set foot in here, and her bewilderment at the ornate skulls and crows, flower murals, and red-leather-upholstered booths took a lot of the sting out of her. That, and the caramel macchiato I slid across the table.

"Soy milk, right?" I said. I was winging it but I was pretty sure she was animal-sensitive—as long as it didn't interfere with her love for leather shoes and purses.

She relaxed her frown a little after the first sip. I nudged a plate of cinnamon cuties over.

She ignored them. "So what's this about, *Martin*?" She said my name like she wasn't sure she had it right. I had to admire the subtlety of her insult.

I scanned the front door and checked my phone. Simon and Frankie were late, and I needed backup. Simon was always able to charm Suzie.

"Simon should be here any minute," I said, stalling for time. I hadn't told her Frankie was coming too.

"I'm meeting the girls at the mall in forty-five." She poked at a cutie with her spoon as if it were a dead bug.

I pointed to the pastries. "They're really delicious. Like a donut met a croissant and jumped in a cinnamon syrup hot tub."

"I don't do sugar," she said. "And I hope this coffee is fair trade."

So much for small talk.

TEENAGE BOY STABBED IN HEART WITH SPOON BY IRRITABLE FASHIONISTA.

Sweat had broken out on my upper lip. I swiped at it and gulped down a too-hot mouthful of black coffee. Two days had passed since Frankie and I had sat in my car in the police station parking lot. My dad was attending back-to-back AA meetings every day. We were smack in the middle of midterms before the wind-down into Thanksgiving. I'd barely had time to come up for air, much less think about how I would entertain Suzie, and how I'd broach the subject of date rape drugs, and in light of the bomb I was about to drop, whether she would want to keep alibying Drew. Frankie had thought about asking Jessa along but decided it would be too painful for her.

When Simon and Frankie finally showed up, I was out of my seat and halfway to the front door before they even had time to spot us.

"Hey, you guys!" I wiped the nervous wetness off my forehead.

They removed their coats and hung them on the twisted branch iron racks near the glowing pellet stove. Suzie had refused to be parted from her fake-fur leopard-print peacoat. She had it draped it over her knees and kept stroking it like it was a live animal.

"Sorry for being late," Frankie said, fanning her flushed cheeks. "Some jerk ran over my bike last night and I had to run."

"Like, accidentally?" I said, cutting off Simon, who was apologizing for not giving her a lift.

"Doubtful. Considering that I left it leaning up against the side of the garage and found it mangled and tossed into the oak tree in my front yard."

"That sounds like an oddly familiar M.O." I told them both about the egging and the tire-stabbing.

"Well, I'd like to ask what kind of asshole would do something like that," said Simon. "But I think we already know."

I nodded. "It's got Drew's fingerprints all over it."

"Yeah," Frankie said, tentative. "But is it a practical joke or an intimidation tactic? Should we be scared?"

"And why is he still messing with you guys?" Simon added. "Is it because the cops brought him in again?"

"That seems likely," I said, shrugging. "Hopefully it's something Suzie can help decipher."

"The princess made it, I see," said Frankie. "She looks annoyed."

"What have you done, Martin?" Simon said in mock terror.

"I bought her treats."

I accompanied them to the counter to order drinks and another plate of baked goods. Frankie got a bag of big muffins.

"Hungry much?" I asked.

She shoved them into her messenger bag without comment. "Hey," she said, "weird question. But do you know anywhere around town where there's red clay?"

I stared. "Umm, up near the creek maybe?"

Her lips set into a firm line. "Yeah, that's what I thought. Let's get this done." She headed to the booth.

There was a moment's hesitation before Simon slid in next to Suzie, giving her a quick hug, which she returned.

"Oof," he said, "that chem midterm was a killer. Feels good to relax."

"Yeah, it sucked, but it's over and there's shopping to be done," Suzie said. "Got to meet my girls." Her eyes lingered on Frankie and then snapped over to me. "So, what's the deal?"

Simon leaned forward on his elbows. "It's about Mal. And Drew. We found out some stuff."

"And? Why bother me about it?"

I was still trying to organize my thoughts, but Frankie beat me to it. "Jessa was roofied at that party," she said abruptly. "But Mal and Drew's plan was to dope you."

I exhaled. Trust Frankie to take the plunge and let me off the hook.

Suzie's mouth dropped open.

"Drew told us everything," Simon said. "Mal was acting like it was big joke but it's obvious he was trying to harm you. Get back at you in some way."

"What are you talking about?" Suzie seemed to have gotten a hold of herself. "Mal and I were over and done with. He'd moved on, clearly. Drew must have got it wrong. He never said anything to me about it."

"Jessa mistakenly drank out of your cup. Check out this photo." Frankie tapped through her phone and zoomed in on the pic of Jessa with the Solo cup inked with Suzie's name. Suzie flicked a glance at it then leaned closer, frowning.

"And Drew would hardly admit it to you," Frankie pointed out. "He was trying to get with you. It would be rape."

That seemed to shake Suzie. She gripped the edge of the table. "How can you be sure there were drugs in my cup? The tox reports still aren't in, right? Jessa didn't say..." Her voice dropped off.

"The police are fast-tracking the labs now, in light of this new information," I said.

"And obviously, Jessa was drugged," Frankie said impatiently. "She remembers only having one beer," she began, counting off on her fingers. "Mal had date-rape drugs on him. She drank from your cup and Drew admitted it was dosed. She lost consciousness."

"Where would Mal even get drugs like that?" Suzie asked. There was an edge in her voice now, and she sat up straighter. "Tell me everything you know."

I told her what went down at the gas station with Coffee Girl, the stolen jacket, the accident. "We found an empty pill bottle of roofies in his jacket pocket," I said. "His father's name was on the prescription."

Suzie drummed her fingertips on the table. "They belonged to Emerson Bradley?" she asked.

"Drew told us Mal had planned it as a joke," Simon said, "But there must be more to it than that."

"It's a hateful thing to do," said Frankie. "Vindictive. And even though the dose was dangerously high, Drew didn't stop him."

"Did anything go down with you two? Something that made Drew angry?" I asked.

Simon took Suzie's hand. "You don't have to be scared. You don't have to protect him."

She was silent for a few moments.

"They argued that night about a girl," I asked. "Was it you?"

Suzie shook her head. "I don't know. Tempers were high. They were both drinking so much."

Her eyes seemed unfocused, as if she were somewhere else, reliving another moment. "What does it matter now? Mal is dead." Her tone was so bitter it curdled in my stomach. "It should end there."

"What is wrong with you?" Frankie leaned over the table, practically spitting the words. "Don't you care? If not about yourself then what about Jessa? Your so-called *girl*." Her face was a brighter red. She seemed to be boiling with rage.

"You don't need to protect him, Suzie," Simon repeated. "We'll all back you."

"I'm not. Just...let me talk to Drew," she said. "He listens to me."

"You might not get the chance before the police haul him in again," Frankie said. "Sooner or later, they're going to find something."

Suzie directed one last glance at Frankie. She looked stricken. Like everything she'd believed in no longer held true.

FRANKIE

As I stood in Jessa's driveway, watching Simon and Martin drive away in Simon's Audi, I paused for a moment, trying to gather my thoughts. Never in a million years would I have believed that I could feel bad for Suzie Jackson, but I did. Didn't mean we were suddenly besties, but I disliked her a lot less. *Mal and Drew.* Their competitive relationship seemed to be where everything hooked together, and poor Suzie had been caught in the middle.

The squad car was gone from Jessa's driveway. They'd put their Halloween decorations up: a plastic skeleton hung from the eaves, and the lawn sprouted both plastic turkeys and pumpkins, some carved by Jessa's brothers into anime characters.

Josh looked up as I walked onto the creaky porch and waved me in. His home office faced the big window onto the front lawn. It was little more than a standing desk and a shelf crammed with design books, but I knew he liked to pace while he worked. He pointed to his phone headset and then gestured to the kitchen.

From upstairs I could hear the thump and clatter of the twins playing one of their complicated games. Jessa was at the counter wearing one of Josh's *Super Dad* aprons and cracking eggs into a bowl.

She gave me a smile when I entered. "Thought I'd make bread pudding out of these leftover cinnamon rolls," she said.

"Your mom's favourite," I said dropping a kiss on the top of her head and gently squeezing her shoulder. "Chocolate chips?"

"You know it." She looked tired but not scary-tired. More like the typical under-eye shadows you'd get from a study marathon. Although she could have been excused from her midterms, Jessa was insisting on taking them, under supervision at the public library. "I'm graduating with the rest of you," she'd said.

"What can I do?" I asked, rolling my sleeves up and easing past her to wash my hands in the sink. I slipped on another apron and eyed a plate of cinnamon rolls.

"Break them up into chunks," she said, raising her fork and watching the eggs flow back in a frothy stream. For a few minutes we talked about regular things like books, Thanksgiving, and whether we'd have an early winter. Bumble went wild on snow, snapping at snowballs and burying herself in it.

"So, any news?" I asked. I could hear Josh striding back and forth and talking to a client just beyond the kitchen. I didn't want to risk him overhearing me. Jessa deserved to know this first and process it in her own time.

She gave me a knowing look. "You fishing for inside

information?" I gave her a weak grin. Before she answered, she said, "I'm told you've been snooping around, Scooby Doo. Going places you shouldn't."

Crap. Eyes downcast, I told her about Cara and her help with Bumble. Her bandana, which I'd washed in hopes of seeing her again, was folded in my pocket.

"Mom told me. Mostly because she wanted me to be clear that going up to that house was strictly forbidden." She tilted her head to catch my eye. "You like her, this Cara? Your face did that little dreamy thing like when I'd catch you staring at Lorelei in gym class."

I felt my cheeks warm although it was so good to hear that teasing lilt in her voice. "I do. She's kind and strong and generous. I'm worried about her though. It's getting colder and they've been staying up near the quarry." I cleared my throat. "I know I should tell your mother. Is it wrong that I want another chance to convince Cara to go to the police herself?"

Jessa pressed my hand. "I know you're a good judge of character. They questioned her friend already. I think it's more a case of whether they saw anything that could prove important. Besides, there's a new lead!"

Grateful for the change of subject, I said, "Tell me all!"

She shot me a tiny smile. "Sergeant Alvarez dropped by this morning. They talked out on the porch but his voice carries like crazy. Apparently Matty LeDuc *was* in the vicinity of the party. They found a bunch of stolen prescription drugs in the trunk of his car, and an unlicensed gun."

My heart leapt to my throat. "What kind of drugs?"

"Oxy, I think."

The wheels started to spin. "Cara said there was a way into the house through the basement. Matty would be pretty hard to miss, but maybe he got in that way?"

"Yeah, Mom said something about that too. The back stairs." She ate a piece of stale roll absent-mindedly. "It was super crowded. They can hold him 'cause of the gun. They're re-interviewing people with his photo. That's what police work is. Slow and steady. Following up every lead." She turned to me. "I can tell you have something to say. It's actually this vibration in the air."

I hesitated. There was a loud thump above our heads, the crash of something breaking.

"David! Michael!" Josh yelled, followed by the sound of his feet as he went up the stairs. "Everyone okay? What did you do?!"

Here was my chance. "I was at the Dead End," I said slowly. "With Martin, Simon, and...Suzie." I heard the clatter of the fork hit the bowl.

"Has the world turned topsy-turvy? Way to bury the lede!" The quip died on her lips as she saw my expression. "Why? What's going on, Frankie?"

"I found something out. About Mal."

"Okay, we've got to sit for this." She linked arms and pulled me toward the stools set up along the kitchen island.

I kept my eyes on her face while I told her everything, noticed the endless play of her fingers with the apron knot, the hunching of her shoulders. She took an audible breath when I'd finished. I broke the silence.

"Did you ever get the sense that he'd do something like that?" I asked. "Controlling? Vengeful?"

"No. I mean, that doesn't even matter. That he would think it was funny..." Her arm jerked suddenly and a glass fell to the floor, shattering. We both stared at it, neither moving to clean it up. I was waiting to exhale, watching Jessa's expression shift from bewildered to surprised to a dawning awareness. Slowly, she looked at me. "I remember a mirror breaking. In the room."

"Yes," I said, staying absolutely still. "There were splinters of glass all over the floor near where you were lying."

"No, I mean I heard the mirror being smashed while I was lying on the carpet, before I passed out. I hit my head on the table. I was woozy but still aware. The person was already there in the room with us." She grabbed my arms. "And Mal spoke to them. Not scared." She frowned. "It was strange. He was angry but he almost sounded pleased. Like he'd won something."

CARA

You know how you'll notice a crow? It lands on a branch above your head and then you see there's half a sandwich on the ground by your foot and you understand. But then another crow shows up and another and another until there's, like, six of them all clawing the tree trunk and you start to freak out a little bit because how did they communicate there was food there?

Well, it's kind of like that with street kids. One knows something and then everyone knows it. Like when the police are doing a sweep at the skate park or the bakery has dumped all their day-old donuts or to look out for the man with the folded newspaper covering his lap on the park bench.

I had no idea exactly where they'd send Toni when she got released from the hospital, so for the past two days I'd been hanging with the skateboarders and the weed-heads. I needed to talk to someone who was in the system. I went home at night to check on Iggy and Shadow and I came down to the skate park during the day. Punk kids liked street kids. I think we made them feel more edgy, more outside the mainstream, like mavericks. I think they romanticized the shit out of it.

Today, I had to threaten Iggy so she wouldn't follow me. She was seething, a mixture of rage and bone-deep worry about Toni. I could see it in her eyes, all skittery, the way she'd started chewing her chapped lips. It was eating away at her. Finally, I handed her the bottle of spiced rum I'd been saving and hoped it would knock her out. "Listen, the cops are looking for us. They have photos someone took at the party," I told her. "It's less likely they'll spot me on my own."

I hadn't shown them the printouts I'd stolen from Frankie. Instead I'd hidden them away at the bottom of my sleeping bag. I hadn't told them about her either. I wanted to hold those private memories in my heart for just a little longer.

"You'll watch her for me?" I said to Shadow, ignoring her unhappy face. "We'll draw attention if we're all together," I reminded her. "Plus, you know you freak out being in town." I laid my hand on her arm, caressed it until she exhaled and some of the stiffness left her body. "If Iggy goes down there, she'll do something crazy, try and bust down the doors to the hospital, stand in the middle of the street and scream Toni's name. We have to be patient."

I was faking it. I felt the same as Iggy. Like we'd swum into a net and it was starting to close around us.

"We should leave town," Shadow said. She'd been repeating this for the last week with increasing urgency.

"Soon," I said. Her jumpiness made me feel like my skin was too tight.

"When?"

"Any day now—but not without Toni. I'll bring her back," I promised, leaving them huddled under the rugs, looks of despair on their faces.

———

SKEETER WAS THIS RAT-TAILED LITTLE PUNK, MAYBE TWELVE, thirteen years old, who spent most of his life on his long-board. His mom was an alcoholic, and depending what kind of a time she was having, he was either at home with her in their bug-infested basement apartment or overnighting in one of the shelters. That's where I'd met him, one town over, on a night when the temperature had dropped so far below freezing that the homeless were dying in the streets. The shelter had been the lesser evil that time.

Skeeter's mom was going to meetings now and things were looking up, so he was home more often than not. Still, the shelter seemed to have an open-door policy as far as he was concerned. I'd asked him to keep a lookout for Toni, described her. His eyes had lit up.

"She sounds hot," he'd said. "Just my type."

"She's gay. And way older than you, toddler."

He'd scowled and blustered a bit.

I softened my voice. "Please watch for me, okay?"

This afternoon, I'd been waiting on the steps for about an hour, growing increasingly impatient, when he finally showed up.

"Where you been?" I said.

He skated right over, grinding on the rail, then popped his board up and caught it. I knew he was showing off and wanted to inform him Iggy was the best street skater I'd ever seen, but I bit my tongue. I could tell he'd discovered something from the way his eyes were gleaming.

"Around," he said. He reached out and fist-bumped me, then sat down on the stairs, spreading his legs wide in that way boys do. I tried not to feel annoyed. "Checking out that new squat in Riverside. A warehouse on the west end by the train tracks. They figured out how to get electricity and everything. It's nice."

"You skated all the way over there?" Riverside was south of Lincoln. Maybe sixty-five kilometres from here.

"Nah. Grabbed a ride both ways. You should check it out. It's mostly girls. Tough bi—" He caught my expression and quickly said, "women."

"Maybe I will," I said, tucking the information away. "So, what did you find out?"

He fingered a non-existent mustache and squinted in a way he hoped was sexy. I pounded his arm until he started talking.

"A friend of mine is in that group home over there on Winchester. Know it?"

I did. It was a wreck of a house with a cracked concrete front yard and a ton of busted-up appliances instead of flowers.

"Mouse says it's over capacity. They just moved a bunch of kids from the adult shelter 'cause they were getting eaten alive over there."

"Mouse?" I asked.

"Yeah, my bro Terrell. He loves cheese."

I'd never stopped to think about how many street kids had nicknames. I guess it was another way we tried to choose our own identities, erase the past.

"Anyway," he said, licking the edge of the joint he was rolling, "they can't handle the overflow. He told me the older kids are getting moved again. Tomorrow night. After dinner."

"Where?" I prayed it wouldn't be on a bus out of town.

"To the Roach for the time being. After that, who knows?"

A grin spread across my face so wide it hurt my cheeks.

I knew the Roach. It was what everyone called the Roosevelt, a fleabag hotel that child services used temporarily for older kids until they could be transferred to a youth shelter. Adult supervision would be minimal. It was even better than I'd hoped.

Before I got too ahead of myself, I asked, "How do you know that Toni is one of them?"

"Mouse said, super cute punk girl. Small. Blond skinhead. Light eyes. Banged-up leg and wearing clothes that were way too big for her." He smirked. "Oh yeah, he also mentioned she had a wicked jab. Sound like your girl?"

MARTIN

G arth was late as per usual but I didn't mind. At least I was working, squirrelling away a portion of my meagre paycheck every week. STUDENT PAYS TUITION WITH A JAR OF COINS. Most of it went to paying my father back for my new tires but Dad didn't seem bothered anymore if we ate out of a box or a can every night and at this point, neither was I. And the cops had left me alone for the last week. Frankie told me they were still looking at Matty LeDuc. Every so often I thought about the reward money Bradley was offering, but that was an impossible dream. It seemed like only people with money made money. The rest of us were doomed to keep struggling.

I figured Dad had taken a step forward in his therapy. He didn't talk to me about it, but he was standing a little straighter, and he was showering daily. I guessed more work had come in. Most nights he was hunched over his computer, tapping away and occasionally exclaiming "ha!" in a satisfied voice. I had no idea how preparing financial reports could be so thrilling, but I was glad to see him occupied. Sadly, his skills in the kitchen hadn't improved.

I was used to the house being dark when I got back from work. The murmur of TV voices and canned laughter coming from Dad's room, a dim light under his door, a sink full of dirty dishes. I expected the kitchen to smell like burned food. Find a lump of something charred or rubbery set out on a plate or in a bowl, fork and knife laid neatly beside it. How exactly did he manage to torch mac and cheese?

So it was a shock when I unlocked the door to find my father sitting on the couch, pale but dressed in clean clothes, tie knotted, hair combed like he was on his way to a job interview. He'd shaved for the first time in months and his skin looked naked without the scruffy beard, his chin small and pink.

"Martin, I need to talk to you." He gestured to the spot beside him, giving me a facsimile of a smile, and my stomach plummeted to my shoes.

I stayed on my feet, afraid that sitting would release a whole bunch of words I was sure I didn't want to hear. Was he sick? Cancer? Could my life get any more tragic?

"Why are you dressed like that?"

"They'll be here soon. I wanted to go in on my terms and they agreed to let me talk to you first." He glanced at the clock on the oven. "That gives me forty minutes."

"They who?" *Martians? Republicans? Stormtroopers?*

"The police. Please, sit down, Martin."

I took the chair furthest away from him and tried to figure out what to do with my hands.

"I have to tell you some things. I've made a lot of mistakes, Martin, and I've lied to you." His voice was steady. I looked for telltale signs that he was drunk—empty bottles, glasses, a cigarette butt floating in half an inch of amber liquid—but there was nothing. In fact, the house looked tidier than it ever had.

He put his hand up, forestalling whatever I was about to say. I'd been about to tell him I didn't need to hear again about his guilt and how sorry he was, that I had forgiven him, even though I feared I never would, and I was ready to move on.

"Hear me out, Martin." Without being aware of it, he raked his fingers through his hair, destroying the smoothness of it. In that instant I recognized my father again, not this calm-sounding stranger who looked like he was about to pull some religious pamphlet out of his pocket. "Let me say everything I need to say. Please, kiddo."

I nodded. I found it hard to meet his gaze. His eyes were burning with a brightness that shone in contrast to the sallowness of his sun-deprived complexion. A horrible thought jumped into my head. *Oh my god, is he about to tell me he killed Mal?* As soon as I thought it, I dismissed it. I definitely would have noticed my own father at that party.

His next words were almost as shocking.

"I didn't only invest your college fund with Emerson Bradley," he said. "I encouraged other people to invest as well. The more people I brought on board, the bigger my slice of the profits. Even though by that point, I'd started to see that things weren't adding up. He was selling people mortgage notes propped up by nothing."

I darted a glance at him. His fingers were gouging the arm of the couch, digging into the fibres, enlarging a tear in the worn fabric.

"Like...a pyramid scheme?" I knew those were scams which only benefitted the people at the top.

"Sort of."

"But the houses went up. They cleared all that land. Hired builders," I said. "It was real."

A hollow chuckle. The rip was the size of a soup bowl now. "Bradley never intended to complete the development. He had some deal with the contractors. He pocketed everyone's cash and made sure the insurance covered his company and protected it from liability. The biggest investors did the same and got a heads-up before it all crumbled. He promised I'd come out of it okay, but he lied."

My father met my eyes. "He knew I wouldn't turn him in, because to do so would be to implicate myself, too. We met more than once. When I confronted him about the numbers, he offered me more value on my investment if I kept my mouth shut. I agreed. Then he went back on his word. Told me he'd taped our conversation and if I ever said anything, he'd release it. Those folks trusted me, but I was a coward, Martin. And I am so sorry."

My mouth was dry, but I was anchored to the chair. "So what now?"

"I'm turning myself in. Whatever happens, at least that man won't get away with what he's done." He sat up and his voice grew stronger. "I've called the newspapers, too. It's going to be a shitstorm."

I felt a tiny flash of pride before my heart sank. "Will you go to jail?"

"I'm prepared for that. I've spoken to a lawyer. I'll go to court in the next twenty-four hours and plead guilty to fraud.

That carries a reduced sentence of three to five years if I agree to be a witness against Emerson Bradley. I can make amends, Martin." He held out his hands, but I leaned further back. I needed the support behind me. His face fell, settling into its old familiar lines of disappointment and sadness. "You'll be better off with me gone, son. You're eighteen. It can be a new start."

I felt a sudden rush of anger. "How can you say that? Ever since Mom died..." He flinched, but I plowed on. "It's like, where've you been?"

He slouched. "You're right, Martin, I haven't been present. But that's why I'm doing this now. Because I can't avoid it any longer."

"So what'll happen to me?" I said dully. "How am I going to survive? You know how much I make at the gas station and landscaping is basically over for the year. There's school. We're barely making it."

"My employers let me cash out my pension plan and put it in an account for you. I've arranged for monthly deposits."

"Won't they grab it? The tax people or the feds or whoever?"

"There are loopholes, and my name is on nothing. I asked Simone Bonneville to set it all up for me." Simon's mother. I looked after her perennials and knew she was a successful investment banker. "She promised me she'd check in with you. Whatever you need." My dad's eyes darted back to the clock. Somehow, thirty minutes had passed. I wanted to slow down time. This whole conversation felt muted, like we were talking under water. Or he was behind glass. Exactly how it would be after he went to jail.

He was on his feet now, his words flooding out of him with more urgency. "There's a class action suit brewing. A chance you might get your money back, Martin. Me signing it over without your knowledge? That was fraud too. I'm willing to pay for that. You said you wanted us to move forward, but I can't. Not until I make it right as much as I possibly can."

He crouched down in front of me with his hands held out again. I took them. Because despite everything, he was my father. He was the only family I had.

CARA

We ate the ramen noodles straight out the package. They were crunchy and tasted how I imagined packing material would. We each had one and then I broke the last square in half and handed a piece to Iggy and to Shadow. I downed my bottle of water in an attempt to trick my stomach into thinking it was full. I don't think any of us had ever been so hungry. When I lay in my sleeping bag at night, my belly was like a bowl, my ribs countable under my skin.

While we ate, I caught Iggy and Shadow up on everything Skeeter had said. Iggy wanted to head out immediately of course, guns blazing, but I convinced her to wait until night-time. From what I'd heard of the Roach, there were only one or two social workers to oversee two floors of rowdy teen-agers. Like, fifty kids. They didn't have the security systems that regular foster homes had, nothing but door locks. Kids in places like that were always sneaking out to get smokes or drink, bed-hopping between floors to hook up.

"Skeeter's getting a note to Toni today. His friend Mouse knows what's up." I'd gotten a description of the kid. He was brown-skinned, tall, and gangly with a retro fade and a homemade panther tattoo on his forearm. "If we're lucky, she can sneak out of there without anybody noticing." It took a while for things to get organized at the temporary shelters. They wouldn't have roll call set up, or bed check. I was hoping for a back door and a quick getaway.

Of course, Iggy was ready to poke holes in my fragile plan.

"And then what?" she said, pushing her lower lip out. She was extra grouchy today. Shadow seemed all in a fog too. They'd finished the bottle of rum I left them the night before. "You don't think that'll hype the cops up even more? Didn't you say they're already looking for us?"

"Then...we'll see," I said, struggling to keep my patience. "I'm working on some ideas." Truth was, I was struggling to think of solutions. Every decision I'd made recently seemed like the wrong one.

"This town is way too hot for us now. They've got her back in the system. Probably photographed her, started a goddamn file," Iggy said. She was right, and it was what I was thinking too, but it pissed me off that she wouldn't let it go. Grumbling about it wouldn't make anything better.

"Calm down," I told her. She kicked a rock. "She can buzz her head or dye it another colour or something. What do they care about an extra girl on the streets? She'll be eighteen in another year."

I slipped my arm around Shadow's shoulders, brushing the knobs of her spine. "You good?"

"She's freaked out," Iggy yelled. "Everything sucks!"

I shot a look at Shadow's pale face, then back to Iggy's, contorted with anger, and forced an edge to my voice.

"Instead of bitching, why don't you figure out what we can take with us. What we can carry on our backs."

MARTIN

It had been hours since they took my dad away, but I was still sitting in the living room, hunkered down in the armchair. His chair. Particularly shabby, it had accompanied us from our old family home and the cushion was caved in from his weight, the brown material shiny from his hands.

I'd sat in the dark, watching lights from passing cars track over the walls and ceiling in this weird hypnotic rhythm that lent beauty to the dingy room, hearing distant sirens that blended into background noise. I wasn't sure how long I'd been frozen in this kind of catatonic state, but somehow it was daylight when I stood up to use the bathroom. One of my feet was asleep and I almost fell on my face.

I peed and then leaned over the sink, washing my hands. The fluorescent tubes in the bathroom cast a grey tinge over my reflection, stubble dotted my chin and upper lip. My hair needed washing badly. I dragged my hand over the scrape of rough hairs, and splashed my face with water cold enough to make me gasp. Grabbing the hand towel, I caught sight of my father's toothbrush in the holder next to mine, bristles splayed and well-used, and it brought a lump of sadness into my throat. I clicked the lights off, poured myself a glass of water from the kitchen sink, and sat back down in his chair.

It had been almost formal. The police officers polite and patient. My dad calm and determined. He'd hugged me, holding on a little longer, squeezing my ribs a little harder, and I'd hugged him back even though it hurt like hell, feeling his newly smooth cheek against mine, breathing in the scent of his clean hair. It catapulted me back to my childhood. I remembered a picnic in the woods. Him gripping my wrists as he spun around in a circle so I could be an airplane and my mom laughing and urging him to slow down; the way the sun beamed through the leaves and made patterns on the pine needles. The knowledge that he wouldn't let me go.

I felt like I'd been drained of all emotion. Like how it had been when Mom died from breast cancer. All that anger and grief I'd been carrying for so long had evaporated, leaving a big hole in the middle of me. I walked around the house, picking things up, putting them down. Trying to figure out how it felt to be here when everything was different. How even when my dad had been at his most distant, passed out drunk in his bedroom, fading a little bit more every day until he was more ghost than man, he'd still been visible in a ton of little ways. A plate by the sink, a piece of toast forgotten in the toaster, the laundry basket spilling over, the smells and sounds of living with another person. And now I was truly alone.

What would it be like visiting him in prison? It wasn't some minimum security they were taking him to—it was

Baylor Creek penitentiary. A place that called to mind gangs with shivs, electric fences, watchtowers, and high-powered rifles. Would I even get to visit him? And what was the protocol?

POP TART–SMUGGLING TEEN TRIGGERS PRISON RIOT.

Sergeant Alvarez had arrived with the uniformed cops. As the guy in charge, I guess. He'd taken me aside while they were helping my dad into the car. "After your father's entered his plea in court, they'll move him to Baylor." He met my worried gaze. "He's doing the right thing."

I trailed after them, thinking of all the things I wanted to say to my dad and not being able to articulate a single word.

The neighbours were out in full force, standing on their porches, peeking through their curtains, until the police car drove off. I could see Dad determinedly smiling at me out the rear window, his hand raised as they took the corner. Every muscle in my body strained to run after them, to beg them not to take him away, but instead I leaned my head against the door frame, fighting the tightness in my chest and the tears stinging my eyes.

My phone buzzed, shocking me out of my dismal thoughts. I checked the time: just after 5:00 A.M.

"Damn, Simon, what is this—insomnia, or a butt dial?" I said, relieved it was him. He was about the only person I could stand to talk to right now.

"Martin, hey. I wasn't sure you'd be up." Voice roughened, words coming in staccato bursts like he was running somewhere. He caught his breath. "I just heard. They found a body up at Heartbreak Homes a half hour ago." His voice dropped to a whisper. "Martin, it's Drew. He's dead."

CARA

Hampered by our bulky bags, we were forced to move slowly. My leg muscles twitched under my skin and I'd broken into a sweat, soaking my hoodie and all three shirts I owned. The few bars and restaurants still open held small groups of people but it seemed like no one other than us was on the street. Standing outside the warmly lit spaces in the cold darkness, it felt as if we were looking through a one-way mirror. Present, mere feet away from everyone, but invisible and isolated.

Every so often, a police siren whooped, scaring us out of our shoes. We kept to the edges, praying their headlights wouldn't pick us out of the dark.

"Why're there so many cops out tonight?" Iggy whispered.

Shadow shifted uneasily, her face screened by her hair. "Something happened," she said quietly.

"So we need to get going then," I said, ignoring the butterflies in my chest.

"Roosevelt Street is up there," Iggy said, increasing her pace. We turned a corner, then another, walking quickly on narrowing streets where the buildings seemed to lean in somehow, creating pools of shadow, and alleyways that screamed of bad decisions. Away from the busy main streets, I was suddenly conscious of night sounds. The wind rattling bare tree branches like chicken bones in a jar, doors slamming, rusty gates groaning, a far-off dog barking, and the oceanlike waves of our breath becoming mist in the cold air.

"There," I said pointing across the street. The Roosevelt Hotel sat by itself on a square of weedy, rocky land as if the businesses at either end of the block wanted to distance themselves. It was a four-storey brick building with a crumbling foundation and small windows draped in mismatched curtains. More than a couple of them were boarded up. The lower windows were barred and the main entrance, illuminated by one bare bulb, was a nondescript street-level door. A few dim lights shone inside, mostly on the second and third floors. The hotel was in worse shape than I'd remembered. The paint was flaking off the window trim like dandruff, and the building seemed like it was sinking into the ground.

I couldn't help but think how much cozier our home had been. The loss of it felt like a splinter in my heart, impossible to remove as it burrowed in deeper.

We picked our way through a river of broken glass to the side of the building. The windows there were even smaller, like hooded eyes. I could smell sewage, ripe garbage, and sour pee, as if every drunk in town were using this place as a urinal. I scowled at the stickiness under my shoes and was careful not to lean against the wall. Beyond was an expanse of wasteland, criss-crossed with railroad tracks. And beyond that was the river; there was enough moonlight to pick out its seething, glassy surface.

"What happens now, Mom?" Iggy said. She said it without sarcasm for once, sounding so young and exhausted that my breath caught.

"Now, we wait."

Pigeons roosted in the eaves above our heads, warbling softly and spattering the walls with smears of white. A car across the road had been completely gutted and set on fire. It was nothing but a charred shell now. I found an old tire to sit on. Shadow crouched on a stack of cardboard. Iggy gnawed her fingernails. A clatter of garbage can lids came from down the street, followed by the god-awful meowling of a cat. We all jumped.

"Who's that?" Iggy said suddenly.

I scrambled to my feet, peering through the murk. "I don't see anyone."

"The window," she said, pointing. "It was a guy, I think. Second floor. He was waving us around back."

"It must be Mouse. Come on."

The back door was looming open when we got there. A tall boy with bright eyes and close-cut hair stuck his head out. He saw us and nodded.

"Cara?" he whispered. "I'm Mouse. I've got your girl. I'm going to help her down the stairs." He propped the door open with a chunk of brick. "Back in a minute."

Iggy stationed herself by the entrance. From inside, we could hear the metallic cranking of an old furnace. The warm, musty air billowing into our faces smelled like cabbage and mould.

Mouse reappeared, backing his way slowly down the stairs, arms held out. "Man," he said, once he got to the bottom, "it's mayhem up in here—no hot water, the electricity is bugging, and the whole damn place smells like soup." He stepped aside, and there was Toni.

She was on crutches, one leg of her green cotton pants sliced to the thigh to allow for the cast. A bandage covered the back of her head, and they'd shaved a patch of her already short blond hair even shorter. The sutures were a black seam. A knitted shawl was draped over her shoulders and she wore gaping jailhouse slippers on her feet.

"Oh, shit," I said. I don't know why I was surprised. She'd been in the hospital; she'd been hit by a car. I guess we'd had so many near misses I'd come to believe we were impossible to hurt. Maybe that charm only worked when we were all together.

"Oh, my baby," said Iggy, rushing up to her. But once she was within hugging distance, Iggy held herself back. "I don't want to hurt you!" she moaned. Toni leaned into her, their foreheads touching, and Iggy gently slid one arm around her waist. I could hear them both crying.

"I'm going to head back in if that's cool?" Mouse said. "Almost lights out. Wanna make sure I get my cot."

"Thank you," I said.

He pounded my outstretched fist. "Good luck out there in the world," he said, looking out at the dark streets, then cracking a wry smile. "You're gonna need it."

MARTIN

"Drew?" I croaked. Feeling dizzy, I held on to the back of a kitchen chair. "What happened?"

"He overdosed, up at the mansion." Simon's voice was ragged. I could tell he was fighting back tears. "They're saying it could be suicide. Why would he do that, Martin?"

An admission of guilt, I couldn't help but think. "Come over," I said.

"Now?"

"Yeah, my dad...won't care. I'll tell you when you get here."

While I waited, I put a pot of coffee on. The milk in the fridge had thickened up like yogurt but black was okay. I wanted something that would wake me up; it didn't have to taste good.

Drew. I couldn't grasp it. I checked the web. There was no official statement yet although a trickle of tribute posts had started. They made my stomach ache. My brain felt dull but an itchy energy permeated my body. I paced and paced, wearing a groove into the carpet from the front door to the back bedroom.

This house had never seemed so much like a box. Beige paint, beige carpet—so faded it was more of a mood than a colour. I was scared I'd never get out. *What if I die here? Like, right here! Mal and Drew had all the money in the world and they—* Thankfully, a knock at the door interrupted my tunnelling thoughts and I let Simon in.

"Dude, what happened to your car?" he said. I'd hosed it down but the congealed egg gunk was surprisingly hard to scrape off and the foul smell lingered.

"Doesn't matter."

His eyes were red and bleary with exhaustion. We went to fist-bump and it seemed so dorky that our hands didn't meet, just floated in mid-air.

"Sit down," I said, pointing to the couch. "I'll bring you some coffee. No milk, sorry."

I placed a mug in front of him and sat in Dad's chair nursing my own, not really enjoying the bitterness of the brew but needing something to do with my hands. I told him quickly what my father had done. When I finished he was silent, didn't jump in with some platitude about doing the right thing, which I appreciated.

It was true that my dad had behaved honourably in the end, but that didn't take away from the fact that he was on his way to jail while Mr. Bradley's legal team would most likely keep *him* out of it.

"Sucks, man," he said finally. "It all sucks. And this...I just can't wrap my head around it. It's so wrong."

The blood drummed in my ears. "How did you find out?" My voice sounded hollow.

"Missy's cousin has a police scanner. We were up texting and she got a message from him. Her cousin knew they were friends."

"Tell me what you heard."

"Booze and pills."

I thought of my father. That was a path he'd tried to take as well. He wasn't better yet, but he'd been on his way. And now this. I was overcome by a wave of loss.

"It happened in the room where..." He took a deep breath. "Mal died. He had candles lit all around him."

I tried to picture it. "Like a Viking funeral or something?" How over the top could you get?

Simon shook his head. "I don't know. Maybe Drew was hoping the house would catch fire again. Maybe he tried to torch it the first time? It's so fucked up."

"Who found him?"

"The cops. I guess he hit the emergency button on his phone and they showed up, called the paramedics, but it was too late."

I felt a wave of nausea. "If he called, then it wasn't an accidental overdose."

"No. He must have panicked or something. Changed his mind, maybe." He rubbed his palm across his forehead. "I could hear the sirens from my house."

I realized that some part of my subconscious had heard them too, even down here in the pit of Lincoln, a moaning soundtrack to my miserable thoughts.

"Jesus." I buried my face in my hands. "I can't believe it." For some reason the image of Drew that flashed through my brain was not a recent one, but of him at eleven or twelve, freckled and gap-toothed, knees scraped, brown hair sticking up like twigs. The Four Musketeers is what we'd called ourselves then; every street an adventure, every stick a sword. There were only two of us left now.

"Me neither," Simon said. "I keep thinking of him with his dogs that last time we saw him."

We sat in gloomy silence for a few moments.

Simon raised his head. "Does it mean what I think it means, though? It can't be a coincidence that he chose that room. He must have killed Mal."

"Honestly, Frankie had him as the number one on her list," I said. "So did I."

"You had a list?!" he yelped.

I grimaced apologetically and checked my phone. It was just past six. Frankie would still be asleep, but I sent her a text anyway, asking her to come over as soon as she could. *I'll explain when you get here*, I added.

"So, this was his way out?" I said. I had my own theories, but Simon was closer to Drew. I wondered if Suzie knew yet. She had to if Missy did. This would destroy her.

"I guess he couldn't go on," Simon agreed. "Face up to what he did. All the drinking pushed him over the edge. Look how he'd been acting. Look what he did to you! That guilt must have been eating away at him."

It made sense rationally, so why was I filled with doubt? Drew was out of control and this just seemed methodical, clear-headed. Not words I would ever have used to define him.

"Maybe the warning signs were there all along," Simon said heavily, "and we chose not to see them."

CARA

I stared at Toni. "What do you mean, you're not coming?"

"Look at me. I can barely walk," Toni said.

Iggy piped up, her voice trembling. "We'll help you. All you'll have to do is lie there and let us look after you."

"What? In the woods? With winter coming?"

They all swivelled their heads towards me. I had nothing. The house wasn't safe with the cops looking for us. And the car at the bottom of the quarry would be too hard for Toni to manoeuvre. We could leave town like Shadow wanted—but go where? There was the squat that Skeeter had mentioned, but squats had weird rules, and there was a trial period before they let you in. *Would they even have room for the four of us?*

"I'll think of something," I said. They all looked miserable and I hated myself.

"Oh, sweetie," Toni said, pulling Iggy close and planting kisses all over her face. "It'll be okay, you'll see. I love you." Their lips met, fused together. I looked at my feet, feeling an ache behind my breastbone. Shadow stared at the river. At least I could let them have these few minutes together.

"It's not so bad here," Toni said when they finally broke free. Iggy sat on the tire and patted her lap, slipping her arms around Toni's waist after she'd carefully lowered herself. "The food sucks but there's a lot of it and it's cooked. Oatmeal, toast, eggs."

Iggy moaned. "I haven't had an egg in years. Don't tell me there's bacon, too!"

Toni mimed zipping her lips. "That kid Mouse is pretty cool. Some of the girls are wrong-headed but these come in pretty handy for knocking some sense into them." She waved a crutch in the air.

"I should have taken better care of you," I said, feeling the ice in my veins lance into my heart.

Toni reached up and pressed a palm against my face. "You did take care of me. And I love you for it, but shit happens. At least I won't be freezing my ass off in a snowdrift."

"If you're back in the system, they'll ship you off who knows where. First, the group thing, but if that fails…foster care again?" I said.

Toni shrugged her shoulders. "I'm too old for fostering. And besides, if I don't like it, I'll take off once I'm one hundred percent again. No place can hold me, you know that!" Her voice sobered. "I can't get up that hill, Cara. Unless you've got something else planned for us?"

I avoided her glance. Even though I knew they wouldn't go for it, I said, "I heard about a squat down in Riverside but I haven't checked it out yet. Girl-run, maybe cool?"

"One of those lentil-stew compounds where they talk about their feelings and write the rules on the wall in big ass letters?" Iggy scowled. "That's worse than a group home."

"Don't make me feel like I'm betraying you," Toni said to me. "This is a sure thing right here. I know how it works. I know how to work it. There'll be a doctor who'll make sure my leg heals up right."

I bit my lip. "We're a family. We're stronger together." They exchanged glances.

Toni stood with Iggy's help and hobbled over. "I know. You're the best, you realize that, Cara?" Tears rolled slowly down her cheeks and I felt the prickle behind my eyes. "You looked after us so well. But you can't fix everything and you can't look after me now." She dug something out of her pocket and pushed it into my hand. It was a jewelled barrette, a dragonfly missing a couple of blue stones.

"I found it at the party. They mean joy, like my tattoo. I know you wouldn't be caught dead wearing it, but it'll remind you of me," she said. "Maybe a good luck charm."

We hugged for a long time and still I didn't want to let her go. Once we broke apart, Shadow said, "Do you know where you'll end up?"

"Some place over in Campbellton. Not so far."

"You sure?" I said quietly. "We came to rescue you."

"I want to carve out a little breathing space for myself, you know what I mean? I can't do it the hard way anymore."

Iggy looked up. In the faint light, her eyelashes glistened. She wiped her nose with the back of a trembling hand.

"Hey, sweetie, what's going on with you? Don't be sad," Toni said. "I can't bear it. This isn't goodbye."

Iggy's voice hitched but she lifted her chin. "I can't leave you. I won't."

"What are you saying, Iggy?" I asked.

"I'm staying with her. They won't notice one more street kid. You heard what Mouse said. It's chaos in there."

MARTIN

It was barely seven when Frankie knocked on my door. Her clothing was rumpled, her hair was sticking out every which way, and she was breathing like she'd just completed a marathon.

Simon looked startled. "Are you okay?"

"Climbed out my bedroom window," she said, pushing her glasses up her sweaty nose. "Bike still screwed...so I ran." She gulped air. "Easier than...telling my grandparents...what was happening. They'll just think I...went to school early."

She waved her hands around. "None of that is important." Catching her breath she said, "Is it true? Drew is dead?"

I filled a glass with water and handed it to her. She drank it gratefully.

"How do you know already?" I asked, a little bit grateful that I didn't have to tell her.

She shot me a quizzical look. "The internet is on fire."

"Already?" Simon groaned. "Why are humans so messed up?" He collapsed back onto the sofa. Frankie lifted her eyebrows at me. I could tell she was itching to give us some news.

"Jessa remembered something."

Sitting down, she filled us in on what Jessa had heard. The familiar way Mal had spoken to his killer.

"So he definitely knew them," I said. "Maybe they had unfinished business."

"That fits with the argument in the pantry," Simon said. "Could be Mal and Drew were interrupted and Drew tried to confront him again later. And killed him."

"The pieces are there, but..." I hesitated, not sure of how to express what I was thinking.

"I think we have to start from the present and work backwards and see if it still fits. You have to ask yourself, is this in character for Drew? The method of death?" Frankie said.

As soon as the words left her mouth, she turned bright red and glanced at both of us. "That sounds so...heartless. I should have worded it better. I'm sorry. He was your friend."

"It was a shock, but we've had a little time to process," I said. "I have to admit, the worst part is feeling so helpless. At least this gives us something to do."

Simon nodded. "Yeah, I'm kind of numb, but in a weird way it helps to have a distraction. A puzzle for us to focus on."

Encouraged, she carried on. "You knew him better than me, obviously. But this just doesn't seem like him, right?"

"That's what we've been talking over," I said. "Trying to match the Drew we knew to this behaviour."

Simon nodded. "In particular, the erratic way he's been acting these last few weeks," Simon said.

"Okay, so where does that take us?" Frankie said slowly. "If Drew didn't act alone..."

"Wait a minute!" Simon said. "Hold up, this is crazy."

"What are you saying?" I could barely process my thoughts. My stomach began to churn.

Frankie shook her head. "We have to think about it logically. Everything has to make sense. If he had never shown signs that he might kill himself, or at least not in this way, then..." Her phone chimed a text alert and she held up a finger. "Jessa. Finally. It'll just take a minute. She was trying to get more info."

I restrained my impatience while Frankie quickly read and responded to texts. My thoughts were a flurry of quesetions and doubts. Beside me Simon picked at a loose thread on the upholstery. The kitchen clock sounded ridiculously loud.

"At least this would give you an alibi," Simon said to me, out of the blue.

"What?"

"Yeah, I mean. The police were here picking up your dad."

Frankie momentarily raised her head from her screen.

In answer to her questioning look I said, "He turned himself in because of his involvement in the Heartwood scam." I looked away from the naked sympathy on her face. I wasn't ready to unpack all those feelings yet.

Simon continued, sounding a little embarrassed. "I'm just saying, you're in the clear this time."

I had to admit that it was a relief, but I was a little hurt that apparently Simon had been listening to the rumours.

He clued into my expression. "Not that I ever—I mean I know you didn't kill Mal." He sunk a little lower in his seat. "But it's nice to have irrefutable proof."

"Yeah," I said, happy to vent a little with sarcasm. "And it only took another one of my friends dying to proclaim my innocence to the world."

Frankie finally finished up and set her phone down. "Get this. Jessa says Drew left a note. Actually fragments of a note. A confession, from the sounds of it."

We all sat with that for a second.

Simon broke the silence. "Why write a note and then tear it up and strew it around? Would Drew even write a note? He'd be more likely to post something on social."

"It all seems a bit...theatrical?" I said.

"I could picture Drew driving off a bridge. Crashing his car into a wall. Something spontaneous," Simon said.

"Yeah, it's almost like he was setting a scene. He did all that, the candles, the note, and then he called for help. Like he wanted to be found. Or stopped," I said slowly.

"We're assuming that *he* called the police? That he wanted to be rescued?" Frankie said. "Was it a cry for help? Or did someone else dial the number, needing him to be discovered as soon as possible?"

I actually felt my jaw drop. Frankie was onto something, and deep down it felt right. "Another person."

"Yes, just suppose someone engineered it to look like a suicide. To implicate Drew as Mal's killer," she said, looking slightly ashamed to be so excited.

I knew how she was feeling though. I'd grieve for Mal, for Drew, for my dad, but right now I needed to actively engage my brain. "Someone who really wants this case closed," I said.

"This is good," Simon said, jumping to his feet and clapping his hands. "We should keep spitballing."

It seemed like the more questions we threw out there, the more answers presented themselves. It was starting to feel like less of a needle in the haystack and more of an Easter egg hunt. I thought of the kind of man Emerson Bradley was. How'd he played my father like a puppet-master, controlling and ruining lives. "Drew could have been following instructions. That might be why this doesn't seem like him at all."

"Let's be thorough," said Frankie. "Attack it like we're researching for a big story. So, what do we have?" She opened her shoulder bag and pulled out a new notebook and a thick stack of photographs. She spread them out on the coffee table, saying, "I think better visually."

They were her pictures from the party. Dozens of them. I'd scrolled through the ones she'd emailed me but it was so much better seeing them like this. Simon leaned forward, examining each one. He paused on a shot of the kitchen crowd. Him and Missy, the punk girls at the table.

"There's something else," Frankie said. "Another piece of the puzzle. I had to reprint these." She looked at me. "That girl I told you about, Cara?" She paused and quickly filled Simon in. "She came by the bookstore. When she left, she took all the photos of her and her girls."

"Why?" I asked. "That sounds suspicious."

"I think it was instinctive self-preservation. They were squatting at one of the other Heartwood houses and they crashed the party, stole stuff, like Mal's jacket. She knows the police have copies of these, but maybe it was too much, seeing their faces blown up like that." She polished her glasses on her shirt hem. "It probably felt like an invasion of privacy."

"But you already said you don't think she killed Mal."

"No. But there was a fourth girl. The aptly named Shadow. She's not in the pictures because she was outside. I'm not even sure if the police know about her."

A *fourth girl*, I mouthed. It sounded like an Alfred Hitchcock movie.

Frankie told us about her weapon theory. "Cara mentioned they'd stolen a bunch of tools. Maybe the murder weapon was in that stash? I think we have to focus there. They're the unknown," she said.

"Unless the police discovered the weapon with Drew?" I said.

"Jessa didn't mention it," Frankie said.

"I think that points away from Drew as well," I said. "I mean, being found with the weapon would be an integral part of his confession."

"The question is, what do these girls have to do with Mal? Or Drew?" Simon said.

"Maybe nothing," Frankie said slowly. "Just a coincidence?"

"Wrong place, wrong time?" Simon said. "There are so many variables."

"Okay, I'll write them in," I said, grabbing a pencil. "What's the best way to do this? Go through everyone who had or might have had a connection with Mal and Drew and then figure out opportunity and motive?"

"Let's not forget the human aspect of it. These are

individuals," Frankie said. "People. We have to ask ourselves what drives someone to murder."

"Wait a minute," Simon said. "Since Drew's dead, who's your number one now?"

"Not sure yet," Frankie said, sounding exasperated.

"May I?" I motioned for Frankie to pass me her notebook. "Let's start with the inner circle and then move out. So, alphabetically, Simon Bonneville."

Simon blinked. "Seriously?"

I couldn't help but grin.

"It'll help to get our thoughts in order," Frankie said. "Why don't you tell us how the night broke down for you."

CARA

A piece of my heart stayed back there at The Roach. I felt better leaving Toni with Iggy to watch out for her, but losing them both was a gut-punch I hadn't seen coming. It was like I'd failed them somehow. The moment that door closed behind them, I wanted to grab it open again, but I'd heard the lock click and I knew it was no good.

"Where do we go now?" Shadow said sharply as we walked away. "We can't just wander aimlessly."

My sneakers slipped and slid in the muck. The cold wet seeped in, setting my toes to burning.

"Back to the campsite. I don't know." I was so tired. I'd put everything I had into keeping our family together only to discover that I couldn't. It should have felt like a weight had been lifted now that there were only two of us to worry about, but instead, I felt a heaviness that threatened to squash me flat. "There's the car in the quarry if the temperatures drop."

"It's not safe there. It's not safe here," Shadow said. "I want to leave."

"And go where?"

"I don't know. But this town is poison and we're falling apart." Her voice was heavy with despair. She was right. What reason did we have to stay?

"Okay, I promise. We'll leave tomorrow morning." I felt an ache at the memory of sitting in the bookstore with Frankie, the warmth of her smile, her hands holding mine like she wanted to look after me. It was an emotion I'd never experienced before. She'd felt like home.

"Swear it."

"I promise. You know my word is always good."

We took the back alleys for as long as we could. There were still cop cars patrolling, driving back and forth, dividing the town into grids they could work. We didn't know what they were looking for, but we knew it spelled trouble for us. Maybe that pizza douche had made a formal complaint? I thought about the photos I'd taken from Frankie. Had she gone back to the cops? Given them details, passed on information I'd revealed when I'd been at my most vulnerable? What was it about those hazel eyes and cute nose that made me break down and tell her things? Made me wish I could kiss her, just once?

A siren blared. Three blocks up, we saw the spinning red-and-blue lights. The loudspeaker crackled as a cop ordered some driver to pull over. We backtracked and took another street, heading in the opposite direction. We paused in a dark alleyway, out of breath, hearts pumping. A pile of cardboard boxes shifted next to a dumpster. It was either rats or someone like us, sheltering underneath. Whatever it was, we gave it a wide berth.

"I saw those photos you have," Shadow said, like she'd read my mind. "From that party."

"You went through my things?"

"Don't try and turn this around on me. Where'd you get them from?"

"A friend."

"We have no friends."

I put up my hands to halt any questions and told her about Frankie. All the while, her lips pressed together tighter and tighter. "Don't be mad," I said when I finished. "We're leaving anyway. We can change our look. They don't know about you."

She started to walk away. I clutched her arm, desperate to keep her from leaving.

"Please, you have to talk to me. Tell me what's going on. You're all I have left."

She kept going and I dug my heels in. I felt the hot sting of tears and tried to hold them back, felt one slip down my cheek and angrily brushed it away with my sleeve. I couldn't remember the last time I'd cried.

She turned back to me. "Cara," she said, touching two fingers to my forehead. I leaned into the contact, searching her eyes, and her face softened. "Someone does know about me. From that party." In the seconds we stood there unmoving, the sharp wind clawed its way through our clothing and set us to shivering.

"Let's find some shelter," I said. We crouched down in a doorway, hands clasped.

"About six months after I was thrown out of my house, I was picked up on a sweep by a social worker and taken to this place for kids who needed help or had nowhere else to go. Like a rehab centre. Anyway, there was a therapy group there." She flicked her eyes away from me. "For abuse survivors, people who had lost hope."

I felt her grief in the deepest part of me, but I forced myself to just listen.

"We were all kids, you know? Boys, girls, some as young as ten. And we'd all been hurt in horrible ways by someone we trusted. By the people we loved most of all." She stopped, and all I could hear were the sirens wailing. Something else had happened. All my senses were screaming at me to run, but Shadow was holding onto me like I was the only solid thing.

"It was my older brother. It started when I was eight years old. They took his side. Said I was sick and I made it up, and that's why I had to leave.

"The foster homes weren't any different. It's like they could tell. How fucked up I was. I ran away, ended up on the street." Her fingers tightened, sending pain through my knuckles.

I pressed my cheek against hers. "That'll never happen to you again, Shadow."

"Eva." Her face was smeared with a combination of dirt and tears, eyes red-rimmed and spilling over." Eva Robertson. It's my real name. I need someone else to know."

"Eva," I repeated, wrapping my arms around her. Never had she let me get so close.

She took a deep, shuddering breath. Then she said another name: "Bradley."

The kid who died in the house that night.

"I heard all about him," she continued. "The things he'd done. Inflicting pain no one else could see. It seemed impossible that there was a connection. I tried to talk myself out of it because the truth was too horrible. I wasn't absolutely sure until I looked at those photos, but that night, I saw—"

The dark alley to our right suddenly exploded into brilliant light. A police siren blasted, followed by a man's amplified voice saying, "Stay where you are and keep your hands where we can see them."

Split up, run, and hide.

Our instincts fired up and in a flash, Shadow and I raced in opposite directions as fast as we could.

FRANKIE

By nine that morning, the notebook was filled with Martin's untidy scrawl. And my own Venn diagrams of motives and arrows linking names. Many of those we'd discussed were easily alibied. Simon was with Missy most of the night. Anabel was with one of the Razorbacks, Glen, who'd spent the evening running the drinking games in the kitchen. We'd organized the printed photos into sequences that made sense to us, plotting a slightly erratic timeline, and figuring out where the holes were. There were a lot of bristling question marks.

We knew roughly when Jessa and Mal had gone upstairs. And we knew that when I went up to find Jessa there'd been two or possibly four unidentified people in two of the smaller bedrooms—the girl who'd told me to fuck off, who we could assume had been with someone, and the passed-out boy I suspected was Drew, with or without Suzie. It was the middle section, just before and after Jessa and Mal had gone upstairs, that we focused on. Tracking where people were or where we guessed they'd been heading—the kitchen, the bathroom, outside, upstairs. The suspects we focused on, those we were sure knew Mal in one way or another, popped in and out, moving from the dancing room to the sitting room, and sometimes disappeared from view for half an hour or longer. If that corresponded with when we guessed someone had murdered Mal, we added them to the potentials column.

By the end of it, we had a list of names circled and underlined and I had that same feeling I got after a night of cramming for a test: suddenly, the elusive answer seemed within our reach.

Martin leaned back into his chair with a groan. "This feels Sisyphean. Maybe Drew *did* do it?"

"You can't quit because the boulder's heavy," I said, trying to ignore the rumbling of my stomach. It must have been audible, because both Martin and Simon looked my way. Simon leapt to his feet. "I heartily concur," he said. "What's the grub sitch, Martin?" he asked on his way to the kitchen.

Martin said something inarticulate and looked embarrassed.

"Yikes," said Simon, withdrawing his head from the cupboard. In his hand he held a box of saltines and a shrivelled apple.

"Yeah, well I usually grab something at the gas station," said Martin defensively.

We shared the crackers and washed them down with tapwater. Simon bravely ate the apple. The effect was negligible but it didn't matter.

Now that we had some kind of a plan I felt energized, anxious to get moving. "C'mon," I said impatiently while I waited for them to put on their coats.

"So, we're decided?" Martin said as we left the house. He and I would go looking for Cara and the other homeless girls. Simon would track Suzie, Anabel, and Missy down at school. Then we'd meet up again, share info, and decide on our next steps together. I'd texted Jessa but she was with her AP Calculus tutor until noon.

"Will your car make it?" Simon asked. It was parked on the street and I couldn't help but notice an odour. Duct tape held the side mirror in place.

"We're not taking mine," Martin said, hauling up the garage door to reveal his dad's car. He hopped in and it started right up. Breathing a sigh of relief, I got in.

"I'll keep you posted," Simon yelled as he pulled away from the curb.

The roads were quiet, morning rush hour over and done with. Martin took my street over to Main and I hunched down low in case my grandfather was outside clipping the hedge.

"The grandparents are going to have to ease up eventually," he said, giving me side-eye.

"Not in my lifetime." If anything, they'd rebuilt the walls higher and thicker.

We parked along the road at the top of the slope, just before it became a bicycle path. To the east and higher up was Heartbreak Homes. And slightly to the west was the creek with the red mud. I remembered it from childhood picnics with Jessa's family. I'd noticed it on Cara's shoes when she came to the bookstore, a thick rusty clay found nowhere else in Lincoln. I knew the quarry was supposed to be in the same general area. My hope was they were camped out nearby.

Martin's phone chirped as we got out of the car and headed up. "Simon can't find Suzie," he said. "She's not at school and she's not answering her phone."

"What about Missy and Anabel?" I asked, already out of breath.

"Nope. Maybe they turned them off to avoid the socials. He says he'll check out their homes and regular hangout spots."

"Not surprising, They must be in shock." Those relationships were complex and ran deep. I could only imagine how devastated I'd feel if I lost Jessa, even if, unimaginably, we were no longer friends. It was something about growing up together. It created bonds stronger than family.

He texted back a reply as we walked.

"Are you holding up okay?" I asked.

He gave me a wry look. "It's impossible to put into words. I just know that I have to keep moving, do something to keep it all from crashing down."

He cleared his throat noisily. "So, what tipped you off? To this mysterious fourth girl?" he said, side-stepping a bush. We'd crossed into the woods and the path twisted and turned through thick shrubs and low-hanging branches. Shards of grey sky were visible through the dense canopy. Eventually, the track would hit the creek and run parallel to it. "Walk me through your detection process, Sherlock." He tipped an invisible hat and I got a flash of what having a slightly annoying older brother might feel like.

"Hardly. It's not more than a hunch, and I'm not saying that she killed Mal. I'm saying she might know something. She's this unknown figure who was there and no one has talked to her. Not even the police. And then there were the tools Cara said they hauled away. We know the killer jumped from the window with the murder weapon. So where did it go?"

"Not with Drew, and not at the scene," Martin said, nodding.

"Yeah, so what if Cara and her girls took the murder weapon with them? Either on purpose or by accident." I remembered Cara's look of surprise when I'd first mentioned my theory. And then what she'd said at the bookstore. *I couldn't find the tools.* "I think Cara suspects the same thing."

"And so, who is the fourth girl?" I could tell he was getting a kick out of saying it.

"I'm wondering if she was the person who was standing in the kid's bedroom early on in the night." I chewed my lip. "And I saw a girl around the side of the house and I think also standing in an alcove near the dining room. Tall, dark-haired. They could have been the same person."

"But what's the connection with Mal?"

"I have no idea." I stopped. "Listen." Over the sounds of our panting I could hear the creek, swollen with fall rains, crashing over the rocks. And faintly, another sound, like the shrill cry of a seagull. "We're close."

The rain had turned the red clay banks into a slurry that made walking treacherous. There were various-sized footprints all around. I placed my boot next to one. A size nine, if I had to guess. No tread marks. I remembered Cara's sneakers. Shredded, held together by the laces, soles worn paper-thin.

I breathed on my glasses to unfog them. Martin shivered against the damp chill, zipped up his jacket, and pulled a wool beanie over his shaggy brown hair. "They're living out here somewhere?"

The creek was exposed to the wind but close by was a thicket of pines. I pointed. "I'm guessing there. Cara also mentioned a car at the bottom of the quarry."

After slipping and sliding our way up the banks, we paused to catch our breath under the shelter of some trees.

Martin shook his head. "I'll never bitch about my crappy house again. Where to now?"

I could still hear the creek waters. They mingled with the hollow rattle of the wind and it almost sounded like voices yelling. "Up there?"

I knew the quarry was a straight shot north of the creek but it was closer than I remembered. A few hundred yards through a dense copse of maple and oak, over a little escarpment covered in brush. We stood on the edge of the quarry, looking down into a roughly shaped bowl with a grove of trees at one end and a deep muddy pond at the other.

"So overgrown it's hard to see anything," Martin said.

Where the solid ground ended was indistinct. I toed the springy vegetation. It was cushion-like, but I could tell that the earth fell away underneath. It reminded me of a tiger trap: plants loosely piled on top of a pit with sharpened sticks at the bottom. I couldn't see any kind of path. "Let's walk the perimeter, see if we can find a way down," I said.

I was beginning to think I'd read this completely wrong. Maybe their home was farther back in the woods? Or perhaps they'd left town already? I remembered Cara saying that Shadow was anxious to be gone. That made me even more certain that she knew something.

Within the tree cover, the quarry pit was deeply shadowed. The earth was scattered with waxy dead leaves and acorns that rolled underfoot. We'd come to the end with the mucky water. A dented washing machine stuck up out of the ooze. I tossed a rock in, listened for the splash, and heard nothing. It was deeper than it looked.

"Pretty good place to dispose of a murder weapon," Martin said.

"Or a body." As soon as I said it, I wanted to take it back. The steep precipice, the trees at our backs that almost felt like they were pressing us forward...it would be so easy to set a foot wrong.

A branch cracked in the woods with a sound like a gunshot. Adrenaline shot through my veins like ice water.

"Animal?" Martin said.

More breaking branches. I glimpsed rapid movement to the right, a person in dark clothing, hair hidden under a hat, bushes swaying as they pushed their way through, running away from us. "There," I yelled. Martin took off in pursuit before I could move.

I waited a couple of agonized minutes until he jogged back, red-faced and out of breath, clutching his ribs.

"I couldn't catch them. Think it was one of those girls?"

"Maybe."

I turned back to the quarry and scanned the undergrowth. Something caught the light. *A windshield? Car mirror?* I pointed.

Someone had pushed a car into the pit decades ago. It looked like a wagon, same as Martin's car, light blue, front end smashed up, side windows popped out, tires rotted away. *How could anyone live in there?*

Martin stepped forward, dangerously close to the rim. I reached out, ready to grab him if he started to slip. "What's that?" he said, indicating something below us. *More garbage, spilled open?* My foot knocked a pebble loose and it ping-ponged down, starting a small landslide.

It was a person.

She was lying on her back, arms and legs flung out. Like a starfish. Like someone falling onto a soft mattress. But this was hard ground covered in sharp rocks. And she'd fallen from a great height.

Cara was suddenly there, pushing her way between us. Her lips were ashen with cold, mud on her face and caked on her clothing. She began to scream, "Shadow! Shadow!" I had to latch onto her, hug her against me, before she fell too.

Martin had his phone out, calling 911. "A girl's hurt. At the quarry," he said. "She fell. She's not moving."

Cara was shaking violently. I shrugged out of my jacket and forced her arms into it. It was like trying to put a coat on Bumble.

She jerked free from my grasp and ran to the head of a hidden narrow trail by a small tree, twisted and shrivelled with disease. Her head disappeared from view and then bobbed up again further down. I followed her as quickly as I dared. It was loose shale underfoot, slick and wet, barely a track, but I did what Cara did, gripping onto the trees and bushes to slow me down on the near-vertical slope. We picked our way hurriedly across the rough ground to where Shadow lay, motionless.

Cara fell to her knees.

I crouched down and pressed my fingers against Shadow's neck, gasping when I felt how cold she was. No flutter of pulse. No puff of breath on the cool air.

Cara made one anguished yelping sound, shoulders heaving with the force of her sobs. I wanted to hold her, but her grief seemed too private, so I sat as close as I could with my whole body waiting in case she needed me.

A long way off came the sound of sirens.

"The police and the ambulance will be here in five minutes," called Martin, carefully making his way down.

My eyes went to the edge of the quarry. And then back to Shadow's body. I imagined the trajectory. She'd fallen backward—not forward as if she'd slipped, but as if she'd been pushed. My head started to jangle with alarm bells.

I noticed a duffel bag a few feet away. The kind of thing you'd take to the gym. I wondered if she'd been holding it when she fell. "Martin," I said, nodding towards it.

Pulling his sleeves over his hands, he knelt and unzipped it. As soon as he raised his head, I knew. It was full of tools.

Cara's sobs had slowed. She rocked herself back and forth, arms snugged tight around her body. "There were four of us and now it's only me," she said. The light had gone out of her eyes. Again I felt that lurching sensation. I heard a voice in my head say, *Four weird girls.* Four; not three, like everyone believed.

"Someone killed her. Someone in your photos," Cara said, breaking in on my thoughts. Her eyes blazed with a silent fury. "She told me last night. It's got to do with that Bradley guy. She saw someone at the party who was hurt by him."

I could hear the sound of heavy vehicles lumbering up the dirt track. The siren whooped one more time and went silent. Five police officers and a couple of paramedics with medical backpacks and a gurney appeared next at the trail head. Slowly, they began the descent.

"Did she say who?"

Cara shook her head. "She didn't get the chance."

It felt like the two of us were inside a vacuum. She was crying silently now and somehow that was even worse. I just sat there feeling helpless.

"And there's this. Toni found it on the ground below that window." She pressed a mangled dragonfly barrette into my hand. I closed my fingers around it, willing my sluggish brain to work faster, to make connections.

A paramedic placed an oxygen mask over Shadow's face, another commenced CPR. Cara watched every move they made. Two of the police officers began examining the ground around her. *The body*, I thought to myself.

I felt dizzy. These little puzzle pieces were slotting together, robbing the breath from my lungs with each click.

"Frankie."

I looked up and met Sergeant Alvarez's dark brown gaze. He helped me to my feet and drew me aside with Martin.

"You two found her?"

"We were looking for Cara," Martin said. "She arrived after us."

"And there was no one else around?"

We told him about the person who'd fled. He called in for backup to search the woods, sent one officer to begin exploring the perimeter. "She had that bag with her," I told him. "I think the murder weapon is in it."

"Johnson." He nodded at one of the uniformed officers who snapped on a pair of gloves and bent to examine the duffel bag. "You touch anything?" I shook my head. Martin looked embarrassed. "I unzipped it but I pulled my sleeves over my hands."

"You'll all have to come down to the station," he said. I glanced at Cara. She seemed so shrunken. Sergeant Whalen was speaking to her. I hoped he'd tempered his abrasive tone a little.

"Can I go to her?" I asked Sergeant Alvarez. He nodded. I made my way over and stood next to Cara. After a moment, I felt her hand slide into mine.

"Do you need to be checked out?" Whalen asked Cara. "Are you hurt? I have to ask you some questions. Are you able to answer them right now?"

She squeezed my hand tighter. "I'm okay."

"Why don't we start with your names?" he asked, his notepad out.

"Cara Bateman. She's Eva Robertson. She went by Shadow." Her voice broke and I squeezed her hand back.

His next few questions were about addresses and phone numbers, next of kin. Cara answered in the negative to each one, her expression becoming more and more wooden.

Suddenly there was a flurry of activity over by Shadow. "We've got a pulse," one of the EMTs said.

FRANKIE

I don't know what I thought would happen. Maybe that we'd all be arrested or the police station would burst into frenzied action, but it wasn't like that at all. Alvarez took me to an interview room, and Cara and Martin were escorted farther down the hall. He led me through everything that had happened, listened and took notes while I shared Cara's information, and then left me to agonize for twenty minutes before finally coming back and beckoning me to the door.

"You're not a suspect," Alvarez said. "This may have been foul play but at the moment, we're treating it as an accident."

"What about everything I just told you? What Cara said? The bag of tools?" I struggled to keep my temper in check.

"We're still questioning her. And looking into it. The forensics team has the bag."

"You won't arrest her, will you?"

His lips firmed. "I can't discuss that with you."

"And what about Shadow?"

"She's at the hospital. She's being looked after."

He read the question in my eyes and relented. "She hasn't regained consciousness yet. She may not. Her injuries are severe."

"So what happens next?"

"We'll do our jobs. We know where to find you if we need to."

"Is Captain Dawson here?"

"Go home and rest up," he said and pointed to the exit sign.

I stared at the entrance doors, frustrated that police procedure moved so slowly.

Martin appeared at my shoulder, rubbing tiredness from his eyes. "That was a let-down," he said. "Come on. I'll give you a ride home."

I shook my head. "Take me to Jessa's." Maybe her mom was around. Maybe I could figure out some way to galvanize the police into action.

I sent her a quick text: *We're coming over*. Ellipses indicated that she was writing me back but no words appeared. Just those three dots blinking, blinking.

My heart started beating faster. "Can you step on it?" I asked Martin.

"I don't think this car speaks your language," he said jokingly, swallowing his grin once he saw my face. He pressed down on the gas. "What's going on?"

I shook my head. It was just a feeling.

When we got to Jessa's, the squad car was gone but a shiny red VW convertible was in the driveway. My body pulsed with adrenaline, my brain screaming *Jessa's in danger* over and over. I was out of the car, taking the steps two at a time and pounding on the door before Martin had killed the engine. *What if she remembered something else and told the wrong person?*

"Frankie? Martin?" Jessa said when she opened the door. She looked startled. "What is it?"

I gave her a giant hug. "You're okay!"

She gently pulled away and turned worried eyes on me. "Why wouldn't I be?"

"You didn't answer my text!"

She palmed her forehead. "I must have forgotten to hit send."

I took a deep breath. "Is Josh here?"

"Yeah, he's in the kitchen making dinner. Are you staying?"

I nodded at Martin, who stared back at me with his mouth hanging open. "We're here to talk to Suzie."

———

"You're asking me if I knew this Shadow person?" she said, repeating my question. She looked to Jessa as if for support, but Jessa was staring at her hands.

"Yes." I placed the dragonfly clip on the table in front of her.

Suzie's eyes flickered up to my face and then down.

"This is yours?"

"Might be," she said. "I have a lot of accessories."

"It is," Jessa said, touching it with her forefinger. "I gave you a pair of these for your birthday."

"It was found below the window of the room where Mal was killed. One of the punk girls picked it up that night, not realizing it was a clue," I said.

"A clue to what?" Suzie said.

"Murder," Martin said. I scowled at him. He was playing it just a little bit too Poirot.

"We just came from the station," I said. "They have the bag of tools with the murder weapon inside. They're doing tests for DNA, evidence. They'll find something for sure." And it would be faster this time. Jessa had told us that with Drew's death, her mom's team had been granted full access to the county labs.

"And you think I killed Mal? Drew? Eva?" Her laughter was abrupt and harsh and I was shocked for a moment. She didn't notice her slip, but we did. Jessa gasped.

"You didn't. *Eva*'s alive," Martin said, sliding to the front of his chair.

Jessa shifted closer to me. My heart was beating so hard I felt nauseous.

It was just the tiniest tremor by her right eye. And then she folded. It was like seeing a mask slip away, revealing the the true person underneath. Pale, panting in quick sharp inhalations as if she couldn't fill her lungs.

"Suzie," Jessa said, moving over to her. "You're my friend. I love you. Talk to us."

Suzie took one last shuddering breath and started crying. Jessa curled an arm around her shoulders and pulled her close. "I didn't mean to. I didn't mean to," Suzie wailed through her fingers.

"Oh, shit," Martin muttered under his breath. I had to agree. My head was in a whirl. It had been guesswork for the most part, a gut feeling. But I didn't feel triumphant. Instead, watching Suzie fall apart, I mostly felt sick.

Once the storm of sobs abated, I got Suzie a glass of water from the kitchen.

Josh looked over at me from his standing desk. His headphones were on. *All okay?* he mouthed. I gave him a wobbly thumbs up and motioned for him to remove his headphones. "Is Casey coming home soon?" I asked.

He gave me a puzzled look. "She's on her way now," he said, before returning to his work.

Back in the living room, Jessa had her head pressed close to Suzie's. She was whispering to her, and Suzie's breathing had slowed down although it still hitched in her chest. I placed the water on the table and took a seat next to Martin.

"Tell us," Jessa said, linking their fingers together.

Suzie kept her head down, her voice low.

"It wasn't the first time we had sex, but after we'd been together for six months," she began. "I thought we were great together. I thought he was amazing. That arrogance, like he could have anything he wanted, achieve whatever he set his mind to. It was in such contrast to how sweet and generous he could be. Such a turn-on." She swallowed hard. Jessa wordlessly pushed the glass of water towards her. After taking a sip, Suzie continued. "He didn't want to use protection. He said it didn't feel as good." She chewed over those words for a second. "We'd both been tested for STIs and he swore he'd pull out in time but I said no. So he... slipped something into my drink."

"Suzie," Jessa said, her face creased in distress. "He raped you."

Suzie shook her head violently. "Don't," she said. "Please, I need to finish." She drank some more water. When she spoke again, the words came faster, carried on a stream of her breath.

"The next morning, I could tell we'd had sex even though I didn't remember anything. And a few weeks later...I knew for sure." The word *pregnant* hung in the air. Suzie's eyes glistened with unshed tears. She rubbed them angrily away. "I didn't tell my mother. Or my friends. I didn't tell anyone. I handled it alone."

"You can't think you deserved it. Oh, Suze," Jessa said. "We would have listened and tried to help. My mom could have taken charge. I can't believe Mal would do this. He should have been punished for what he did to you."

Suzie shielded her face with her arms, her shoulders shook. Was she crying? Another thought crossed my mind. *Laughing?*

She raised her head, eyes glittering. "Mal?!" Her voice was like a knife. "Mal was just a way to get back at him. Emerson Bradley's the one who drugged and raped me and paid for my abortion. He's been giving me an allowance. He bought me that car sitting outside on your driveway. *A sweet little car for a sweet little girl.* All to keep me quiet."

I sucked in a breath. A loud thud sounded as Martin fell off the arm of the couch he was perched on. He got to his feet, rubbing his elbow.

"I thought your parents bought you the car?" Jessa said. "Wouldn't they wonder?"

Suzie grimaced. "Perks of a vicious divorce. I told Mom it was from my dad and vice versa. They always try to one-up each other."

"What he did to you was criminal," Jessa said. "There are laws to protect—"

"Don't rattle off all that legal shit," Suzie interrupted. Tears began to spill from her eyes, but it was as if she didn't notice. "You know how it is. It's the girl who's ruined. So I took his money. And to really fuck with him, I started dating his son. And then, Mal fell in love with me." She looked down at her lap. "I couldn't do that to him. Pretend. I broke his heart."

She wiped her face with her sleeves. "I thought I was on top of it but I was losing a lot of weight, hardly sleeping, my hair was falling out. Remember when I said I was in Cabo for the month? My mother sent me to a place where they fix you." She uttered a bark of laughter. "I saw them arrive the night of the party, those punk girls. And then later, I couldn't believe it when I realized one of them was Eva. Her hair was different, but I recognized her immediately. We'd shared a room, spent so much time together, talking, crying. She understood. I didn't open up to any of the therapists; they would have had to make a report. Only her. I thought I could go on with my life, pretend like none of it had ever happened, but when I saw her that night, I knew I couldn't. She knew everything about me."

"But why kill Mal?" Martin asked.

She turned those flat eyes on him, mascara streaking her cheeks. "Shut up," she said. "I'm not telling *you* this."

He retreated into a corner of the couch.

Suzie stared at her clasped hands. "I searched all over for her. I went upstairs, hunting in all the rooms. I was in the master when you and Mal came up. I was trapped." She shook her head. "He was so angry that whole night. He was drunk and he kept trying to corner me to talk. I didn't know why. I thought his heart was healed. I wanted to get out of there but the window wouldn't open. There was a pile of tools nearby and I tried to lever it loose with this big screwdriver, but there wasn't enough time. I freaked out and hid behind the curtains."

She turned in the chair and faced Jessa. "You could barely walk, and he was snatching at you, telling you all this sweet stuff. You slipped off the mattress. You lost your balance and fell hard against a small table and broke it. I tried to help you, but you were totally out of it so I just left you there. You curled up on the floor like an animal and the whole time Mal was just lying flat on his back on the bed, calling you *baby, sweet beautiful baby*, telling you how much he wanted you, how good you two were together. All the things Emerson used to tell me."

"You killed him because of his father?" I said.

Suzie startled, almost as if she'd forgotten I was there. She shook her head violently. "Mal saw me hiding. He thought I was there for him. He'd found..." She paused for a breath. "Photos of me and his father in Emerson's desk. He said I sickened him. He said he would tell everyone, destroy me, destroy his father. I couldn't take it. I had to shut him up."

She shuddered. "I was close to the bed. And then I was on him. I was still holding the screwdriver. He was blinking, trying to focus, and his hands felt like slabs of hot meat when he grabbed my arms. I couldn't stand him touching me. I stabbed down, once, and it went in so easily. No blood. None at all. Not until I pulled the screwdriver out."

She was quiet for a minute, staring at her trembling hands, turning them over as if they were no longer a part of her. I saw scratches on her wrists as if she'd clawed at herself. She pulled her sleeves down and raised her head. Her eyes looked huge, blank, as if she were reliving it all. "I saw myself in the mirror afterwards and I couldn't bear the sight. Who was that person? Who am I now?"

Somewhere a wall clock ticked off the seconds, each one sounding like a hollow heartbeat. It was almost a whisper but she said, "No one would save me, so I had to save myself."

There was a heavy silence, thick as smoke, hanging in the air. Then Martin spoke. "What about Drew?" he said. "Did he have anything to do with it?"

"Drew was so drunk and high at the party he barely remembered anything. He got handsy with me, aggressive, like he expected something. He blacked out," she mumbled and stared at the floor. "It wasn't until afterwards that I realized I could use him. He was furious; he needed a target to lash out at and I filled his head with all kinds of possibilities. I thought that if he was going ballistic it would deflect attention away from me. I encouraged him to keep drinking, to go after you two. All those stupid pranks."

"How could you?" Jessa asked, pulling away. "You tortured him. You took advantage of his grief, his confusion, his sickness."

Suzie's face paled. I could tell that in that moment, she knew she'd lost Jessa.

"He was my alibi. He said he'd do anything for me. But I couldn't count on him to stick to our story, that we'd been together that night. After he passed out, I left the room to hunt for Eva. He remembered waking up in that room alone. And he knew I'd started the fire up at Heartwood. He showed up at my house, just after I got back. The smell of gasoline was all over me. I convinced him I'd done it because I couldn't bear the reminder of Mal's death. That the house symbolized everything that was wrong. But it seems he *insisted* on calling in an anonymous tip."

"You started the fire to conceal evidence," Jessa said quietly.

Suzie nodded. "In case I'd left DNA in the bedroom. That was my biggest fear. It was supposed to spread from the front hallway upstairs to all the bedrooms, but instead the ceiling caught fire and I had to get out quickly. Because of Drew's meddling, the fire department got there early enough to contain it. As soon as I could, I went back looking for the screwdriver but it was gone. I'd buried my jacket under a bunch of leaves and dirt. There was blood...I had to wash my hands in the swimming pool."

"Bumble slipped her leash and dug it up." Another piece of the puzzle clicked into place. "It was you in the house when I was there. Upstairs," I said.

"I needed to see the room again. I couldn't stop thinking there was something that might tie me to it." For an instant, her lip quivered. "Your dog got loose. She grabbed the jacket from me. She wouldn't let it go. I had to—and then I heard you coming." Her voice dropped to a whisper. "I'm sorry."

I shook my head. I could deal with my rage later. Right now, I needed the truth.

"Emerson Bradley didn't suspect you?" I asked.

"He just thought I was his golden doll. Completely under his control."

"And what about Drew?" Martin asked fiercely. "At the end. Did he know?"

Suzie's mouth contorted. "No, the stupid—it never even occurred to him. He was fixated on you. And then those punk girls. If he'd kept his mouth shut. If he'd only..." Her eyes glassed over. It was like seeing cracks appear in a dam.

"So you killed him, too," Jessa said. Tears trickled down her cheeks.

"I didn't want to." She reached out for Jessa's hands. "You have to believe me. The drinking made him unreliable. The police kept bringing him back in. Every time they did, I was at risk. He was a liability. I couldn't control him."

Martin's jaw was clenched so tight I could hear his teeth grinding. "He was my friend."

"How did you do it, Suzie?" I asked, trying to keep my voice steady.

"It was easy. I lured him up to the house. I brought plenty of booze and I put a bunch of oxy in his drink. I used his phone, his thumbprint to send the emergency alert. He just fell asleep. I didn't want to hurt him but I had to. Don't you see? I had no other choice. I thought that would be the end."

I shuddered. She made it all sound so easy. Like she was the victim of these unfortunate circumstances, not the people she'd killed.

"I'm not a murderer," she whispered.

"You're forgetting about Eva," I said, sickened but determined to get through this.

"That was an accident." The tremor by her eye had started up again. "We fought over that bag and she fell. I didn't want any of this to happen."

"What about Drew's note?" Martin asked. He couldn't even look at her, fixing his furious gaze on a kid's drawing on the wall. "That took planning."

"He'd written this crazy letter to Emerson about how he was innocent. That he never would have killed Mal. That he loved him." Her face turned ugly. "Emerson Bradley doesn't understand love."

FRANKIE

The smell of cinnamon and coffee wrapped itself around me like a hug. Jessa and I hung our coats up on the wrought iron coat tree by the front door. It was shaped like an actual tree and someone at the Dead End had garlanded the higher branches with baby pumpkins and shiny plastic apples that looked straight out of *Snow White*. It was ten o'clock on a Sunday, too early for the lunch crowd. There was still a short line, so we got behind a cute couple with matching haircuts, their hands in each other's back pockets.

"I like it," Jessa said, taking in the red leather banquettes, the checkerboard floor, and the collection of velvet zombie paintings. "Shades of debauchery."

"Indeed. I'm thinking of hiring them to do my bedroom."

"A little romantic boudoir for you and Cara?"

It was good to see a sparkle in Jessa's eye, but unfortunately I had to disappoint her. "Alas, I'm pretty sure her heart belongs to another." I tried to manifest wounded but brave, and failed miserably. Maybe I was more like Heathcliff than anyone out of Austen.

"Relationships are overrated," she said quickly, but then she kissed her fingers to my cheek. "Oh Frankie, you shine so bright."

I kissed mine to hers.

As I placed our order, Jessa's phone pinged. She looked down, tapping a response. "Mom. Making sure we've arrived safely." It had been three days since Suzie's confession and arrest, but the gauntlet of parental protection hadn't loosened yet.

"My grandmother asked me *exactly* where we were going and when I'd be back. She also said she'd pray for us." The grandparents' newfound concern felt strange. It was like they were seeing me for the first time and appreciating me more. "Last night I had to dodge a bunch of questions at the dinner table," I added.

"How come?" She looked surprised. She knew how silent our meals usually were.

I swallowed hard. It still seemed surreal. "I came out to them." In fact, I'd just blurted out "I'm gay" when my grandfather asked whether Suzie had ever demonstrated sociopathic behaviour at school. "I had it all planned, this grandiose speech about love being love, but then it just slipped out." Maybe it was because Cara had been on my mind so much.

Jessa squealed and pinched my arm. "I'm so proud of you! How'd they handle it?"

I detached her powerful fingers, caging her hand with mine. "They took it well. Well-*ish*," I amended. Mostly they'd looked confused and a little aghast that I'd felt the need to overshare, but I was pretty sure my grandfather appreciated the fact that teen pregnancy was off the table. I just felt like I could breathe finally.

Martin, already commandeering one of the booths, caught sight of us and waved. Jessa and I collected our cappuccinos and a plate of assorted pastries and joined him and Simon.

"Any news?" Martin asked.

"Suzie's out on bail. Both her parents are back," Jessa said, "and they've hired the biggest law firm in Campbellton."

"Eva hasn't woken up but they moved her out of Intensive Care and she's stable now," I said. Cara had been down there every day during visiting hours.

We all knew there was a low probability that Eva would regain consciousness; the trauma to her body had been severe. But still we hoped. If the worst happened, I wasn't sure Cara would survive it. I blinked back tears and concentrated on shredding my paper napkin.

"I'm still confused about a couple of things," Simon said, snagging a cinnamon roll. "So hopefully, you're here to enlighten me."

"Yeah," said Martin. "First of all, how did you figure out it was Suzie?"

I lifted an eyebrow. "You mean, once I stopped suspecting you?"

"Yeah, but that was never serious...I mean..."

"Just a fleeting thought," I assured him, lying through my teeth. He'd had big motive.

I'd spent most of last night staring at my bedroom ceiling, going over everything in my head. It would feel good to share my process with other people, get my thoughts in order.

Martin still had the notebook and he flipped through the pages. It was half filled now with his meticulous notes. He checked his pens, selected one, and looked at me inquisitively.

Cringing a little from all their eyes on me, I began: "Suzie's movements were the hardest to pin down. No one could really say where she was at certain times. And her alibi with Drew was muddy. Once I really looked at my photos, I found big gaps of time when she was out of sight."

"Hunting for Eva," Martin said, nodding.

"What about the roofies? Did she know that's what they planned?" Jessa asked.

"No," said Simon. "Suzie seemed genuinely shocked when we told her."

"I think Mal planned to drug her out of revenge. He wanted to hurt her as much as she had hurt him," I said. "He wanted her powerless. Seeing her of all people lose control was probably an attractive scenario."

"How terrible to find out that Mal used the exact same drugs his father had used when he raped her," Martin said quietly. "I mean, what would that do to a person?"

Jessa cut in: "I'm not saying it wasn't criminal of him, but I think he loved her, and being dumped and then finding out about his father just broke him."

"It must have felt like the ultimate betrayal," I said.

"I'd noticed he'd seemed withdrawn. And he was definitely drinking more. I just wish he'd confided in me," Simon said.

"And what about Drew and the roofies?" I asked Martin.

"He swore he thought it was just a prank. He also admitted he saw it as an advantage to himself if Suzie were to be more...pliable."

Jessa and I flushed red with anger.

"I don't want to speak ill of the dead, but that was so wrong," Jessa said.

Simon nodded. "Agreed. So then, what next?"

"After Suzie killed Mal, she jumped out the window," I said.

"It's a fifteen-foot drop," Martin pointed out.

"She's a gymnast, remember?" Jessa said. "Vaulting. Uneven bars. She knew how to land on her feet."

I continued. "She threw the screwdriver into the bushes at the side of the house, not realizing that Cara and her girls were tossing stuff back there too. I figured Suzie meant to recover it later and dispose of it, but unfortunately for her, the girls unknowingly took it with them. I think Eva discovered the screwdriver later on, noticed that it was"—I struggled for a word—"suspiciously dirty, and put two and two together." We all exchanged queasy looks. "At the same time she ditched her jacket, which was stained with blood. Cara and I found it next to Bumble, but I didn't make the connection that it was a clue until later, and when I went back to look for it, Suzie had already retrieved it."

I searched my photo prints until I found a group shot of Suzie with Missy and Anabel. All of them in matching black jean jackets with their hair pinned up.

I pointed to the dragonfly barrette Suzie was wearing. "She also dropped this outside the window. Toni picked it up that night and later gave it to Cara as a keepsake."

"So, she's just committed murder and fled the crime scene. Then what?" Martin asked.

"She couldn't leave. That would be suspicious. She came back to the party, still searching for Eva. I think she was in a rage."

"Or shock," Simon said.

"Both. She'd tried so hard to keep her secrets," Jessa said. "She must have felt desperate."

I thought about what Suzie had said. That the girl was always blamed in some way. It was *so* not cut and dried. There was not one bad guy, there were many, and other than Eva, no one in this scenario was purely innocent.

"So what started you thinking about her?" Jessa asked.

"At your house, she mentioned four girls. She knew about the fourth: Shadow, Eva. I didn't realize the significance of that until later, but her words stuck in my brain."

"Such a small mistake," Simon said. "How did she hold it together under constant threat of discovery?" There was a note of sympathy in his voice. My own feelings about it were a knotted mess.

"Was she the person you saw standing in front of the mirror in the girl's bedroom?" Jessa asked.

I hesitated. "Too tall. I think it *was* Eva. Cara believed she'd stayed out of the house that night, but I think she must have snuck up from the basement." There was that one photo I'd taken that showed her inside standing in a corner. I found the magnified print I'd made and pushed it forward. "Maybe she just wanted to remind herself what comfort and home felt like."

"If she hadn't, Suzie would never have known she was there," said Jessa.

"And if Drew hadn't caught Suzie after setting the fire, he'd be alive too," Martin said.

"Plus, he was cracking up. She knew that at any moment he might tell the truth—and remember, she wasn't with him in the room," Simon said.

"Suzie had to keep going," I said. "Because to stop meant discovery."

"One murder led to the next and then the next," Martin said. "An escalation."

I let out a long breath and heard it echo around the table.

"I can't forgive her for what she did to Drew. Messing with his head like that, using him to cover her tracks," said Jessa.

"Yeah, she has to own that," I said.

"It was evil," Martin said.

Jessa spoke up, distress evident in her voice. "I realize now that all those times Suzie was checking in with me, she was actually trying to find out about the investigation. Where the police were looking, possible suspects." She looked at me miserably. "I think I might have told her where to find Cara and the girls. Where they were hiding out."

I shook my head. "None of us suspected Suzie. It's not your fault. Don't you blame yourself for that."

"Do you believe Eva's fall was an accident?" Simon said.

"The screwdriver *was* the murder weapon," I said. "Suzie knew that and she had to get it, and Eva was standing in her way. She forced a confrontation. The sad part is that I don't think Eva would have turned her in. She'd already hidden the tools from Cara. All she wanted to do was leave town."

"Clear motive," Martin said, sounding all Poirot again. "Premeditated."

"Not to be a downer," Simon said, "but Suzie's lawyered up. And even though she confessed, she might still walk away from this. Especially if Eva doesn't wake up."

"Mom got a call last night," Jessa said, sounding more like herself again. "I only heard a snippet of the conversation, but she was talking about some DNA samples they found under Eva's fingernails. I have a feeling Suzie isn't walking anywhere."

MARTIN

For the tenth time, I re-folded the instructions Dad's lawyer, Rachel, had given me and placed them back in my pocket. "The penitentiary is not a place to flout the rules," she'd warned. "You sneak in contraband and you'll end up in there with him." I'd been so nervous I'd emptied my pockets in the car, afraid that somehow I'd forgotten something illegal. Like, was gum okay? Or could a wily MacGyver type break out of jail with it? How about my belt?

MASS PRISON EXODUS OCCURS HOURS AFTER GUM-CARRYING, BELTED TEEN VISIT.

I was sweating bullets even though I'd been waiting in the chill morning air for two hours. And my jeans kept slipping down in an annoying way.

Behind me, along the front of the building, snaked a long line of people, mostly sitting or leaning like I was against the wall, nursing cups of gas station coffee. The parking lot was full now, but when I'd arrived this morning at five-thirty, it had been nothing but a few floodlights and a couple of lone cars.

Truth was I hadn't been able to sleep last night, and finally at three in the morning, I'd started driving. The jail was a few hours north of Lincoln, near a small town that boasted nothing but motels and bail bonds offices offering *Zero Down* and *Easy Repayments!* The only vehicles on the road had been long-distance truckers. It felt eerie and surreal being awake in a world when most people were still sleeping.

Finally, after a sweep of a metal-detecting wand and a serious pat down, a small group of us were escorted down a maze of hallways into a large hot room filled with round tables and slippery chairs that were bolted to the ground.

Dad was sitting over by a row of vending machines. He looked sad and tired in his bright orange jumpsuit with *BCP* across the back, but when he spotted me, his face cracked into a wide smile. We hugged for the full thirty seconds we were allowed, and I sat down across from him. I removed a plastic baggie filled with quarters from my pocket.

"Are you hungry? What do you want to eat?" I asked. A whole side of the room was taken up by the snack dispensaries. Chips, candy, instant noodles, oatmeal, coffee, and hot chocolate. It was far better stocked than our cupboards had ever been.

"I want to sit here with you," he said. "You eating enough? Is Simone checking in on you?" I noticed a watery glint in his eye. *Oh no.* It seemed like just hearing my voice was enough to set him off these days. We'd had a few exceptionally sobby collect calls.

"I'm great. Tell me about your cell. Your cellie. Your days," I said swiftly, trying to distract him. If he cried, I'd cry, and I couldn't imagine how that would go over with the guards and the other prisoners. This did not seem like the kind of jail where they offered morning yoga.

Dad nodded at a tall, stoop-shouldered man with a shock of white hair sitting with a sweet-looking old woman. "That's Shupe over there. I lucked out with him. He's got all kind of tricks up his sleeve."

"Oh yeah, like what?" I stared at the man, sliding my eyes away when he looked up. He didn't look like a violent felon serving a life sentence. But then, neither did Suzie. "Nothing dangerous, I hope?"

"How to heat up food in our cell. How to get first dibs on the books on the book cart. Plus, he got me a job in the library."

I relaxed my spine. Other than the intimidating presence of the guards, this felt like some weird family reunion where no one knew each other very well.

COUSIN SHUPE'S PRISON CELL POTATO SALAD IS THE HIT OF THE PICNIC!

"And your midterm results were good?" he asked.

"Yeah." I couldn't control my grin. Surprisingly, my grade point average was hovering around 3.8. "I'm working with the guidance counsellor on my college plan." I'd already sent in early applications to my top picks but I didn't want to tell my dad until I received a response. He'd go from over-the-top excitement to misery that he was stuck in here.

He told me he'd seen his lawyer a couple of times already. "The DA is taking on the Bradley fraud indictment. I guess Heartwood wasn't the only scam he had going. She says

I'll be called up as a witness." His mouth tightened. "And I heard about the new case against him. Suzie Jackson's family is going after him with everything they've got. He won't be able to avoid jail for much longer."

"That's great, Dad. One for the good guys." I was trying to calm him down. He was sweating profusely and his hands were dancing across the table like frantic mice.

"I heard they charged her with both murders," he said. "I can't believe it."

"They have." Naturally it was the hot topic in Lincoln, but I'd become a master at avoiding the subject. I'd gotten together with Simon a few times to talk over everything. It still didn't sit well with me. Especially since it looked like Frankie and I might be getting the reward money after all. Emerson Bradley had set it up as an independent trust. We'd decided that if we did receive it, we'd share it with Cara.

He hesitated. "How's your article going?" An online news blog had reached out to me for the inside story. It was a great opportunity, everything I had ever dreamed of, but I wasn't sure how to answer my dad's question. I'd thought that finding out who killed Mal was everything. It would prove my innocence once and for all, and there'd be a peace in that. The killer exposed and arrested. A well-defined ending. Instead, the whole thing was a series of tragic events that led to a double murder and an attempt on another life. All shades of grey. *People, don't forget it's about people*, Frankie had said. Mal and Drew were gone. Eva might never wake up. Suzie was a murderer. Our town was never going to be the same. And we all had to live with that.

I exhaled a little too noisily and my father, who'd been studying my face intently, covered my hand with his. "It's not only about what happened," he said. "That's never neat and tidy. The only way you can find some kind of truth is by giving the victims a voice, too. The human angle. Mal, Drew, and Eva. Make sure their stories are told."

CARA

The bell chimed as I pushed the door open. Frankie popped up from between two bookshelves, beaming when she saw me. "Oh, Cara," she said. I guessed my expression gave it all away. "Tell me immediately." She'd frozen in place holding a teetering stack of books that reached her chin.

"She woke up. She recognized me." The relief and joy sang in my voice.

For a second, a whisper of sadness crossed her face, but it was immediately replaced by another wide smile. It felt like the sun taking root in my chest, replacing some of the lingering emptiness with warmth.

"I'm so happy for you, Cara. For you both," she said, looking for a place to put the books.

I trotted over and took the top half of the pile from her, placing it on the table. We were inches apart. Now she wouldn't meet my eyes. The silence between us crackled with electricity.

"You must be so relieved," she continued. "Will you go to that women's squat or the nearest big city or just hit the road? The weather is holding still. No snow yet." Her mouth snapped closed as if she realized she was babbling.

"Eva's getting help in Cambellton. Physio and therapy. We need to be close by. Simone Bonneville says she can stay with me at the apartment once she's released. I'm moving in next week." I still couldn't believe that people were reaching out. Making sure we got what we needed. Simone was keeping tabs on Iggy and Toni at their small group home. They were doing good. The kindness made me well up a dozen times a day. And I almost dared to believe that if I blinked, it might not all disappear.

"That's wonderful. Great. Fantastic," she said. She put the rest of the books down finally and pounced on Higgins, burying her face in his thick fur. He let out an indignant meow.

Her smile slipped a little. "Everything will be all right now." She seemed so sure of it. Me, not so much. I was wary. So far we hadn't been charged with theft or trespassing but who knows what would happen once this charitable feeling wore off.

"Can't count on the future," I said, more offhand than I felt.

"You look good."

I rubbed a hand over my head, pleased by her compliment. They'd arranged for a fresh cut before I left and I'd gelled my bangs the way I liked them. "They gave me some clothes too." The jeans were stiff and the sweater was so big I felt I was drowning in it, but they were the newest clothes I'd ever had and I was finally warm.

"At the shelter?"

"Yeah."

"It will be really nice to get to know her. Eva, I mean."

"Frankie," I said, determined to make her look at me. She was acting so weird. I'd thought she would be as happy as I was. Maybe it was nerves. My stomach was tumbling.

"Yes." She peeked at me over Higgins's head.

"It's you, Frankie. A big part of the reason I'm staying is you."

"Oh." She gave me a friendly smile.

I grabbed her wrist. I could feel her rapid pulse. Surely she could hear my heart?

"I *like* you."

Her cheeks flushed bright red. "I like you too. But you and Shadow..."

I shook my head. "Shadow and I are family."

"Oh." She laughed nervously, and she still wouldn't look at me.

I moved closer. And closer still. I could smell cinnamon on her breath, count all her freckles. She let Higgins jump back to the floor. I heard her inhale and all of a sudden, she threw her arms around me.

I hugged her back, feeling all the tension I'd been holding melt away.

I cleared my throat against her neck. My lips were chapped. My hands were calloused even with all the showers I'd had recently. I was scared to touch her. We pulled away just a bit, staying in the circle we'd made with our arms.

Finally she raised her eyes. The air fizzed like it was made of ginger ale. I found myself praying that no one would come in, that someone would come in. *Am I ready for this?* Something Tick Tock once said to me resurfaced. We'd been getting ready to hop off a freight train. It had picked up speed and my head was spinning with equal parts excitement and fear. *Sometimes it's best to just close your eyes and jump*, he'd said.

"Okay?" I asked. Because nothing good ever stays good, right? And maybe I shouldn't risk it.

Now, she smiled. She leaned in. Kissed me so lightly I felt only the warmth of it. I shivered, my lips wanting more of her.

I jumped.

ACKNOWLEDGEMENTS

Conceiving of and writing a novel during these past two pandemic years was both a blessing and a curse. A blessing because it engaged and entertained my brain and gave me a place to focus my energies. A curse because sometimes said brain didn't want to cooperate. I spent a lot of time staring at the sea. Thank you, Ocean, for being there in all your wild beauty! How you refresh and delight!

The reason this book exists comes down to some very special and talented women. My trifecta: Ali McDonald, literary agent beyond compare at 5 Otter Literary; Diane Terrana, fantastic author and generous and incisive editor; and Whitney Moran at Nimbus Publishing, who took over at the last, applied her ruthless clarity, helped me tighten all those loose ends, and guided me to the heart of this story. Thanks, Whit, for giving me far more than 10 authorly moments! I'd also like to thank proofreader Penelope Jackson, publicists Kate Watson and Karen McMullin, designers Heather Bryan and Rudi Tusek, and everyone at Nimbus for all they do.

I'd be less of a writer and less of a happy person without the support, wisdom, advice, and accommodating shoulders of a number of fine authors, in particular the amazing writers who work and create here in the beautiful and inspiring Maritimes, my adopted home for the last twelve years. There are too many to mention but you are all amazing and thank you!

Thanks to retired RCMP constable Patrick Moran for clarifying all things procedural. Also Simon Hatherley and Paula Cardinell for the informative chats about police work.

My family and friends deserve special thanks for listening quietly when I, on occasion, have to vent. I wouldn't be able to do this without you. Thank you all, especially Mum and Dad and Silvia, who have to put up with me because we are closely related.

I feel such extreme gratitude for the booksellers, librarians, and book bloggers out there. Thanks for putting my books in the hands of readers. Special shoutout to Anne-Marie Sheppard and the bookstore, Block Shop Books (Lunenburg, Nova Scotia), that we own together. Best business decision I ever made!

My kids have grown up in the years since I was first published. They inspire me every day and I am so proud of the loving humans they have become. I have no doubt their generation will save the world.

To Kirsten, always and forever, the reason behind all my books and why I am compelled to put pen to paper again and again.

And in memory of the best dog, Princess Deli Ancho, my precious marshmallow gargoyle.

Madeleine Kendall

JO TREGGIARI was born in London, England, and raised in Canada. She spent many years in Oakland, California, and New York, where she trained as a boxer, wrote for a punk magazine, and owned a gangster rap/indie rock record label. Her books have been nominated for numerous awards, including most recently a Governor General's Literary Award and a Crime Writers of Canada Award.

jotreggiari.com